Praise for PHILLIP TOMASSO III

"(Tomasso) takes the standard fare of the private investigator genre and adds twists and turns to make it anything but standard. Tomasso's writing is crisp and clear . . . thoroughly enjoyable." —Joseph Nassise, author of *Riverwatch*, editor of *Fear of the Dark*
"(Tomasso) crafts an engrossing and 'edge of your seat' tale of deceit, betrayal and murder. The story line and Mr. Tomasso's writing held my interest until the very end. He weaves a tale of mystery and suspense with dark threads of the supernatural . . . a well-written novel with wonderful characters that come alive on the page . . . I'll be waiting for Mr. Tomasso's next novel."—Nancy Mehl, *The Charlotte Austin Review*

"A highly original idea for a mystery series . . ."—Pamela G. Ahearn, *The Ahearn Agency*

"Phillip Tomasso's supernatural tale develops three-dimensional characters for a different style of detective series . . . where the unexpected prevails."—N.B. Leake, *Write Time Write Place*

"Fast-paced and deftly told—Tomasso knows his craft."—Olivia Boler, author of *Year of the Smoke Girl*

". . . His prose is adept and visually evocative. Like a sculptor, Tomasso deftly handles the psychological thriller genre, hewing out a mystery rolling with suspense and empathy . . ."—Matthew Butler, *Table Hopping*

"Tomasso has a talent for building consistent characters and bringing them through some fast paced scenes."—Judi Clark, *Mostly Fiction Review*

". . . A brilliant concoction of suspense, thrills, action, and love all mixed into a book you won't want to put down!"—Amanda Mueller, *MyRochester.com*

"Tomasso stands as a master conductor, bringing in one exciting movement after another . . . This might be your first time hearing

Phillip Tomasso's name. Be assured, however, it definitely won't be your last."—Jack Pantaleo, author of *Mother Julian and the Gentle Vampire*

". . . Meticulously detailed in both setting and character depth. The story will pull you in, shake you about, disturb you, keep you guessing and always wanting more. It delivers!"—Keith Rommel, *BookReview*

Advance Praise for JOHNNY BLADE

"Phillip Tomasso understands what drives people who live on the edge. His characters are three-dimensional and they engage your sympathy and your anger. A taut tale of deceit and rage, Johnny Blade is well crafted and gripping. It was my first Tomasso book . . . it won't be my last."—William Meikle, author of *Watchers of the Wall* and *Island Life*

"The story is absolutely riveting; I could not stop reading for even a second. However, the biggest lure in this book was the interactions between Michael and the quirky customers who frequent Jack's Joint. The other side to the book, Martin's murderous streak, is also written with elaborate narrative that was not only believable, but also fast-paced and it flowed smoothly. There were no slow parts in the story. From start to finish, Mr. Tomasso grabbed the reader's attention and my focus never wavered once. I look forward to more by this talented author in the future."—Tracy Farnsworth, *The Romance Readers Connection.com*

"Johnny Blade quickens the blood. Tomasso's compelling characters lure you in and then lock the door as the screams begin!"—S.J. Gaither, Co-Author of *Black Moon*

"JOHNNY BLADE is a serial killer novel. If you're the type of reader who groans at another serial killer book, I highly recommend that you don't walk away from this new thriller. Phillip Tomasso slices and dices through this sub-genre's trappings and comes up with one helluva a gutsy ride. The characters crawl under your skin and don't leave. I'd like to see more of Detectives Cocuzzi and Cage. JOHNNY BLADE will keep your heart thumping and your brain engaged. Another winner from Tomasso."—Patty G. Henderson, author of *The Burning of Her Sin* and *Blood Scent*

"As a retired police officer, I felt that Mr. Tomasso had a law enforcement background because of his depth of police knowledge. This is cleverly written and displays a true writing artist. This book should easily fall into the classification of 'Best Seller.'"—Bobby Ruble, author of *Have No Mercy*

Praise for THIRD RING

". . . a well written fast paced thriller with more than a few twists and turns. The characters are convincing and there is just enough magic to make the story interesting without it becoming a Dennis Wheatley-style novel."—The Eternal Night

"P.I. Nick Tartaglia has a knack for attracting cases out of the realm of normalcy. In THIRD RING, what started out as a case of burglary and murder seven months ago, ends up pulling Tartaglia into a nightmare involving The Talisman, three books titled "Heaven," "Earth," and "Hell." He who possesses all three, possesses unspeakable powers of black magic. Just as in TENTH HOUSE, Tomasso expertly blurs the line between real and surreal, and knows how to flush out the dark side in chilling detail. An excellent follow-up to a promising series."—Sandra Tooley, author of the Sam Casey Mysteries (written as S.D. Tooley), and the Chase Dagger Series (written as Lee Driver)

"Phillip Tomasso breathes new life into an old genre – an EXCELLENT read!"—M. R. Sellers, Author of *Harm None* and *Never Burn a Witch*

"A burglary gone bad draws Rochester PI Nick Tartaglia into a race for possession of three apocalyptic books. Tomasso executes a plot that is a chilling reminder of how insidiously Evil can infiltrate the commonplace, the secure and the familiar."—Jane Rubino, author of *Homicide for the Holidays*, and *Plot Twist*

"Third Ring is a tightly written, fast-paced private eye novel. Nick is an enjoyable character who relies on his instincts and street smarts to help keep a level head during an investigation."—Jennifer Monahan Winberry, The Mystery Reader

"Tomasso has created a hero you will root for—Nicholas Tartaglia may be small in stature but he has great heart and courage in the face of unspeakable evil."—Jamie Katz, author of *A Summer for Dying*

"Tomasso weaves a fantastic tale of supernatural proportions in *Third Ring*. This book keeps you at the edge of your seat, makes you question what you really believe, and entertains, all at the same time. I enjoyed reading this novel because it had just the right amount of characterization to make me feel like I know Tartaglia (the protagonist) but not so much that it took away from the plot."—John Misak, Jr., author of *Time Stand Still* and *Soft Case*

"Tomasso has a hit with his Nick Tartaglia series. His writing is real and flows just the way a detective novel should . . . THIRD RING is a frightening ride, full of twists and turns. But when the ride is over, all you want to do is buy another ticket and go again."—Nancy Mehl, author of *Graven Images* and *Sinner's Song*

JOHNNY BLADE

A Novel By

Phillip Tomasso III

Published By
Barclay Books, LLC

St. Petersburg, Florida
www.barclaybooks.com

PUBLISHED BY BARCLAY BOOKS, LLC
6161 51ST STREET SOUTH
ST. PETERSBURG, FLORIDA 33715
www.barclaybooks.com

Printed and bound in the United States of America

ISBN: 1-931402-29-9

This is for my brothers and sister,
Peter, Paul, and Maryjean . . .
You are the best, and I love you.
What more can I say?

Special Thanks too:

I may continue to write stories, but without the love and support of family and friends nothing else would ever get done. I cannot forget, even for a moment, that Greg Palmer, Corrine Chorney, and Marian Gowan have suffered through relentless drafts of this novel. Their insight is, as always, invaluable. I appreciate their time and editorial advice. And who needs a PR manager when you have a great friend like Christine Wrzos-Lucacci. She is unstoppable and has been since the release of my first novel. Some of the ideas she comes up with, let me tell you . . . well, let's hope the police don't come knocking at my door.

Then there is my wife and kids, my true inspiration. Though my wife often reads books I write and looks and says, "We inspire you to write this way?"

Lastly, but not least, I want to thank Barclay Books, Becki and Brantley. They work hard putting in long, long hours, reading whining e-mails and phone calls—not from me, mind you—and put out some high quality books by top notch authors that I feel fortunate to share company with.

www.philliptomasso.com

Contact the author: ptom3@hotmail.com

To Sharon—

Glad you made it to the event!

Hope you enjoy!

Best wishes,

[illegible signature]

8/2002

Prologue

Rochester, New York—One Week Before Christmas

The city resembled a freezer in desperate need of defrosting. Ice and snow spotted the walls of buildings, homes, cars, and anything else unfortunate enough to be outside. The chalky white build-up on everything made the city look dingy and dirty. Several inches had accumulated in the last few hours and the snow falling from the bleak sky showed no sign of letting up. The temperature felt frigid at fifteen degrees. The wind blew hard, strong, and constant. Anyone outside would swear it felt more like fifteen below.

City salt and plow trucks could not keep up with the weather dump, and the roads looked neglected because of it. Cars parked on the street became more and more buried with each pass the plows made.

Martin Wringer saw, barely visible in the slate sky, the Kodak tower with the Kodak name in red lights. He felt warm and secure in his white conversion van as he drove north on State Street and right by Kodak without as much as a second glance. The tower was as commonplace in Rochester as snow during the winter.

Along side the tower stood Manson Chemical Technologies. He once worked for MCT, but they decided to terminate his employment two months earlier. He had punched his supervisor and broken the man's nose. The fight was provoked. For nearly a year, the supervisor had hounded, teased, and harassed Wringer.

At the beginning of a night shift, when Wringer showed up late for work, the supervisor accused him of being drunk. Things were said, and names called. It became a heated argument. Wringer could not take anymore and threw a punch that connected with his supervisor's face, knowing instantaneously that he had just jeopardized his job. Satisfaction, however, had filled him.

It was the loss of his job, though, that wound up costing him the rest of his life.

But that did not matter right now. It was all in the past. All of it. His wife—soon to be ex-wife—his kids and his home. All of it was in the past where it belonged.

The bottle of vodka was in the coffee cup holder on the center console. He had already swallowed a fifth of the contents. His throat felt raw. His stomach burned. His head—his mind—he knew reeled in a whirlwind full of neurotic, obsessive-compulsive thoughts, all having to do with his planned destination.

He continued north toward Lyell Avenue, a road that intersected State. Once he crossed over Lyell, State became Lake Avenue. The difference between State and Lake could easily be compared to night and day. While prestige lined the banks of State, poverty and depravity lined those along Lake.

His vehicle was equipped with a twin-size bed, a stocked college refrigerator, and a complete entertainment system that was his home on wheels, literally. His wife lived in the house with everything that had been his. She would wind up keeping it all, too, but not the van. His attorney fought to keep the van. Now he lived in it, spending nights in vacant parking lots. No one bothered him. Only once had he received a parking violation. He paid the fine and nothing ever came of it.

Jack's Joint was before the next light, on the right. The place was a hole. He had never eaten there. The thought of some dirty cook making meals disgusted him. However, he had been there one other time. Not for the food, though. He had gone there for a woman. There was a part of him—the controlling part of most men—which desired satisfaction, pulsing and throbbing in anticipation of release.

The whore, who called herself Casey, stood in front of Jack's. Her long blond hair with its black highlights hung over her shoulders. It was her trademark, he supposed. Tonight she wore a knitted cap.

He stopped at the curb and lowered the passenger window from the control on his door. He took another long swig from the bottle of vodka.

Casey came over and stuck her head in the van. "I remember you. Back again, huh?" she said, snapping on chewing gum. She wore too much make-up. He hated that, but liked the heavy application of lip-gloss. She looked stoned. Her eyes were barely open. Two slits stared intently at him. Stoned, but not too wasted to work.

"Can hardly get enough," he said, smiling. "Hop in?"

"Sure." She opened the door and sat in the captain's chair. "Same thing as last time?"

"You remember what we did last time?" he asked.

"You were a big, um, tipper. I remember the big tippers."

"Then I'll drive while you go to work."

She swiveled her chair to face him as he pulled away from the curb. Slowly, she undressed. He took as many chances to glance at her while attempting to concentrate on the road. She was being naughty, undressing while he drove, and this excited him, but not nearly as much as the rest of his plans for the evening.

* * *

Wringer parked the van in a semi-vacant lot, farther north up Lake Avenue. Casey giggled as they went to the back of the van. Wringer closed curtains that hung directly behind the captain chairs and switched on a small desk lamp.

Casey crawled like a panther onto and across the twin-sized bed. She kept her rear high in the air and craned her head over her shoulders, watching for Wringer's reaction.

Wringer stripped and stood on his knees. He could not help but smile. He had spent many hours planning for this. Once the idea had come to him, he saw no other way around it. He liked to think he felt inspired.

After copulating, Martin Wringer stayed on top of Casey. He outweighed her by over one hundred pounds. She could try, but he did not believe she would succeed, in throwing him off.

After a few moments of silence and no activity, Casey's smile faded. "You can get off me now."

"Where's the smile, doll?" Wringer asked, showing her his grin.

"We're done." She looked suddenly nervous—scared maybe. Wringer loved it.

"In a manner of speaking. I think, you're done."

"What the hell's that supposed to mean?" She raised her arms, trying to use her elbows and forearms to push him away.

He stopped her, pressing his own forearms onto hers, pinning them to the mattress. Wringer had the blade between the mattress and the plywood he used for a box spring. He slid his hand in to retrieve it. "When you're a whore," Wringer said, "people don't expect much from you. Do they?"

Casey's eyes, wide open, stared intently into his face. The fear in her expression spoke volumes. "You want me to answer that?" she finally asked.

"Do you think I'm talking to you to answer my own questions, whore?" Wringer screamed. His body was pressed flat against hers. He knew he had to be crushing her.

"I forgot your question," she said in a whisper. She did not cry. Wringer knew she wanted to. He could see the tears brimming. Somehow Casey managed to contain them. *Strong whore, but I'll break you*, he thought.

"People don't expect much from a whore, do they?"

"I'm not sure what you mean," Casey said.

He continued to keep the knife his secret—for now, anyway. "Let me put it to you another way. If you had to wager a guess, what might be the one thing people expect most from you? Huh? Can you figure that one out?"

"Discreetness?" Casey asked. She sounded as if she might be gasping for air. It had to be hard to breathe with Wringer's weight on top of her.

"Good. Damned good. But no. Wrong answer. Try again," Wringer demanded.

"Great sex?"

Laughing, Wringer said, "Not even close. I don't think anyone expects great sex from a street corner slut. John's like me are just looking for a release and a tramp like you is where we find it. Try again."

The tears started. Her lips quivered. "I don't know," Casey said. "I don't know what you want. What do you want from me?"

"See, you're almost on the right path," Wringer informed her. "You're this close to the answer, but can't see it."

She started to cough. Breathing had to be getting more and more difficult the longer he stayed on top of her. He pictured her ribs snapping under his weight. She did not struggle—perhaps knew better—though Wringer was surprised at her passivity. Disappointed. He expected her to fight—to try and gouge out his eyes. He had prepared himself for that kind of scene. In a way, he wanted her to fight back.

"See, it's not what do I want from you, as much as what you gave to me." He showed her the knife.

"Ah, dear God, help me," Casey said, crying suddenly. "Don't do this to me. Please. Please, don't do this."

"It felt refreshing when I pulled up tonight and you remembered me. I was afraid I might have to remind you of who I was. So if you remember me, and you remember the last time we were together, then you must remember giving me a freaking venereal disease. So in answer to my initial question, 'What do you think people expect from a whore more than anything else?' The answer would be . . . as long as you don't mind me jumping in here with the answer . . . for them to be clean of diseases!"

Wringer raised himself up like a walrus, then stuck the blade into Casey's belly. He knew his behavior was highly psychotic. Shooting someone would be far less personal, less intimate and deranged than physically driving a blade into another human. It felt weird, yet riveting. Her flesh, though soft to the touch, resisted the sharp point of the blade when he pressed it against her skin. Only when he pushed hard, did the knife pierce the thick layers. It had a distinct sound, too—one Wringer would never forget. It sounded like a knife plunged into a crisp head of lettuce. Once inserted though, the blade slid and sliced smoothly, reminding him of cutting open a summer-ripe watermelon.

With her free hand, Casey clawed for Wringer's face. One fingernail scratched under his right eye, drawing blood. So Wringer twisted the blade in her gut. She arched her back, as if attempting to buck him off her, but Wringer knew it was only intense pain from the blade making her spasm with such strength. She reminded him of a Bronco, and this caused him to laugh at her. Aside from that futile movement, there was no fight in her. He removed the blade, and stuck her one more time.

He pulled the blade out and lay back on top of her. The warmth of her blood spilling from the wound excited him. He felt it, warm against his fleshy middle.

When she started gasping and moaning, he punched her in the head, knocking her out cold—that—or she passed out. Then, using the blade like a finger, he touched all of her, tracing every curve and exploring every orifice, leaving a blazing trail of split flesh as he did so.

Chapter 1

Thursday, January 10

Michael Buzzelli watched Jack Murphy look over the completed job application he had just handed in. Murphy, who owned Jack's Joint, kept an unlit cigarette between his lips. Michael thought Murphy might be the exact opposite of everything he was. While Murphy looked to be in his early sixties, Michael was just twenty-five. Murphy seemed to tower at six-one, since Michael was merely five-eight. Compared to Murphy's two-hundred-and-forty-pounds of fat, Michael weighed in at a lean one-eighty. Whereas Murphy's balding head was lined with wisps of thin gray hair, Michael wore his almond-colored hair closely shaved to his head, with a little extra at the bangs.

"I can work weekends," Michael blurted, not wanting to miss this opportunity. He thought Murphy might be losing interest. This job was important to him and he wanted Murphy to understand as much.

"That's good, kid. I need someone weekends. Nights mostly. See, but I'm talking about every Friday, Saturday, and Sunday night. Not just when you feel like coming in, know what I mean?" Murphy asked. "I had a guy here, lasted less than a month. He told me he could work weekends. I think he worked one Friday night, then called in sick all the other times."

"I wouldn't do that, sir," Michael said.

"Sir?" Murphy snorted and looked at a fat man sitting at the counter. "Sir," he repeated for the fat man's benefit. They both laughed.

Michael ignored them. "I can work all weekend long. All night."

"What about during the day?" Murphy asked.

"I can work Saturdays and Sundays during the day. Other than that, I can't." He had a day job at The Rochester City Chronicle. He had it listed on the application.

"Says here you have experience . . . four years?"

"In college, I worked thirty hours a week at a diner. I was the night manager within the first six months. I have my supervisor's number there as a reference. You can give him a call," Michael said.

"I just might do that," Murphy said without conviction. "I'm getting old, Michael. Too old for the kind of crap I have to put up with running this place at night, know what I mean? I can stomach it during the day, but I'm too tired to have to put up with it long into the night, every night, as well," Murphy said. He pulled a lighter out of his apron. He lit his cigarette. "Man's got to relax a little. I've been working hard all my life, and I'm ready to do a little relaxing."

"I can't blame you," Michael said.

"You can't blame me? Hell, boy, you don't have any idea what I'm even talking about," Murphy said. "What are you? Twenty, twenty-one?"

"Twenty-five, sir," Michael said, and again ignored the snickering exchanged between Murphy and the fat guy at the counter.

"Twenty, twenty-five, huh? Makes little difference."

Next came a long silence while Murphy smoked his cigarette and continued to stare at the application. "Well?" Michael finally asked.

"Job pays a dollar more than minimum wage, for starters, and seeing as tomorrow's Friday, I expect you to be here by ten." Murphy kept the cigarette between his lips, allowing the smoke to billow into his eyes. He did not blink away the smoke, as if his eyes were callused to it.

Michael held out his hand, and they shook on the deal. When he left, he felt good. Jack's Joint was a small diner on Lake Avenue, on the bottom floor of a vacant building. The structure resembled a plain dark red brick version of the hotel pieces found in the board game Monopoly—very nondescript. It was the fire engine red awning over the sidewalk with Jack's Joint scrawled in white cursive letters that brought attention to the place.

The thought of spending his weekends earning next to nothing did not bother Michael Buzzelli as much as it bothered his girlfriend, Ellen. They both worked more than forty hours a week now. Seeing each other was difficult enough already. Taking this second job, they both knew, would make seeing each other next to impossible.

Chapter 2

Friday, January 11

Murphy told Michael a few things before going home for the evening. "Be consistent. If you cook a burger and put two pickle slices on it, be damned sure every burger you make thereafter has two pickle slices on it. The menu ain't complicated. Most of the regulars order the same thing night after night, anyways. Soon enough, you won't even have to ask them what they want. Some of them you'll be able to set your watch by. I've never been robbed. There ain't no safe. Someone tries to rob the place, give them the cash out of the register. No big deal there, know what I mean?"

Michael knew what he meant. He found it hard to believe that Jack's Joint had never been robbed. The place had been around for as long as Michael could remember. The area was never considered a good or safe neighborhood.

Standing behind the counter, Michael tied a white apron around his waist while taking in everything surrounding him. The counter was L-shaped. It ran longest from east to west, then rounded at the front door, and went south some. There were eight booths along the wall with orange Formica seats and brown tables. Shabby green curtains hung over each of the three windows along the row of booths. Four tables, each with four chairs, separated the counter from the booths. In the one corner, near the door, stood a silent jukebox. In the other corner, at the end of the shorter run of counter length, sat two pinball machines next to a large window. They made noise—sounds to attract potential players. Murphy assured Michael he would get used to the games and not hear their constant rings and bells, but the sound of the pinball machines did not bother Michael in the least.

The fat guy who had been at the counter the other night was still sitting at the counter this evening, as if a permanent fixture. Michael lit a cigarette while watching the man sip his coffee and read the paper.

"Anything interesting in there?" Michael asked.

The man shrugged. "Hardly ever is."

"You think?" Michael asked. "I usually find some good stuff."

The fat guy put down his paper and stared at the new cook. "You read this today?"

"Some."

"And you found something interesting in it?" It was a challenge.

Tentatively, Michael reached over and picked up the fat guy's newspaper. Keeping his eyes on the man, Michael almost methodically flipped through the sections. The fat guy held his stare.

Michael laid the paper back down. "Right here."

The fat guy looked at the paper and smiled. "The funnies? That's what you found interesting?"

Michael leaned his elbows on a napkin dispenser and smiled. "Read 'em every morning. Every one."

The guy laughed and held out his hand. "I'm Fat Joe. It's a nickname that found me in high school. I never could shake it. Then one day, it sounds like some guy is calling me Fatso . . . but he's really saying Fat Joe. Say it fast enough, sounds like Fatso. So believe it or not, my nickname has a nickname. That's what most people call me . . . Fatso."

Shaking hands, Michael introduced himself. "Michael Buzzelli, and it's a pleasure to meet you, Joe."

"Nah, kid. It's all right. You call me Fatso. No disrespect taken. As a rule of thumb, my friends, that's what they call me.

Fatso."

Michael did not feel comfortable. Calling someone fatso made him uneasy. Regardless of the man's own testimony, Michael thought in doing so, he would sound rude.

"Know where that came from?" Fatso asked.

"Where what came from?"

"Rule of thumb . . . the expression. Any idea how it got started?" Fatso asked. When Michael shrugged, he continued. "In England, a long time back, they used to say that a husband could not beat his wife with anything wider than his thumb. Go figure. Rule of thumb . . . that's so funny."

"Maybe not for those women," Michael replied.

* * *

Fatso had retired from a post office job nearly five years ago. His wife had died a year later. They had no children. At fifty-nine, Fatso had suddenly found himself orphaned.

"What do you think of Old Man Murphy?" Fatso asked.

"Seems nice enough."

"He's a good man. Hard worker. Man never has a day off. Not that I can remember. Seven days a week the guy goes. He's had people like you before," Fatso said.

"People like me?"

"Yeah. You know? You come, you go. Hard to find dependable help these days." Fatso always made eye contact when he talked. Michael figured he liked being observant and aware of his surroundings.

"See what he's paying?" Michael asked, smiling.

"So why you here, then?"

"I need this job."

Nodding, Fatso said, "Man's got to do what a man's got to do."

"My father says that."

"Mine did, too."

Despite the cold temperature outside, Fatso sweated profusely. He was obese with a fat face highlighted by swollen looking eyes, a pug nose, and no sign of a chin bone. His neck resembled one large roll of flesh. The site of him left Michael feeling claustrophobic.

"You following that case, the prostitute murder story?" Michael asked. There had been some activity around Lyell Avenue the last few weeks. After Christmas, and day by day, the news coverage had become less and less.

"Hard not to. Casey used to stand right here on that corner," Fatso said. He motioned with his thumb over his shoulder, toward the street.

"So you knew her?"

Fatso shrugged. "Get to know most of them when you're here as often as I am."

Michael crushed out his cigarette in the ashtray near Fatso's coffee cup. "More coffee?"

"Yeah, sure. I ain't going nowhere soon."

Chapter 3

The place got busy for an hour before settling down. People came in and ordered a lot of take-out burgers with fries, or hot dogs with a bag of potato chips. Jack's Joint sold a lot of coffee to go.

"See that guy there? That's Marcus," Fatso said, while Michael topped off his coffee for the sixth time that evening.

Michael casually glanced at the guy in the smart black suit taking a seat in the last booth in the back of the place. Fatso had the low-down on everyone. Whenever someone entered, Fatso would spew off a synopsized biography.

Lighting a cigarette, Michael said, "He looks like a mobster, with the dark suit and the thin tie."

"I suppose he thinks he's in the mob," Fatso said. Though he spoke with an air of sarcasm, almost mocking, Michael thought he detected a trace of a tone of respect.

"Is he?"

"Like I said. Thinks he is. I can't say for sure, truthfully, but I wouldn't count on it. He's just a two-bit hood, you ask me." Fatso added a packet of sugar to his coffee and stirred it in. "He's here nearly as much as me. We nod hellos, very cordial, little else. We talked once."

"He always come in alone?" Michael asked.

"Usually comes in alone, not always. Different people come to see him. I hear he does . . . how would you put it . . . odd jobs?" Fatso said, questionably. Michael gave him a look indicating he did not understand.

"Let's say the neighbor's dog keeps crapping in your yard. You try over and over to get the dog's owner to keep the mangy mutt on a leash when they let him out. Try as you might, they don't listen and all the while your yard looks like crap and they have a lawn that could be featured on the cover of Better Homes and Gardens. With me so far?"

Michael nodded, getting the picture. "So maybe you visit with Marcus and explain to him about this problem you're having with the neighbor's pet . . ."

"You catch on quickly, Michael," Fatso said.

"Sounds like mob work."

"Taking out a dog? Get outta here." Fatso waved the comment off with a hoarse laugh. "Taking out a dog is not Mafia business, trust me."

Michael noticed Fatso's reaction. The tops of his ears reddened. "Was that the one time you talked to Marcus, when you told him about the neighbor's dog?"

"What the hell's with you, kid? Anyone ever warn you about minding your P's and Q's?" Fatso asked. "Huh?"

Michael knew he had just put his new friend on the defensive, so he held up his hands and backed away from the counter. "Don't blame me if I catch on quickly." He leaned closer and said more softly, "I ain't judging you, not by a long shot."

"Who the hell would care if you was judging me?"

"Fatso, you're telling me a story and I put one and one together. Your story might as well have started with you saying that you have this friend."

They stared at one another for several seconds before Fatso smiled. He reached across the counter and patted Michael on the cheek. "You're all right, Michael. You know that?"

Michael laughed and wiped his hands on the dishtowel slung over his apron's tie string. He stood up straight. "I like to think so."

"Hey, ever hear that one before . . . the thing I said about the

P's and Q's?" Fatso asked. Michael cocked his head to one side and raised his eyebrows, as if encouraging an explanation. "It's an English saying. They have all them pubs over there. Well, those English pubs sold beer . . . still sell beer, I'd imagine . . . in pints and quarts. You know how it is in bars. People get a little crazy and rude. The bartenders would tell the drunk rowdy patrons to mind their Pints and Quarts, P's and Q's."

The small bell jingled as the door opened. Michael was relieved some for the intrusion. He turned and was startled to see a beautiful woman enter. She had long natural-looking burgundy-red hair with big loose curls. Fiery. As she looked around Jack's Joint, Michael could not help but notice her large gray-blue eyes. The milky-white complexion made her striking hair and stunning eyes so much more visually vibrant. She entered Jack's slowly, almost cautiously, but with a level of comfort that suggested familiarity. She looked like she might only be nineteen years old.

"One of the whores," Fatso whispered a little louder than was necessary.

Michael, annoyed by the rude comment, went to the end of the counter. "Coffee?"

The woman with dark colored hair and penetrating eyes regarded Michael with an assessing stare. "Please," she said, finally, relinquishing a faint smile made with large lips under layers of lipstick that closely matched the color of her hair. "New here?"

From under the counter, Michael fumbled with a cup. "First night." He removed the pot of freshly brewed coffee from the warmer and filled the cup. He put out a napkin with a spoon. "Need a menu?"

She laughed. "You *are* new. Unless something's been added to Jack's delicacies, I think I can manage fine without one. But for now, the coffee's fine. Thanks."

She took the cup, spoon, and napkin and went to the first booth by the front window. She sat with her back to them, choosing to instead watch the traffic.

"Michael," Fatso said. "Come here a minute."

Michael did not realize he had been staring at the woman.

"What?"

"Not for nothing, kid. A word to you. Felicia . . . she's a prostitute. She makes her living screwing people. You don't want any of that. Don't let yourself get mixed up in that," Fatso said, pointing his thumb over his shoulder. "She may look good, kid, but she's pretty well used up."

"Thanks for the tip, Fatso. I don't mean to disrespect your opinion or nothing, but I don't see it that way," Michael said. "Anyway, you're talking like I'm about to fall in love with the girl. She just walked in. And you're right. She does look good. Beautiful. But I'm not here to get involved. Just looking to increase my income."

"Smart, kid. You're a smart kid. Look at the situation any way you want, but as long as you keep yourself clean, you'll do all right," Fatso said, smiling.

Monroe County possessed strict smoking laws. Jack's Joint allowed smoking. As the cook, Michael knew it would be against the law for him to smoke while behind the counter. Michael leaned his back to the wall and lit a cigarette anyway. This infraction was serious and Murphy could wind up in a lot of trouble, but during his interview, Michael watched Jack smoke while behind the counter. Monkey see, monkey do.

Though Felicia sat facing away from Michael, he watched her sipping coffee. Then, just before the door to Jack's opened again, he noticed her reflection in the front window. She appeared to be watching him, too.

Chapter 4

By two in the morning, Michael was feeling the effects of a long day. He knew working two jobs would not be easy. He planned to keep at it. Ambition and desire were the driving factors behind his need for a second job. He could endure this lifestyle for a given length of time. *How long might a given length of time be*? Michael hoped not too long.

"Tired kid?" Fatso asked, munching on the few remaining French fries. The burger had disappeared in large bites moments after the meal was set down in front of him. Now, using the fry like a mop, he sponged up the ketchup to clean his plate.

"Adjusting," responded Michael. With his hands on his hips, he leaned back and listened for the satisfying sound of a crack. When he heard it, he sighed. "Now that feels good."

"Sounds disgusting," Felicia said. Michael turned to see her sitting at the counter with an empty cup in her hand. As Michael refilled it, she removed a cigarette from a pack and placed it between her lips. She did not attempt to light it. She watched Michael as he set down the pot, then raised an eyebrow at him. Getting the point, Michael fished his lighter out and did the honors. Then he lit one for himself.

"My name's Felicia," she said.

"I'm Michael." He put out his hand.

She did not shake it. Instead she took a long drag on her cigarette and exhaled. "Michael. Not Mike, or Mikey?"

"Sometimes. I answer to any of those."

"And kid," Fatso added. "He answers to kid." He slid off the counter stool, then rolled his newspaper and tucked it under his arm.

"I'm pretty sure he's not a goat." Felicia looked over at Fatso, but did not smile. She turned her attention back on Michael—all smiles. "Enjoying your first night?"

"It's been all right, kind of boring," Michael said. "Been talking with Fatso, mostly."

"Thanks for the compliment, kid," Fatso said, reaching into his slacks for a wallet.

"I don't mean you're boring," Michael said, laughing. "You know what I meant."

"We know what you mean," Felicia said. "Don't we Fatso?"

"No offense taken. Still, this place has its moments," Fatso said, agreeing. "What do I owe you, kid?"

Michael gave him a check. Fatso paid and left a healthy tip. "Enjoy. It's big because it's your first night . . . and you put up with the likes of me longer than anyone should have to."

"I enjoyed talking with you," Michael responded, putting the cash into the register, his tip into the apron.

"Sure you did, kid. Sure you did. I'll see you tomorrow?"

"You say it like I might not be here," Michael said.

"You never know," Fatso said, pulling open the door and letting a gust of frigid cold air in. "Take care."

Michael felt the goose bumps appear on his arms. A sudden chill tingled its way down his spine. "Yeah, you too. I'll see you tomorrow night," Michael said, promising.

When the door closed, Felicia called Fatso a lard-ass.

"Why's that?" Michael asked.

"When he gets here tomorrow, ask what he does during the day."

"Do you know what he does during the day?"

"Sure I do," Felicia said. She had not looked away from Michael's eyes. Or he could not look away from hers. They captivated and demanded his attention.

“So why should I wait until tomorrow if you can tell me tonight?” Michael asked.

“It’s much more rich coming from him,” she said, then walked back to her booth where she resumed staring out the window. Their conversation ended.

Chapter 5

Martin Wringer hated his new job—hated everything about it. The foreman was an asshole. He seemed to be standing over Wringer's neck all night just watching him work, as if waiting for him to make a mistake. For a few dollars over minimum wage, screw it. He did not need it. Wringer knew he could find another job making the same crap pay, but with none of the management hassles.

"How those parts coming, Martin?" The foreman handed Wringer an envelope.

"Good, boss," Wringer responded. "What's this?"

"You're first pay check. For last week."

"Right, thanks," Wringer said, folding and sticking the envelope into his back pocket.

"I want to tell you, you're doing a very competent job, but some of the parts sent down the line are questionable. None of the parts have been rejected, mind you . . . but they're questionable. We'd appreciate if you could, maybe, just take a little more time double-checking the quality of your work. Your quantity is great . . . no problem there. You clip along like a pro. Still, the company strives to be recognized for the quality of its products. All right?"

"Sure boss. You want me to slow down and concentrate on the quality aspects of the job. We want these parts to last and last. If bad parts are assembled into the machines, and the machines crap out after a week of operation, customers will not be happy. The last thing we want is unhappy customers," Wringer said, tilting his head to one side and smiling. "So, if I focus my attention better, and build high quality assemblies, the machines might last a lifetime. Am I on your wave length here, boss?" Wringer asked. He noticed the odd look the foreman was giving him—the way he furrowed his brow and wrinkled his nose. "Did I misunderstand you?"

"No. No. You understood me," the foreman said. He backed slowly away from Wringer's workstation. As if forcing himself to smile, he said, "Keep it up, and thanks."

When the bells rang, signaling break time, Wringer took his coat and keys, and left the building, walking by the people forced to smoke outside. "Hey, where you headed?" Someone shouted.

Wringer did not respond. Why should he? He climbed into his van and pulled out of the parking lot without taking the time to brush the snow off his windows, and instead ran the windshield wipers on high. "Screw that place," he mumbled.

The digital clock on the dash displayed the time: 3:00 A.M.

More wound-up than tired, Wringer wondered how he might spend the day. In the deeper recesses of his mind, he knew he needed another job. For now he just needed a place to cash his paycheck and find an open liquor store.

Chapter 6

By three in the morning, Michael thought he might fall asleep standing up. He had hoped to talk more with Felicia. She spent most of the last hour in the back of the joint on the pay phone, while the rest of the place became empty. At some point, Marcus, the mob-wannabe, had slipped out. Though the man had left enough cash at the table to cover the bill and a generous tip, Michael felt slighted for not noticing the man leave. He knew he would need to become more observant.

The door opened and two women stumbled in, giggling obnoxiously. They staggered up to the counter. The one to Michael's left was an attractive black woman with a heavy layer of blue make-up covering her eyelids. The brows were drawn on. Her lips were full and alluring. When the woman smiled, all was lost. The incomplete rows of teeth, an even shade of Post-It yellow, stood crooked and uneven in her mouth. "Hey, sugar," she said. "I'm Vanessa. John's call me Venus. What do you want to call me, sexy?"

Michael smiled. He reached under the counter and produced two coffee cups. "Coffee, Vanessa?"

The other woman with Vanessa laughed and jokingly shouldered her friend. "Stuffed!"

"Stuffed, my ass," Vanessa said, attempting to produce a

seductive smile for Michael's benefit. "Night's young. And what is your name, cutie?"

"It's Michael," Felicia said. She was off the phone and making her way to the counter. "Not Mike or Mikey. Anyone calls him kid, and I'll knock 'em upside the head."

"Michael. Works fine for me. I'm Sandy," the other woman said. She wore her long stringy brown hair straight. It looked greasy and unwashed. Sandy's skin was pitted. Purple acne spotted her cheeks and forehead. She had thin colorless lips. The complete package made her look old, though Michael would guess Sandy to be in her early twenties.

"Coffee, Sandy?"

"Please."

"How about you, Felicia, more?" Michael asked.

"Nah. I'm set," she said, looking at the clock over the door.

"When'd you start? Tonight?" Vanessa asked Michael.

"First night," Michael answered.

"Like it?" Sandy asked, next.

"So far I do."

"That's what most of them says on their first night," Vanessa commented. "Murphy can't seem to keep any help behind his counters . . . not at night. Too much always going on. Last guy was stealing cash out of the register. Marcus caught on to the scam and told Murphy. You meet Marcus yet?"

"Meet him? Not really. He was here tonight. Left just before you ladies walked in," Michael pointed out.

"Ladies," Sandy snickered.

"Michael, you didn't meet Marcus, so how'd you know he was here?" Vanessa asked.

Before Michael could reply, the three women looked at each other. At the same time they said, "Fatso." They all broke down laughing.

Felicia sat at the counter next to Vanessa. "Still freezing out?"

"Hell yeah," Vanessa said. "I was down on Ambrose Street shivering my ass off like a damn fool. Made seventy dollars. I was out there since eleven. Damn. I had the last john drop me off here. No way I'm standing out there in this cold-ass weather."

"Don't know why you were in the first place," Sandy said. She hooked a finger onto an ashtray and slid it close as she lit a cigarette. "After December, the weather is too unpredictable to be standing out in it. Tonight's a perfect example. We ain't going to make anything."

"Says you," Felicia said. To Michael, she said, "You know how witches have a witching hour, midnight? We have hours, too. It's between the hours of three and seven in the morning. See . . . bars close at two. The johns spend another hour debating if they want to pick up a whore or just go home and sleep it off . . . you know? And, in the winter, anyway, it's still pretty dark up until seven. While some johns are going to work they enjoy a little before the workday starts, it's almost like how some of us need a cup of coffee before we can function properly. See what I'm saying?"

Michael just nodded. The candid talk around their profession shocked him. He may have secretly hoped for it, but did not expect it. Wanting to become a "star reporter" for The Rochester City Chronicle one day, he knew meeting people and hearing them talk would enhance his insight. He would be able to generate compelling articles. He had questions, but kept quiet. Being a good listener was one of the affable qualities he proudly possessed.

"Yeah, I better at least bring in another hundred and thirty bucks, or this Friday night was a total waste," Vanessa said.

Sandy quietly sipped her coffee, ignoring Vanessa's complaint.

Michael chewed on the numbers. Vanessa expected to make two-hundred-dollars tonight. Twenty-five an hour. Aside from standing in the cold between jobs, how much time did she spend actually "working" for the money? To boot, the money earned was tax-free.

Felicia sat with her back to the counter. Sandy stared at the counter. Vanessa chewed on her lower lip and looked around Jack's Joint anxiously. Michael just tried to blend with the background, smoking a cigarette.

He could not help but wonder about what might be passing through their minds. Could they all just be enjoying the break before business picked up? Did they wish they could be doing something else with their lives, instead? Did they fear going back out on the streets because their friend Casey had been viciously murdered by a customer?

Vanessa broke the silence. “I’m gonna use the bathroom and then I’m going to work. I can’t afford to be sitting around with you all. Love all of you and all that, you know, but I’m not here for the company,” she said, smiling and touching both Sandy and Felicia on their shoulders. “Unless Michael . . . you want to take me for a ride?”

“Don’t get paid until next Friday,” he said, smoothly, shrugging his shoulders in mock-defeat.

“Uh-huh. Fine thing like you? You can test drive Venus for free. Think about it,” she said as she made her way to the restrooms in back.

Sandy let out a quick short laugh. Felicia was grinning. “What’s so funny?” Michael asked.

Sandy and Felicia laughed out loud.

“What?” Michael asked again.

“Just trying to imagine what a free test drive with Venus might be like,” Felicia explained.

“Same here,” Sandy said, still laughing. When Venus returned, the laughing only grew louder and more intense. Immediately the black prostitute knew the joke was on her. She acted tough and shrugged it off. Without a word, she took her purse from the counter and sauntered outside. Once she was gone, and to Michael’s disbelief, the laughter reached an even greater intensity. He found himself laughing right along as loud as the others by that point.

When a van pulled up to the curb, he watched Vanessa climb in. He assumed she would be taking the frustration out on her john. Shaking his head, Michael went about his business of topping off coffee with freshly brewed hot coffee.

Chapter 7

Getting a second wind at six, and with only an hour to go, Michael knew he would make it. He could hardly wait to get home and climb into bed. He was not used to being on his feet all night. Imagining how it would feel to remove his sneakers brought a smile to his face while he washed down the counter top.

A few people had wandered in, ordering breakfast, filling the booths along the window.

It closely resembled midnight outside. The sky looked black. The streetlights, still on, cast an iridescent glow that accentuated the large puffy falling snowflakes. Glancing out the window, now and then, Michael saw Felicia work the corner. Coming and going and coming again and he wondered how close Vanessa would come to meeting or exceeding her monetary goal before seven a.m.

When the door opened, Michael expected to see Felicia, or perhaps, wanted to see her coming in out of the cold. Instead, a young rail-thin black man entered, flashing a wide grin and revealing two rows of the straightest whitest teeth Michael had ever seen before.

"Man it's cold outside. Capitol C, cold. Know what I could go for?" the man said, clapping his hands and vigorously rubbing them together to generate warmth.

"Nice hot cup of Murphy's coffee?"

"Murphy's coffee. You're funny. Nah, I'm in the mood for a Coke. Can I please have a large Coke with very little ice? I ain't paying for ice. I'm paying for Coke. If the Coke's warm, I'll fill the glass with some snow. You see what I'm saying? You put two scoops of ice in the glass and there's no room for the Coke. I won't pay the price Murphy charges for a large Coke when three quarters of the cup is ice. You see what I'm saying? So a Coke . . . some ice . . . not a lot of ice . . . some ice . . . got it?"

Smiling, Michael filled the order and set the glass down on the counter before lighting a cigarette. "Hungry?"

"Could eat a cow. You new here, huh? What's your name?"

"Michael." They shook hands.

"Mike, huh? Great. You cook?"

"But of course," Michael said, and bowed in a most gracious mockery. "Hamburger and fries?"

"Damn, Mike. It's six in the morning, you know. Six A.M. Burger and fries? Man, I don't think so. Stomach can't handle that this early. No, I'll take three eggs. Two scrambled, one over easy. Two strips of bacon. Well done. I hate those strips of white flabby fat along the sides of bacon. I see that, I can't eat a bite of the stuff. My appetite will be ruined."

"Got it," Michael said.

"Wait, man. Mike, that isn't it. I'd also like two sausage links and a side of hash browns. Have wheat bread? Nah, never mind. Rye. That would be perfect."

Michael checked the bread. "I don't see rye. We have wheat."

"No. I always say wheat, but what I mean is rye. And Murphy knows it, but orders the wheat instead. All right, forget about it. I'll have a burger roll. Slice it, butter it up good and thick, and grill the bread. You know, make a hard roll out of it?"

"I can do that," Michael said and could not help but smile. He liked this man. The guy had an inspiring and upbeat personality. His eyes looked wide, bright, and clear, so he did not think the man was on drugs. He seemed to be soaring on more of a personal high, as if he might actually enjoy life. "What did you say your name was?"

Stopped cold, the guy said, "I didn't. Why?"

Michael sensed sudden tension build between them. "Just being friendly," Michael said, cracking a shell on the side of a bowl. He dumped the egg into it, then added another.

Without staring, Michael casually watched as the black man laughed and shook his shoulders. "Mike, man, I don't know why I jumped on you like that."

"What jumped? Forget about it."

"You know what people call me? I mean if you had to guess what people called me, what kind of nickname might I have. It's pretty easy. An obvious choice, if you ask me. Got an idea? Go on ahead and give it a shot. What do you think people call me?"

Michael smiled as he flipped over the egg frying on the pan. "I don't know . . . No-Dose?"

The man slapped the counter. "No-Dose, I like it. That's a good one. Funny and fitting. Close, but no, man. No, Mike, they call me Speed."

Michael put out his hand. "A pleasure, Speed. And you're right. The name is fitting."

Without letting go of Michael's hand, and while tightening the grip between them, Speed asked, "Are you a cop?"

The smile was gone from Speed's face. His large brown eyes seemed to grow larger. He stared intently at Michael. "See, if you are, Mike, you have to tell me. The law says so. When someone asks, and you're a cop, you have a legal obligation to say so. So I'm asking, are you a cop or a police officer? Do you work for the FBI, CIA, or any other branch of the government that deals in any kind of law enforcement? Do you . . ."

"Speed, whoa! I'm not a policeman, or a cop. I do not work for the FBI or the CIA. I do not like green eggs and ham. I do not like them. Sam I am," Michael said.

Speed seemed to regard Michael for a long moment. "You're funny, Mike. You're a real funny guy."

When Michael served up Speed's order, he said, "Enjoy."

Michael poured a cup of coffee for himself, lit a cigarette, and went to the end of the counter. He did not want to smoke near Speed while he ate.

"Hey Mike," Speed said. He waved him over.

Reluctantly, Michael left his cigarette burning in an ashtray where he'd been standing and walked down to stand in front of Speed. "Need something?"

"Kidding? Everything tastes great. I mean great. No, what I was going to say was, you ever need anything, you let me know."

"Like what?" Michael asked.

"Like, anything. Because, you ain't a cop right?"

"Told you, I'm not a cop."

"Exactly. So I got things like car stereos speakers, clothing, jewelry . . . anything. Got kids? I can get you the latest video game system. Stores can't even keep them on the shelves. The demand is greater than the supply, you know? Those digital places do that kind of thing on purpose. They make like two hundred systems and tell the world about it. They get orders for millions and then jack up the prices until they eventually flood the market. But I got two, brand new and still packed fresh in their boxes. So if you need one for your kids, you let me know," Speed said, slopping his toast in the yolk of the over-easy egg.

"No kids, but thanks Speed. I'll keep the offer in mind," Michael said.

"You do that," Speed said and went back to devouring his breakfast with the same amount of energy he used for talking.

Chapter 8

Saturday, January 12

Michael slept the whole day away, waking up after eight. He could not help but question his motives for wanting to work two jobs. His first night went well, in retrospect, and he enjoyed meeting an array of people.

While showering, he thought of Felicia. He knew women did not just become prostitutes for the sake of becoming them. Assuming each had a unique story, Michael decidedly wanted to hear whatever tale Felicia might have to tell.

Knowing most people were private people, getting Felicia to open up would take some doing. He could not imagine her reasons for choosing her profession, but felt intrigued at the prospect of finding out.

Of course, Sandy and Vanessa were not to be ignored. In truth, he wanted to hear stories from them all. In time, he hoped to have an inside line to each of them, including Speed and Fatso. Marcus might make the most fascinating person of them all—so quiet and sneaky. Michael wondered about any existing mob ties.

Most people thought the Italian Mafia was dead and gone. It was not. It just wasn't as active as it had been back in the 1960's, 70's, and 80's when the Rochester Mafia was home to the likes of Joe Bonanno, Stefano Magaddino, the Luccheses,' and Sammy

G—the Hammer. At some point Michael entertained the idea of writing a book based on those historically infamous characters.

Michael dressed in jeans and a white T-shirt, then sat down at his computer. He typed up three pages of notes. He used a bulleted list under each name, then saved his work. He received a message informing him that Ellen was on-line and wanted to chat.

He turned on his messenger and typed, "Hey, Ellen."

"Where have you been?" she wrote back, her message instantly appearing on his monitor. Ellen and Michael had met at a college party. He had been a senior at the State University of New York at Brockport, while she had been visiting from SUNY Buffalo, where she was a law student. They hit it off immediately, and had been dating ever since. She lived in Spencerport, a village on the outskirts of Rochester, while Michael lived in Greece, a large suburb. They were maybe eight miles away from each other.

"Sleeping," he typed back. "Why?"

"I've been calling. No one answers. I keep getting the machine."

Michael looked at the answering machine. He had no new messages. "Did you leave a message?"

"No. I hate talking to those things."

"I had the ringer off. I didn't want to be disturbed," he typed.

"I would be disturbing you?"

"The ringing of the phone would."

"Even if it were me?" she wrote back. "Want to get together?"

"I have to leave for work in a little while."

"I don't like you working two jobs," Ellen wrote.

"We talked about this."

"CORRECTION. You talked about this." She wrote "correction" in capital letters to imply that she was yelling.

"I need to do this," Michael wrote. "And I have to get going."

"When can we see each other next?"

"I'm not sure. Monday?"

Ellen wrote, "MONDAY????? How about dinner at TANTALO'S?"

"Six?"

"See you then."

Michael switched off the computer. Deciding he would cook something to eat at Jack's Joint, Michael left the apartment with two fresh packs of cigarettes in his coat pocket.

Michael's car had at least four inches of heavy snow on it. He used a gloved hand to brush away the snow on his door. He found the lock, and inserted his key. The wind had a bite in it. It gnawed at Michael's ears and cheeks. He started his car, and while the windshield defroster tried to melt the ice on the glass, Michael used a brush and scraper to assist in cleaning off the accumulation.

* * *

Jack's Joint offered limited parking in the rear. Michael pulled into the tiny lot, parking in between the large green Dumpster and Murphy's car. He turned off the engine, got out of the car, locked the doors and rang the bell by the back door. Murphy kept the back door locked. Aside from Murphy's own keys, a spare was inside, under the register.

With his shoulders hunched forward, and his hands stuffed into his coat pockets, Michael wondered what the temperature might be. It felt colder today than in the past several weeks. Though he had only been standing by the door a few seconds, he literally felt nose hairs freezing.

Murphy opened the door with a smile. His apron was covered in grease. "Come on in, come in," he said, stepping aside.

"It's freezing out there," Michael said.

"And packed in here. You're going to have a busy night."

"I can handle it," Michael said, enjoying the heat in the diner.

"From what I hear, you did pretty well last night."

"It was a good first night," Michael said, curious about who might have provided Murphy with a progress report. He suspected Fatso, but, at least for now, decided to let it go. "I met a lot of interesting people."

"Ah, and there are still so many more interesting people to meet," Murphy said. "I guarantee it. Listen, it's not quite time for your shift to start, but I was planning to have dinner with a lady friend tonight . . ."

"Mr. Murphy, are you asking me for permission to leave early?" Michael said.

"Hardly. I'm just telling you that as soon as you strap on a clean apron, I'm out of here," Murphy said, hardening his shell, after an exposed moment of softness.

Michael smiled, shrugging out of his coat. He hung it up on a hanger, tied a clean apron around his waist, and transferred his cigarettes to the apron's pouch. "Mr. Murphy, I'm all set."

Jack Murphy laughed, undid his own apron, and put on his coat. "I'll see you in the morning. Oh, in the middle booth are a couple of teenagers. They've been good, sipping coffee for a while. If they get loud or anything, I want you to throw them out. I know them, they're good kids, but sometimes they get loud, you know? Be nice about it, but don't take any of their crap. Got it? And, if they sit too long, throw them out. This is a business. Not a coffee shop. If I have a customer who comes in and wants to eat, and there is no where for him to sit . . . and some guys have a booth for several hours with little more than a few bucks on their tab . . . hear what I'm getting at?"

"Loud and clear," Michael said.

He pushed through the swinging door and stared in awe at the mass of people gathered in booths, at the tables, and sitting at the counter. There had to be at least thirty people in Jack's Joint. Even after sleeping like a rock, Michael suddenly felt exhausted. "Holy crap."

Chapter 9

The heat from the grill worked to warm Michael's bones. He knew after being outside scraping ice off his car and then waiting for Murphy to let him in the back door, it would take a while to thaw his bones. He thought he would never warm up.

The orders came in fast. Hamburgers, hot dogs, chili and French fries. Those were the top items being ordered. While things grilled, he filled coffee cups. While he cooked, he tried to be mindful of who was in the place. He did not want to let someone skip out without paying a bill. He saw no way to prevent it from happening, if someone decided to do so. So far, people were paying.

Michael kept an eye on the two teens in the center booth. Both were white, and big. They looked like football players. He watched them now and again. Each time, the teens seemed engrossed in conversation. They animatedly talked, using hand gestures. Here were two young guys hanging out, drinking coffee and staying out of trouble. He saw no reason to throw them out into the cold, even if they were nursing coffee and taking up customer space.

Michael glanced out the front window. Sandy, with her long, straight hair, stood with one hand in her pocket. The other cupped a cigarette to her lips. She noticed Michael and waved. He waved back.

"Can I get more coffee?" a man at the counter asked.

Michael filled it, and many other cups as well. Eventually, the place became less and less crowded. Soon enough, only small groups of people remained. At midnight, Fatso came in. He looked happy, wearing a big smile. He sat at the same stool he sat at the night before. He set his paper down on the counter. "How are you, kid? Sorry I'm late."

Without being asked, Michael poured a cup of coffee for Fatso. In a stern, yet playful voice, Michael said, "We're still going to have to dock your pay."

Fatso laughed. "Dock my pay? You're funny, kid."

"Fatso, you're free to come and go as you please. I'll do my best to save a stool for you," Michael said. He lit a cigarette, then put a hot dog for himself on the grill.

"Yeah, well, I passed by earlier and didn't see a place to sit," he said, explaining why he was "late ."

"When I walked in, the place was hopping. You know, for your benefit, you might want to consider calling ahead for a reservation." Michael put a slit down the center of his dog, and toasted his bun roll. "Quieter now."

"Cold nights. People don't want to be home . . . they come here."

Michael thought of what Felicia said. She wanted him to ask Fatso why he spent so much time here at night. "So what do you do during the day?"

"Sleep," Fatso said, adding sugar and cream to his coffee.

Michael waited.

"I sleep most of the day," Fatso said with a shrug. "I do whatever running around needs doing, don't get me wrong. Like, I go to the bank and doctor visits. Since I've retired, and since I don't have any family, there isn't anything to do really. I like it here. I like the people and the excitement here. Once in a while I show up for breakfast or lunch . . . especially on days where I know I'll be driving all over the city. But the nights here are so much more interesting than they are during the day. Murphy's got his day clientele, who I find boring, but his night customers . . . well, they're another story all together. I could stay home and watch television at night, but what's the point? This is real here, kid. I love it," Fatso said.

Michael wasn't sure he'd agree with Felicia about Fatso's "story." Fatso had an interesting explanation, but it left Michael feeling sorry for the man. His life had been reduced to something just short of pathetic.

"Feel like making me up a burger and fries?"

Michael stubbed out his cigarette and slapped a hamburger patty onto the grill. "Coming right up."

While eating his hot dog, Michael was aware of the fact that Felicia had not shown up. He had to admit he was looking forward to seeing her again. Yes, he wanted to hear about the road to prostitution, but he also wanted to hear about her.

He found it odd and a little disturbing to think he might have feelings for a woman like Felicia. He tried not to think of her as a whore. He did not even care for the term prostitute.

When the door to Jack's opened, he looked up expectantly. Sandy entered, hugging herself. She shivered so hard that her teeth chattered loudly. "I'm freezing so bad. I'm so cold," she said. She sat at the counter near the door.

"Slide down here, away from the door," Fatso said. "Heat from the grill will warm you up some."

"Good idea," she said, moving down a few stools.

The two teenagers stood up and put on their coats.

Marcus entered. He wore his, apparently traditional, long black winter coat over a black suit. While the two teens paid their bill, Marcus stood behind them.

As they left, Marcus placed an order.

"I'll bring the pop over to you," Michael said.

"Thank you," Marcus said. "I'd appreciate that."

"Not a problem."

"Felicia been by?" Sandy asked.

"Not yet," Michael said, then cringed. He knew he had responded too quickly, too anxiously.

Fatso laughed. He did not seem to miss anything. "Can't follow advice, can you son?"

"You the one giving the advice?" Sandy asked. To Michael,

she said, “Then you’re better off, Michael.”

“Let me ask you something,” Fatso said. “You been a prostitute how long?”

Sandy shrugged while lighting a cigarette. “Since I was sixteen.”

“How old are you now?”

“None of your business,” Sandy retorted. “Where are you going with this?”

“In the years you’ve spent as a working girl, how many serious relationships have you had?” Fatso crossed his arms over his chest. He seemed eager to hear Sandy’s reply. Michael knew immediately what point was being made. Still, he waited.

“Two. Maybe three.”

“Two. Maybe three, you say. These relationships . . . were you monogamous in them?” Fatso asked.

“I still worked,” Sandy said.

Michael cocked his head to one side. “Did these guys know what you did for a living?”

“It’s how I met each of them,” Sandy said, somewhat deflated. “And you know what, Fatso? You can go screw yourself.”

Fatso held up two hands, as if he were backing off. “All I’m trying to tell the kid is not to get involved emotionally.”

“With who? Felicia?” Sandy asked, looking at Michael. “I think they’d be cute together.”

“Murphy’s only paying him a few cents more than minimum wage,” Fatso pointed out. “How long could ‘cute’ last on that type of income? Twenty . . . thirty minutes a week . . . tops?”

“You’re a pig,” Sandy said. “Asshole.”

Michael went around the counter and set Marcus’ drink on the table with a straw. “There you are.”

“Thank you, Michael.”

Michael did not think it odd that Marcus knew his name, but wondered why the man used it when they hadn’t been formally introduced. “Food will be right up,” Michael said.

Chapter 10

When Felicia showed up at Jack's Joint, she and Sandy sat at the front booth, side by side, staring out at the street through the window. Michael watched them, watching their faces in the reflection. They were talking quietly. At any given moment, Michael would have sworn that he might have been the topic of their discussion. He could almost slap Fatso for embarrassing him.

"You know, Fatso," Michael said, scraping down the grill, "I never once expressed an interest in Felicia."

"Sure you did," Fatso said casually.

"I did not. In fact, I resent you bringing that up to Sandy."

"Resent it? Why? All I did was ask her some questions, you know?"

"You did more than that. You almost flat out told her I wanted a date with Felicia."

"And don't you?"

"I don't. No," Michael said. He stopped scraping, and put his hands on his hips.

"Not very convincing, kid. Not at all."

"Well, for your information, I don't need to convince you of anything." Michael lit a cigarette and poured himself a soda and drank some from a straw.

"They're people, just like you and me, but different," Fatso said. "They are less fortunate, if you think about it."

"And what's that supposed to mean?" Michael asked. He wanted to sit down. It had already proven to be a long night, and it was not even one in the morning yet. He knew if he sat, it would be hard to get back up again.

"Look, I don't think these women are capable of being in a relationship . . . in the kind of relationship that you and I might consider genuine. Only way I see it happening is, if some rich guy picks them up and never drops them off again. Like in that movie about that rich guy, the one with Julia Roberts," Fatso said.

"Pretty Woman," Michael said.

"That's the one. See? But that was a fairytale. Things like that don't happen everyday, I'll bet my ass it never happens to whores. What guy in his right mind is going to want to get serious and settle down with some hooker?"

"So what was your point?"

"I feel bad for them," Fatso said. He sounded more sincere than Michael could have thought possible. "Hey, I do. I razz them, you know, but I still feel bad for them. I know what my wife and I had . . . that was special. When she died, a large part of me went with her. A large part. I can't imagine anyone else ever being able to fill that emptiness inside me. But I will tell you this, kid, from the bottom of my heart, that old saying 'it's better to have loved and lost, than never to have loved at all?' It's true. It's so true, and that . . . that is why I feel bad for these girls. They will never experience the kind of love and warmth and intimacy that I experienced with my wife."

Michael stared at Fatso, thoughtfully. He would never have expected such sensitivity. Fatso's perception was deep, touching, and heartfelt. "Good point."

Michael took the pot of coffee off the burner and filled customer coffee cups on his way over to where Felicia and Sandy were sitting. "Can I top off your cups?"

They nodded, smiling. The smiles looked curious and mischievous, but Michael ignored the feeling and just smiled back as he filled their cups. He wanted to say something to them. After what he and Fatso had been talking about, he could not help but feel sad for them, too. Instead, he turned and went back to the counter. As he walked, he heard the ladies giggling.

The door opened, and a gust of wind entered ahead of two large men in Halloween masks. One mask resembled the Grim Reaper. It was a black hood with a black mesh face guard. The mesh was thick enough that Michael could not see through it. The other person wore a rubber mask shaped like a baseball, with oversized goggle-eyes on the seams of the ball. Everyone in Jack's Joint immediately recognized the situation for what it was—a robbery.

Michael saw the guns in their hands and felt his heartbeat increase rapidly. The tiny fist-sized organ slammed wildly behind his chest. Could it explode? The fulminating sound of it thudding and pounding into his ribcage rhythmically boomed like thunder in his ears. He felt as if his head might be swelling.

The gunmen pointed their guns at Michael. It was obvious what they wanted. "What do you want?" Michael asked.

"Empty the register," Reaper said, tossing Michael a dark knapsack. "Fill it with everything in there."

Michael could not see clearly. He blinked hard, hoping to wash away the blurry vision as his fingers stuttered over the keys on the cash register.

"Sit back down!" Baseball shouted at someone who attempted getting up. "Anybody moves, we'll blow your head off!"

"Fill it," Reaper said.

Michael felt captivated by the unfolding scene. He found the right key on the register and hit it. The thing chimed as the money drawer slid open. The allotted slots were full. It would have been a good night for Murphy. Reluctantly, Michael began to fill the bag.

"This should take seconds," Reaper said, aggravated. He pushed the barrel of his gun into Michael's chest, knocking him backwards. Then, with his other hand, he grabbed the money out of the slots and stuffed them into the knapsack himself.

Baseball addressed the crowd. "Put your wallets and purses onto the tables. Now!" No one moved. "I mean now!" Slowly, people put belongings on the tables. Everyone, Michael noticed, except for Marcus. He watched the scene unfold with arms crossed and an amused look on his face.

Great. The place has never been robbed and here it is only my second night on the job, Michael thought, as Reaper, the man with the knapsack, went to the tables and collected the items. At Felicia's table, the man stopped. "Where are your purses?"

"We don't carry them," Sandy said. "So get lost."

Obviously taken aback, Reaper appeared stunned. He flipped the gun around in his hand with a flick of his wrist. Holding the barrel of the gun, he moved to strike Sandy with the butt.

"Stop right there, and throw your gun down," Marcus said. He had a gun drawn and aimed at the Reaper. The gunman looked too startled to move. Michael wished he could see through the masks. He would have loved to see the expression on the man's face.

"Screw you, mister," Baseball said. He pointed his gun at Marcus. "Drop your gun or I'll put a bullet in your head."

Ignoring the man who made the threat, Marcus walked toward the front booth where the Reaper still stood poised as if ready to strike Sandy. "I said throw your gun down."

Baseball walked around a table and stood behind Marcus. This did not seem fair. In one of the customer's laps Michael saw a cell phone. The person had it on. Michael did not think cell phones could be traced. Hopefully they had dialed 9-1-1, and the police were listening.

Michael took a chance. "Look," he said, loud and clear, but not so loud as to be obvious that something might be up. "This is Jack's Joint, you know? The place has never been robbed before. The both of you have all the money . . ."

"Shut the hell up!" Baseball said, turning and aiming his gun at him. "Shut up. Just shut up!"

Marcus moved like a bolt of lightening, spinning around and chopping the gun out of Baseball's hand. He stepped on the man's foot with the heel of his shoe. Marcus boxed Baseball's head, slapping his palms against Baseball's ears. Baseball covered his ears and began screaming. The sound came out muffled. Marcus turned back on Reaper, who seemed to be watching in disbelief as the robbery began to fail miserably.

Reaper tucked the gun away, slung the knapsack over his

shoulder and backed up toward the door, as Michael heard sirens approaching.

Baseball seemed still to be in agony, and wearing the mask had to be driving him crazy. He ran for the door, though, knocking his thigh into the corner of a table. The table shifted, and Baseball grunted. Reaper opened the door and ran out with Baseball close behind him.

Michael went around the counter and to the front door in a hurry. Everyone else seemed frozen in place. One of the police cars did not slow as it came upon Jack's Joint. Perhaps having seen two men run across the street and around the corner, the driver must have decided to follow them as possible suspects.

The other car switched off the siren, kept its lights flashing, and pulled alongside the curb. The police officer on the passenger side had the window down. "Was that them?"

"Yes, the two of them. They were wearing masks. One has a gun for sure," Michael said, describing the masks. The driver of the police car talked into his radio.

"We'll be back. Have everyone stay. No one leaves," the police officer said. The squad car pulled away from the curb and turned back on the siren as it joined pursuit.

Chapter 11

"Where are you going? You can't leave," Michael said.

Marcus just smiled. Everyone in Jack's Joint remained silent. "What the hell you mean, I can't leave?"

"I mean, that police officer just told me not to let anyone leave." It came out sounding like a challenge. Michael deeply regretted his choice of words. He watched the expression on Marcus' face change. It went from a slightly annoyed look to a, "you better get the hell out of my way" look.

Michael stepped aside. "Marcus . . ."

"How do you know my name, Michael? Huh? Just how in the hell do you know my name? I never told you my name, did I? You never asked me my name, did you?" Marcus poked at Michael's chest with his finger. "You know my last name? Do you?"

"No. I . . ."

"So how do you know my first name?"

Michael could have asked him the same question. It would make him slick smart-ass, though, and he was not about to say Fatso provided a synopsis on most everyone walking through Jack's doors. "I heard someone call you that, maybe."

Marcus laughed. "The hell you did. I've been sitting alone the two nights you been here. No one talked to me at all. I've ordered food, but other than that . . ."

Marcus looked across the room and stared intently at Fatso.

Damn, no one here wants anyone else to know their name; Michael thought about the way Speed had reacted when they introduced themselves the other night.

"I'll tell you what, Michael. Forget you know my name, and forget I was even in here tonight. Got it? And that goes for all of you," Marcus said, addressing everyone in Jack's Joint. "Nobody saw me in here tonight, see what I'm saying?"

Marcus left.

Fatso let out a long sigh. "Man I thought he was going to pop you, kid."

Sandy stood up. "I got to use the john."

Felicia slid slowly out of the booth. "Are you all right?"

Michael smiled. "Me? I was just about to ask you the same thing."

"I'm fine. Those guys weren't going to shoot anyone," Felicia said. She smoothed her skirt against her thighs with the palms of her hands. Michael could not help but watch. He liked her legs—long tone and smooth looking.

"Maybe they weren't going to shoot, but Sandy there came this close to getting pistol whipped," Michael said, holding his thumb and finger close together.

"Yeah. That was a little unnerving," Felicia said. "But what was the big deal with Marcus? I've never seen him so uptight before."

Fatso, still sitting at the counter, said, "He was acting a little weird."

"Why would he want to leave? I mean, he handled two robbers . . . saved the money. And look at this," Michael said, bending over to pick up the gun Baseball dropped.

"Freeze," two policemen yelled at the same time from the front door. They had weapons drawn and aimed at Michael.

Michael dropped the gun and put his hands up in the air.

* * *

Murphy parked in front of his restaurant, behind the two police cars. He walked into Jack's Joint wearing flannel, navy blue and maroon red plaid pajamas under his winter coat. His gray wisps of hair spiked out of his head with static electricity as he pulled off his wool cap.

Michael sat on a counter stool between the two officers, and gave the owner an acknowledging nod. Murphy stood silently by the doorway and listened as the police officers talked with Michael. Most of the people in the place were questioned first. They all seemed to tell the truth, but when it came time to talk about Marcus' roll in foiling the robbery, they became nondescript. Michael was doing the same thing now. "Yeah, I'd never seen the guy in here before. It's my second night," he said.

"But what did he look like?" one of the officers asked.

"I really can't recall."

"Was he short?"

"He could have been."

"Tall?"

"Sounds right," said Michael.

"In relation to the robbers, you saw them, right?"

"I saw them. They were big, strong-looking guys." Michael's mind replayed the robbery in slow motion. "I could even identify their voices, I'd bet."

"That's good. That's great," the police officer said. "Now you're telling me that this mystery man was sandwiched between the two of them. He karate chops the gun out of one guy's hand, steps on his foot, boxes his ears, and then scares the hell out of the other guy without touching him?"

"Right," Michael said.

"And you can see this in your mind?"

"Clearly."

"Think hard, now. In relation to the robbers, would the guy in the middle be taller than them, or smaller?" The police officer asked, sounding hopeful.

"I'm not sure," Michael said.

"Damn," the other police officer said, closing his notebook.

"Hey, I have a question," Michael asked. "Did the officer at dispatch hear me say the name Jack's Joint? Is that how they knew where to send you guys?"

"Yes and no. The person who dialed nine-one-one and left an open line on their cell phone was smart. It's a lot harder to trace a cell phone, but it can be done. Satellites make it easier. We were zeroing in on the transmission. Then the officer heard your tip and dispatched two units. You and the lady with the phone did nice work," the police officer said, smiling.

Murphy introduced himself, and the police talked with him for a while by the counter.

"We're going to need to take the knapsack with your money in it, and the wallets and purses. It's all evidence. The other officers apprehended two suspects we believe may be responsible for the attempted robbery, and attempted assault," the police officer said. He looked at Michael. "Tomorrow, first thing in the morning we'd like you to come down and file a complaint and maybe look at a line up."

"I can do that. I'll come right from here," Michael said. He walked away then, letting the officers go back to talking to Murphy.

Fatso sat in the booth Marcus seemed always to sit in. He had his coffee and newspaper with him. Another couple sat at a table near the back of the room, by the payphones. Sandy and Felicia sat at their front booth, in opposite sides this time, facing one another. Michael went outside and lit up a cigarette.

He propped a foot up behind him, placing it on the building, and leaned back. It was freezing outside, but he thought he could use the fresh air. The sky looked brilliant with the stars and moon standing out, highly visible in the pitch-black heavens. His breath mixed with smoke when he exhaled, and it all blew away with the wind, reminding Michael of an old train. Childish as it may seem, he pictured his mouth as the smokestack on the train's engine. Chug-a-chug-a-choo-choo!

"No coat?" Felicia asked. She leaned against the building next to him. "Your arm is covered in goose bumps." She ran her hand down his arm.

Her touch felt electrifying. Michael watched her as she stared at the goose bumps on his arm. "I just wanted some fresh air. I've never been in a situation like that. I ran through a gauntlet of emotions. I guess right now I feel a little shaken up and overwhelmed."

"I can't blame you," Felicia said. Michael had his hand in his pocket. After running her palm over the goose bumps, she latched her arm around his and snuggled in close, like a cat trying to get warm.

Michael was not sure what to do. He did not know how to interpret her behavior. This, hanging out with a prostitute, was something entirely new in his life. It was hard not to couple Felicia's work with her person. Yet, he did not want her to let go of his arm. "How about you? You don't even seem upset."

"I'm not," Felicia said. "Tonight? That wasn't so bad. I've been in situations much grimmer than two high school boys trying to hold up a diner."

"Oh my God."

"What?"

"The robbers. It was those kids who sat in that booth drinking coffee for hours, and hours. That's what they were doing. They were plotting, casing the place," Michael said. "I should have known them right off the bat. They were big and strong looking."

"Oh, I knew it was them. I'll bet Marcus did, too."

"What was with him? He comes in, sits at the same booth, and says nothing. He eats his food and just sits there." Michael shrugged to punctuate his confusion. "I just don't get it."

"Not my place to know what his business is about," Felicia said. She reached up and took the cigarette out from between Michael's lips. She took a long drag on the end, all the while staring into Michael's eyes. When she slid the cigarette back into Michael's mouth, the end was covered in cherry-red lipstick.

"But that doesn't mean you don't know what his business is though, does it?"

"I might. I might not. Marcus is an interesting one, you might say. I think he is, or was, Mafia. I'll guarantee if he was in with the mob, he wasn't anyone big in the family. He's always here, never with any buddies, and Italians just aren't that way. They're worse than ladies all going to the restroom together, if you get what I mean. What do they call each other, *Pisan*? Well I don't know that Marcus has any Pisanoes."

"Nice accent," Michael said, smiling.

"Eh-oh, you talken' to me?" Felicia said, in an openly mocking Italian accent.

"That don't sound Italian," Michael said. "You sound like you're from Brooklyn." They started to laugh.

They were still laughing, huddled close, when the police officers came out of Jack's Joint. One of the police officer's said, "Hey, if you pay more than twenty, you're paying too much!" Both officers burst into laughter as they climbed into their squad car.

Felicia and Michael felt their own laughter killed. Their smiles disappeared.

As the car began to pull away from the curb, the same officer yelled out his open window, "And for the love of Pete, where a helmet, soldier!"

You could hear the officers laughing as the car sped north up Lake Avenue.

Felicia's arm slid out from around Michael's. She hugged herself and turned around. Michael tossed his cigarette butt to the sidewalk, then ran his fingers through his hair. "Hey Felicia," he said just as she was about to go back into Jack's. She stopped walking but did not turn around. "Why didn't you say something to them?"

"Why bother, besides, why didn't you?"

Michael had no idea what to say. Calling out to her might have made things worse. It let her know for sure that he was aware of her embarrassment. "Forget about those assholes."

She stood with her back to him for a moment longer before going back inside.

Chapter 12

After the police left, Murphy closed the place. There was no money in the register, so it would be hard to make change for customers. Michael thought Murphy looked depressed and tired. He planned to return at seven and try to start the day out fresh.

Michael locked up the back room. They exited Jack's using the front door. "Sorry about tonight," Michael said with his hands in his coat pockets. He felt and was sure he looked defeated.

"Sorry? About what? You didn't rob me. Forget it. When you go down to the police station tomorrow, you file a complaint or whatever, and tell them whatever you know. What do I care if you leave Marcus out of it or not. They got my money, and eventually, I'll get it back," Murphy said.

"You know about Marcus?"

"What I heard in there, it could only have been Marcus."

Michael felt intrigued. "I think I can identify the guys who tried to rob you."

"Was them two high school kids sitting at that booth, am I right?"

"That's what I think, yeah."

"Good. Then you can confirm my suspicions with the police. I told them the same thing. I told them how they came and just sat in a booth. At the time I thought they were harmless, you know?

Looking back, I think they must have been here just watching everything. They knew how busy I was. I wouldn't doubt if they were trying to add up everyone's orders . . . get a better idea of how much might have been in the till," Murphy said, walking up to his car parked alongside the curb. "Go home. That's what I'm going to do. I still got a few more hours before I have to be back here."

* * *

Michael walked around the side of the building to the back parking lot. Felicia stood, leaning against his car's rear bumper. She smoked a cigarette and watched him slowly approach. "You know what I hate about winter?" she asked, tilting her head back, exposing her neck and throat, while exhaling and sending a large plume of smoke into the night sky.

"What?" Michael asked. Though he had both hands in his coat pockets because he felt cold, his palms felt suddenly sweaty.

"The slush. It's gross. It's hard to walk in and it's sloppy. I think that's what I hate most."

"Not the cold?"

"That's bad . . . unbearable at times . . . but I don't hate it."

Michael nodded. He had never thought about it. "Yeah. I guess the slush is a pretty bad thing. Hell, look at its name. Slush."

"Exactly," Felicia said, moving away from the car. "Heading home?"

"I was going to," Michael said. He had his keys in his hand. Standing in the secluded back parking lot of Jack's Joint felt a little surreal. Everything was snow covered, but nothing looked pretty, the way snow sometimes made things look. The backs of buildings were the backs of buildings. Everything was dark, gloomy, and gray. Then there was Felicia, a splash of color on an otherwise drab and dreary canvas. The air was cold and burned his lungs. He knew his ears were turning red, could feel the heat in them.

"Have a good night, then. You working here tomorrow?"

"I'll be here," Michael said, smiling.

"Me, too," Felicia said as she turned away.

"Still gonna work? Tonight, I mean?"

She stopped and turned back to look at Michael, then shrugged. "Nah. Night's shot."

"Heading home? Do you need a ride?" Michael asked. The conversation was headed somewhere. He did not know what kind of answer he was looking for, or hoping for, but felt an opportunity approaching.

"No thank you. I was thinking about going home, but I doubt I will. Too early," Felicia said. She smiled and waved. "I'm something of a night owl. Have a good night."

When she turned around, Michael closed his eyes and thought hard. He did not want to go home. He wanted to spend some more time with Felicia. Why did he want to spend more time with her? He wanted to hear her stories. Was that really all? What about Ellen? Ellen. "Yeah. I'm not very tired either."

Again, Felicia stopped walking and turned around. "No?"

"Know anyplace that serves a good cup of coffee?" Michael asked.

Walking back toward him, she said, "I know of a place, but it closed early tonight. Mind if I join you?"

Mixed feelings spread throughout Michael and seemed to congregate in his chest. He thought his hands might be shaking, but dared not look. The last thing he wanted to do was call attention to the fact that he was nervous. "I'd love to have you join me."

Michael unlocked the passenger door and opened it like a gentleman. Felicia climbed into the car. "This place you know of . . . why did it close?" Michael asked.

"Place was robbed," answered Felicia, grinning.

Michael shut the door, went around to his side, and got in. He started the engine and let it run while the car defroster kicked on, blowing hot air onto the windshield. "Robbed, huh? Maybe we should go somewhere else, then. What do you think?"

"I know just the place," Felicia said with a curious grin.

Michael backed out of the parking spot. "Tell me which way to go, and we're out of here!"

Chapter 13

Felicia had Michael drove west down Lyell Avenue. The city of Rochester ended at the Erie Canal Bridge. Just past the bridge, to the right, stood a large sports bar and restaurant. Years ago the place had been a party house. When business decreased drastically, and ownership changed hands from father to son, the place underwent major renovations.

Michael had come to the club before. He liked it. The food was good, the prices fair, and there always seemed to be a good crowd, though you never had to wait long for a table.

"It's too late to have drinks served, but I like it here," Felicia said as Michael parked. "Ever been here before?"

"A couple of times." They got out of the car and walked toward the sidewalk. Felicia immediately coiled her arm through his. Michael felt relieved that Felicia did not dress, or look like, some stereotypical prostitute. This was Rochester, New York. The working girls did not dress like the women portraying hookers on television shows, or like the ones out on the busy streets of L.A. No one would know he was on a date with a streetwalker.

He opened the door and Felicia thanked him. A hostess in tight jeans and a red and black striped company pullover shirt led them to a cozy booth in the corner. "Your server will be right with you," she said, and sauntered away.

Sitting across from each other, Michael was given an opportunity to stare into Felicia's eyes. He took advantage of his position and studied her face. Her eyebrows were thick, a feature he found himself attracted to. Her nose was small, with a tiny hump at the bridge. And her lips were so full, so sensual, they held his attention, and he watched them move while she talked. "I'm kind of hungry, too. Are you going to eat? I'll only get something if you will."

Michael patted his belly. "I can eat. They have the best Buffalo Chicken Sandwich I've ever had." It consisted of chicken strips, breaded in a beer-batter, served on a roll, fully dressed, and doused in Buffalo style chicken wing sauce and with blue cheese.

"Sounds fattening. I usually get the salad."

"Salad," Michael repeated as if insulted by the suggestion of a salad over a sandwich.

Felicia laughed. "It's that good?"

"It's better than a . . . a salad," Michael said. "If you can't finish it, I'm sure someone at this table will." He smiled.

The server showed up. Michael ordered for them.

"Anything to drink?"

"A water," Felicia said.

Michael grimaced. "I'll have a large vanilla milk shake, please."

Felicia raised her eyebrows at him. While staring at Michael, she said, "Make it two shakes."

"You little piggy," Michael teased as soon as the server walked away. Felicia reached across the table and playfully slapped his arm.

* * *

The server cleared away the plates while Michael slurped up the rest of his shake from the straw. "I can't believe you ate all that," he said.

"It was good," Felicia said. "I gave you most of my fries."

"Most . . . ha! You gave me a few." Michael wanted a cigarette. This place did not have a smoking section. Most places did not, unlike Jack's Joint which claimed to be seventy-five percent smoke-free. Non-smokers were more than welcome at Jack's, but an ashtray was readily available on every table.

"You look nervous," Felicia said.

"I want a cigarette."

"Me too. Want to leave?"

"Lets." Michael picked up the check. "This is mine."

Felicia put money on the table. "Then I'll take care of the tip."

Outside, they both lit up and walked slowly back toward Michael's car.

"Doesn't seem as cold out," Felicia commented.

Michael looked around, as if assessing the weather. "Not nearly as cold as it was." An awkward silence followed, and grew. Michael felt apprehension building within him. He thought he should say something. Nothing worthwhile came to mind. He didn't want to just blurt out anything and risk sounding stupid.

Before he could think his next thought, she was standing directly in front of him, staring and chewing on her lower lip. "Kiss me?"

Felicia sounded insecure, fragile. Michael could not resist. He leaned forward, kept his eyes open, and kissed her. Once their lips were pressed together, she closed her eyes first. When he closed his, an explosion of desire and satisfaction was set off in his heart. He wanted the kiss to last, but he also wanted more of her.

When the kiss ended, they both opened their eyes slowly. "That felt nice," Felicia said.

Michael could only swallow. Every urge flowing inside him grew more and more intense with each throb of his heart, with each surge of swift moving blood. "I better get you home," he said. He looked at his watch and smiled an ironic smile with arched eyebrows. "It's early."

"I'm not tired," she said, lazily. She continued to stare at Michael. She licked her lips. "Want to go somewhere where we can be alone?"

Yes. "Not tonight. No." There was no other way to put it. "I mean . . . I want to. I can't."

"A girlfriend?"

"You could say that," Michael said. He could see Ellen's face in his mind's eye. He knew the kiss had been wrong. Guilt ebbed its way through his system. The throbbing he felt quickly descended into a steady and more normal pulse. "Felicia . . ."

"We can be discreet?" she asked. He thought he could sense her hunger and wondered if it came close to comparing with his own.

"It wouldn't be right. Not at this point," Michael said. Even as he spoke, he began to question his own words, and the meaning surrounding them. Were they just talking about having sex, or making love? Would things change if he left Ellen and started seeing Felicia? He knew he would not be able to stay with Felicia if she did not change careers. Would she change careers for him? "Besides, I want to get to know you better."

Felicia let out a loud laugh. "Ha! You're a guy," she said. She took hold of his coat lapels and pulled herself in close to snuggle. "Don't tell me you'd rather talk than make love."

"I never said that," Michael said. He kept watching her lips, then looked into her eyes. "I never said . . ."

And she kissed him. This time it was a deep, hard, and passionate kiss. Her tongue slid through his lips and darted around inside his mouth. Her arms snaked under his coat and around his back while her fingers kneaded and massaged his muscles.

Unable to resist the affection, Michael hugged her tightly, pressing her body against his. He felt amazed at how perfectly they fit together, in awe at how natural it felt holding her, and mesmerized by how completely turned on and aroused he had become.

He stopped the kiss. As firmly as possible he said, "I can't."

They both knew the reason revolved around Michael's girlfriend. "She's lucky, you know."

Not really. "I suppose she is," Michael said. "I'm sorry."

"Don't be. I understand. I admire you and envy her," Felicia said. "And I'm ready to go home now, too. Mind giving me a lift?"

"Felicia, you know I'm going to drive you home. Get in the car," he said. The drive was silent except for Felicia calling out left and right turns. Michael pulled into the driveway of a small Cape-

Cod home. The front step light was on. "Nice place."

"Thank you. I rent it. I'd love to buy a house some day. It's hard to do that when you can't get a mortgage. Banks want you to show them you have a steady job, you know? At least like a year with an employer. If I told them how long I'd been at my job and how much I made weekly, I'd be living in Pittsford." She opened the door. Before closing it, she leaned in. "Want to come in?"

"I do."

"But you won't?"

"I won't."

"See you around, Michael," Felicia said and closed the door.

Michael watched her walk carefully to the front step. The snow appeared to be several inches deep. Large icicles hung like dangerous crystal stalactites along the gutters. It took every bit of strength and will power for Michael to remain in the car.

When he arrived home, he took a long cold shower. He knew he only had a few hours to sleep since he told the police he would be down first thing in the morning. He wanted to sleep and not think about Felicia. Yet, once asleep, Michael found himself confronted by a brigade of sensual dreams, revolving around a pretty burgundy-hair-colored prostitute.

Chapter 14

Sunday, January 13

Michael did not feel at all rested. He felt as if he had been awake for forty-eight hours straight, and going to the police station proved an ordeal. The police officers from the past night produced a line-up. Michael immediately recognized the two young men from the restaurant, but could not confirm as fact that they had been responsible for the hold-up. He told the police time and again that the robbers wore masks, and although he thought it might have been the two in the line-up, he could not say for sure.

He filled out a complaint before leaving.

Knowing he should go home and get some more sleep before his third nightshift at Jack's Joint, Michael did not think he would be able to sleep. He instinctively knew it would all catch up with him, especially Monday morning, when he went right from Jack's to his job at the paper.

Hungry, and having skipped breakfast, Michael wanted to eat lunch. There were many places to go for a good meal, but he decided on Jack's. He found a good parking spot along Lake and went in. Murphy, behind the counter, waved.

"Hey, Murphy," Michael said.

"Hey Michael," Murphy said with a grin. "Hungry?"

"Like a bear," Michael said. He sat down at a counter stool and ordered. He was sitting one over from Speed, who was more than half way through his lunch. "How are you, Speed?"

"Feel like I'm running behind. This place opening late had my entire day off-kilter. I get here around seven, like I always do, and the place is closed. I stood in front of the door for like three minutes, just standing there like an imbecile. I'm thinking, closed? Jack's don't close. It's one of the things I love about it here. The Joint is always open. So then I have to find somewhere else to eat breakfast. There's that place a few blocks down. They have okay food and all, but it's not the same. So by the time I finish eating, it's later than usual, and time is money. Ever hear that expression before, that time is money? Well, trust me, it couldn't be any more true. Not enough hours in the day for me to amass the kind of money I want. So when lunchtime rolls around, I'm stuck, you know? I have to debate, do I come back here and risk seeing the closed sign hanging on the door, or just go somewhere else to eat?"

Michael just smiled and shook his head. "Murphy put you in a real tough spot, didn't he?"

"Don't encourage him," Murphy said, giving Michael his soda. "Did you go to the police station this morning?"

"Police?" Speed asked. "Why would you go see the police?"

"I went," Michael said. "Place was almost robbed last night."

"Damn," Speed said.

"And?" Murphy asked.

"It went okay," Michael said. He didn't feel comfortable discussing the situation in front of everyone. "I'll tell you about it after, all right?"

Seeming to catch on, Murphy agreed.

Michael stuck a straw between the ice cubes in his drink. "So what was your day like, Speed?"

"Busy, like I said. Busy. Today's my father's birthday. It's his fiftieth. My mom's having a big surprise party for him tonight. She called me late yesterday to remind me. She knew it would slip my mind, and it had. So I spent the morning finding a gift for my father," Speed said.

"With work you don't have time to go shopping?"

Murphy laughed as he served Michael his meal. "No time to go shopping? Speed, hear that one?"

Michael looked from Speed to Murphy. He did not get the joke.

Murphy said, "You might say Speed here is in the merchandise business."

Speed smiled. "Screw you, Murphy."

Michael ate a French fry while he added ketchup and mustard to his burger. "I'm listening."

"Anyway, I get to the mall as it opens, right? I walk in using the entrance by men's clothing. The place is always unorganized first thing in the morning. People are setting up still, and talking about what they did the night before. So I go right over to the sweaters and shirts. While I look at one I like, while I look at the price tab . . . Know how those tabs have the perforated edges? And with my thumb I bend and then gently tear off the price. I drop a few of those items into my bag and walk briskly to the men's counter.

"As I suspect, no one is at the counter, or anywhere near the men's apparel, as they call it, so I stand there waiting. When this teenage girl arrives, she's all apologetic for keeping me waiting. So I tell her I'm in a hurry, and that I bought these items just the other day. I set the bag on the counter and she removes them. I tell her they are a gift for my father . . . which will be the truth . . . and that my wife told me I got all the wrong sizes. I ask her if I can just exchange them," Speed said, smiling. He's into his story. "The girl says sure, so I, in a round-about way, get back over to the sweaters and shirts and pick the extra-large sizes that I want. I bring them back to the counter. And the girl tells me I'm all set."

Michael just laughs. "You've got to be kidding me?"

"Mike man . . . no wait . . . you haven't heard the best part," Speed explained. "I then tell the cashier that I had the items gift wrapped . . . because the store does that stuff free if you have a receipt. I told this girl that in order to return the stuff for the right sizes I had to tear open the gift-wrap. She tells me not to worry about it. She gets on the phone, calling over to customer service, and tells the girl over there to re-wrap my gifts for me. At no charge." Punch line delivered.

"What if you get caught?" Michael could not help but ask.

"Part of the risk. It's all part of the risk. But see, you're missing the point. I just got a store to give me a few sweaters and shirts free . . . but not only did they give them to me free, they also wrapped them in beautiful birthday paper with bows."

Michael got it, all right. When Speed left, he ate his burger and contemplated what he had been told. He wished he had his notebook handy. He did not want to lose any detail of the story in his own rendition.

Though it was after noon, Michael wondered about Felicia. Did she spend her days sleeping, and only come out to play at night?

He looked around the room. He did not recognize any of the people. Some of the customers seated at tables and booths wore suits. Michael would have sworn he was in the wrong place without Fatso sitting at the counter to serve as a kind of landmark.

Chapter 15

Martin Wringer filled his tank with gas using a credit card which he had never used before. It was equipped with a ten thousand available line of credit. The bill would be sent to his wife at the end of the month. Wringer knew she would call the company and tell them he no longer lived at the address. Wringer figured he could squeeze a month of usage, maybe two, out of the card before it was canceled on him.

He remembered back to when immediately after losing his job with Manson Chemical Technologies, he had applied for Unemployment Insurance Benefits. He would never forget the long, drawn out, over-the-phone application. He had to listen and respond to over eighty automated questions by pressing a corresponding number on the keypad of his touch-tone phone.

A week later, he had received in the mail the determination handed down by some ass-face Claims Examiner with New York's Department of Labor. The Determination told him that he was not eligible to receive benefits. The reasoning was based on the information his former employer provided. The Department of Labor believed his actions rose to the level of misconduct within the meaning of the Unemployment Law.

"Get the hell out of here," Martin Wringer had said out loud, standing alone by the mailbox as he read the form. He had stuffed it into his pocket, wanting to hide it from his wife.

He had decided to call the Department of Labor. After being placed on hold for nearly an hour, and after supplying someone with his social security number, Wringer had found himself talking to the ass-face Examiner that wrote the determination.

"This is Brian McCollough. How can I help you?"

Wringer had taken a deep breath and exhaled before explaining his situation. "I received a determination from you today, informing me that I am not eligible to receive unemployment checks. I'm out of work, you know. I have a wife and kids to support and a mortgage that needs to be paid. We're coming on the holiday season. Listen pal, I spent twenty years with that company. All the while, I've been paying into unemployment. That money is mine. I don't know who you think you are telling me that I'm not eligible . . ."

"Sir," McCollough had said, "according to New York State laws, you were terminated from your job for reasons that rise to the level of misconduct. If you are unhappy with the determination, all you need to do is request a hearing."

"Yeah, and how do I do that?" Wringer had asked.

"All you need to know should be on the back of the determination you received in the mail."

Martin Wringer had turned the form over in his hands. His wife had entered the kitchen and watched him expectantly.

"That's all I have to do is request a hearing and I'll get one with some impartial Administrative Law Judge?"

"In writing, sir. Send it to the address on the front of the document."

"And how long will I have to wait before I get a court date?" Wringer had asked.

"Not long. The cases get assigned quickly."

"Quickly? We'll see about that," Wringer had said, and hung up.

The hearing regarding Wringer's Unemployment Insurance had been set for Tuesday, November 20th at 10:00 a.m. Wringer's wife had made him wear a shirt, tie, and sport coat. He arrived at the office on South Union at 9:30, but spent fifteen minutes trying to figure out where to park.

He had signed in with the security guard in the lobby and took an elevator up to the 3rd floor. He had entered a room manned with two secretaries, and the lady sitting furthest from him made eye contact.

Unsure, Wringer had approached her and handed over the Hearing Notice he had received in the mail. She smiled and posted his notice on a corkboard under the Administrative Law Judge's name. "You can just have a seat. We're running a little behind today," she had said pleasantly.

Wringer knew he had a doctor's appointment at noon. It took him more than two weeks to schedule the visit. He did not want to risk missing the appointment. "Thank you," he had said simply.

He had turned around and shook his head with disregard. Seated in the back row of chairs were his former supervisor, a woman in a smart gray suit, and a large man wearing a white dress shirt and black tie.

His former supervisor had nodded a hello. Wringer had ignored it and sat down in the front row of chairs.

At fifteen minutes after ten, the secretary had called their case and led them into the judge's room. The large man in the white shirt and tie remained seated in the waiting room. Wringer had found this curious.

The Administrative Law Judge was perched behind a large steel desk. Jutting out from the desk was a six-foot long table with two chairs on both sides. Wringer had sat across from his former supervisor and the woman in the smart-looking suit.

Aside from his degrees and a few plaques from a college fraternity hanging on the walls, the room was bare, save a large window with a view of the Strong Museum.

The judge had introduced himself, then had each person present introduce themselves, for the record. The hearing had been recorded.

"Stan Engler. Supervising Team Leader for Manson Chemical Technologies."

"Kathleen Parsons. I'm an Unemployment Insurance Hearing Representative. I work directly for Manson Chemical

Technologies."

"Martin Wringer. I used to work for the Charlie Manson Company. I don't work anywhere right now," Wringer said, smiling at his joke. He did not care that no one else found him amusing. It felt a little intense sitting there. He felt isolated. He wanted to lighten the mood, and felt he had done so the only way he knew how. Humor.

Testimony was taken under oath first from the supervisor. The judge did a thorough job of examining the witness and extracting a side of the story. When he felt confident enough with the answers he had received, he allowed the employer's representative to question the witness.

When Parsons finished asking the supervisor questions, the judge said, "Mr. Wringer, do you have any questions for the witness?"

"I have some," Wringer had said. "But this is new for me. I don't have the skill that this woman has to ask questions."

"That's all right, Mr. Wringer. I will assist you in any way I can to ensure that you are allowed to ask whatever relevant questions you have," said the judge.

Wringer had smiled nervously. "Isn't it true that you have a problem with me? That you never liked me since the first day we met? Didn't you have it in . . ."

"Sir," the judge had said, holding up his hand. "You need to ask one question at a time, and then allow the witness to answer the question. All right?"

"Sorry, your Honor," Wringer had said.

The judge had said, "I think Mr. Wringer's first question asked if you had a problem with him. Can you answer that, Mr. Engler?"

"I never had a problem with Martin. He's always done good work. He never caused any trouble before. We work in a high-stress area, as I testified to. Our operation runs twenty-four, seven. We don't even shut down for holidays. But no, I've never had a problem with Martin," Engler responded.

"That's bullshit," Wringer had said.

"Mr. Wringer," the judge had warned.

"Sorry, your Honor. Can I ask another question? Why were

you always taunting me at work and harassing me? I can't remember a shift where you didn't . . ."

"Mr. Wringer, one question at a time, please."

"Sorry, your Honor."

Stan Engler had stared at Wringer. "Martin, I never taunted you. I can't honestly figure out what you're talking about."

"Can you be more specific, Mr. Wringer?" the judge had asked.

"Specific? How?"

"Can you tell us a specific instance where you believe you were taunted by your supervisor?" the judge had said, clarifying his question.

Martin Wringer had sat quietly, thinking.

"Mr. Wringer?" the judge had prompted.

"I can't think of anything off the top of my head. I feel like I'm being put on the spot here." He had cupped his hands over his face. "The night we argued . . ."

"Which night was that, Mr. Wringer?" the judge had asked.

"The last night I was there . . . the night of the fight," Wringer had said.

"Continue."

"That night we argued. Didn't you call me a drunk?"

"I said that I thought you smelled of alcohol. I did not call you a drunk."

"Didn't you mean to imply that you thought I was a drunk?"

"No."

"But it is what you were thinking, wasn't it?"

The judge said, "Mr. Wringer, I don't see . . ."

"Sorry, your Honor. After you said I was a drunk," Wringer had said.

"Objection," Kathleen Parsons had said.

"Sustained," the judge had agreed. "Mr. Wringer, the witness has already testified to the fact that he did not call you a drunk."

"Sorry, your Honor. You said, when the judge was questioning you, that I smelled of alcohol. You said that you wanted me to go to medical and submit a blood and urine sample. You wanted to prove that I was unfit for work. Why?"

"We work with chemicals, Martin. If your judgment is even slightly impaired by drugs or alcohol . . ."

"Objection," Martin Wringer had said. "No one has mentioned drugs before."

"I believe a point is being made, and that no one is accusing you of drug usage at this point, Mr. Wringer," the judge had said.

"Oh. Sure. Sorry, your Honor."

"As you were saying," the judge had said to the supervisor.

"If your judgment is even slightly impaired by any substance, then there are safety hazards that need to be considered. Not just your own safety, but the safety of those working around you . . . and to the community," Engler had said. "When I asked for you to come with me to medical for testing, it was because I needed to be sure you were fit to work."

"Any more questions?" the judge had asked.

"Yes, your Honor," Wringer had said through clenched teeth. "How'd it feel when I slammed my fist into your face?"

The judge took testimony from Martin Wringer next. Like before, the judge took the liberty of asking questions first, before turning loose Manson's representative.

"Mr. Wringer, when your supervisor asked you to go to medical for a fit for work test, what did you say to him?" Parsons had asked.

"I don't remember."

"Did you tell him to screw himself?"

"I don't remember."

"Did you tell him to go to hell?"

"I don't remember."

"Do you remember punching him in the nose?"

"Clearly."

"When you broke your supervisor's nose, did you think you might risk losing your job?"

"I guess."

"Did you remember thinking you might lose your job if you punched him . . . before you actually threw the punch?"

"I can't remember. I don't think so. It was a heat of the moment thing."

"Heat of the moment? Can you tell me what your supervisor might have said to you that caused you to assault him?" she had asked.

"He called me an alcoholic."

"Objection," she had said.

"Sustained," the judge had agreed. "Your former supervisor has already testified that he did not call you an alcoholic."

"Yeah, well, I remember him calling me one."

"And that has been noted," the judge said.

"Did your supervisor ask if you had a problem?"

"No."

"Did he ask you if you needed help?"

"No."

"Your supervisor testified that he wanted to help you . . . to get you into a program where you could . . ."

"The hell he did," Wringer had shouted.

"Mr. Wringer, please control your language and those outbursts, or I will close this hearing immediately," the judge had said.

"Sorry, your Honor."

Kathleen Parsons had spent the next fifteen minutes introducing documents into evidence, for the record. They were company policies on behavior and treatment of others. She even submitted the company's handbook, indicating sections where it explicitly explained the penalties for violence in the work place. Each document had an annual date and Wringer's signature, proving that he was well acquainted with company rules and policies.

"No further questions," Parsons had said.

The judge allowed for the woman to make a closing statement on Manson's behalf. "Your Honor, the claimant knew, or should have known, that striking his supervisor would cost him his job. Credible evidence clearly establishes the fact that the claimant was aware, or should have been aware, of company rules and policies that prohibit workplace violence. The claimant was terminated for reasons of misconduct and should be deemed ineligible to receive benefits. Thank you, your Honor."

Wringer had declined to make a closing statement. He saw no point. The company screwed him. He lost his job. He lost this hearing. In his mind, little else could go wrong to make matters worse.

Wringer, the first out of the hearing, had ignored the people in the waiting room and headed for the elevators.

When at last the rep, his ex-supervisor and the man in the shirt and tie appeared, Wringer stood ready for them. The tension had built inside him. He could not keep his fingers unrolled. It felt as if the tips were bound to his palms—indefinitely clenched in a fist.

"Did you enjoy that, bastards?" Wringer said, speaking to her, to him, to all three of them. "Making me look like an ignorant jerk? If that judge denies me checks, how in the hell am I supposed to support my family? Have any idea how I'm supposed to do that?"

"You should have thought . . ."

The man in the shirt and tie had stopped Stan Engler from talking. "Mr. Wringer, please turn around and proceed to your car."

"And who the hell are you?"

"Please, Mr. Wringer." The man had his arms bent, keeping his hands non-threateningly in front of his chest.

Wringer had recognized the defensive stance. "You're a cop? Corporate security, or something?"

"I'm with the company, yes. Now please, go to your car."

"Freaking undercover security. I'm not dangerous, assholes. Do I look dangerous?" Wringer had asked, staring at Engler, whose skin around the nose and under the eyes was still dark and bruised-looking. Frustrated, Wringer turned and walked away.

Wringer had then gone to the doctor's appointment, despite his pissy mood. After the doctor examined him, and after some blood work, the doctor told Wringer that he had a venereal disease. Wringer could remember the embarrassment he felt. He had known right away how he had contracted the disease. There really was no surprise.

"You're going to need to tell your wife," the doctor had explained.

"Of course," Wringer agreed. He had no intention of telling her. He could not remember the last time they had been intimate—not since him losing his job. His encounter with the disease-infected whore came after losing his job.

When he arrived home late that afternoon, however, he was appalled to learn his doctor had called home to let his wife know that he had contacted the pharmacy about a prescription, completely destroying the confidentiality of a doctor-patient relationship. Wringer felt certain the act was illegal, too. *When someone can't trust his or her own doctor . . . what does that tell you about society*? Wringer thought, bitterly.

And his wife played it cool, too, before she had let on. "How was the hearing? . . . How was the doctor's appointment? . . . When were you going to tell me you'd been screwing a prostitute? . . . Get out of my house! Get the hell out of my house you sick, perverted asshole!"

Casey, the whore, had deserved to die. She had ruined his life.

Chapter 16

Michael Buzzelli spent the rest of the day at home, writing. He set up columns in the spreadsheet on his computer. He put the name of each person as a header over each column. Under each column, a cell per item, he listed what he knew about them. He started everyone off with a description. He recounted the events of the previous night, and wrote many things under "Marcus" The last thing he entered was the story Speed relayed to him about shopping for a birthday gift for his father.

In a Word document, Michael took careful time to document his narrative, recapturing his own thoughts and emotions. He wanted the reader to be able to see all that he saw, without overdoing the descriptions. He wanted readers to enjoy the crisp dialogue that he listened to, without having it sound contrived. *Less is more.*

Before going in to work Sunday night, and despite feeling completely rejuvenated and freshly inspired, Michael knew he needed to consider his work at Jack's like an assignment and not as a second job.

Upon arriving, Murphy and he discussed in the back room what took place at the police station. "I told them the truth, Murphy. I told them I was pretty sure it was the two young guys in here the other day, but because they were wearing masks . . ."

"I understand. Don't worry about it. I'd have done the same thing," Murphy said. "Besides, they didn't get the money."

Was that all? They didn't get the money? Michael thought about how close the one thug had come to pistol-whipping Sandy. The creeps had aimed guns at all the customers. Anyone could have been hurt, or killed. Murphy seemed content knowing the money was recovered, though, and Michael was not here to argue. Not to mention, no one was hurt. What else should Murphy say? There was nothing more that Murphy could do.

When Murphy left, Michael attempted to settle back into a routine. He tied on his apron and lit up a cigarette before even going out into the dining area.

As though he had never left, Fatso sat at the counter reading through his paper. Sandy was on the payphone in back. Marcus was not around, but his booth sat empty as if waiting for him to show. There were many more people in the room, eating and drinking coffee—all of them talking. The loud murmur of conversation felt calming, and Michael could not ignore the sense of peace that overcame him.

When Sandy hung up the telephone, she approached Michael. "You see Vanessa last night at all?"

"No, why?"

"She hasn't been around since Friday, and I've been calling her at home, but no one's answering," Sandy said. "No big deal. If she comes in, and I'm out, tell her to get in touch with me. Will you do that for me?"

"No problem," Michael said. A question for Sandy burned inside. He wanted to ask her if she had seen Felicia. He bit his lip, and tucked the question away.

As the night wore on, Felicia did not show. Michael wondered where she might be. He found himself trapped talking with Fatso. He did not mind listening to the man, except that tonight he felt highly distracted.

Where might Felicia be?

Chapter 17

Monday, January 14

Michael drove along Ridge Road on his way to Tantalo's, a wonderful Italian restaurant in the suburban town of Greece, a few miles west of The Mall at Greece Ridge Center. Traffic at any given time felt dense on Ridge Road. Drivers in the area seemed to enjoy riding the ass of the car in front of them. Keeping his road-rage temper in check, Michael refrained from honking his horn when the driver next to him changed lanes in front of him without using a directional signal.

He pulled into the parking lot, saw Ellen's car, and parked as close to it as he could. When he walked in and did not see Ellen, he knew she already had a table. He checked his watch to make sure he was not late—and he was not—before looking around the restaurant.

"Can I help you, sir?" The hostess asked.

"I'm here to meet a friend. She might already have a table."

"And your name, sir?"

"Michael Buzzelli," he said.

"Your friend is at the bar, right around this corner," the hostess said.

Michael thanked the young lady and made his way to the bar. He took off his gloves and stuffed them into his coat pockets. He shrugged out of his coat and hung it over the back of an empty, black leather seat next to Ellen at the bar. "What's a pretty thing like you doing all alone in a place like this?"

"Starving," Ellen answered. She leaned over, and they kissed. Michael tasted sweet liqueur on her lips, and smelled it on her breath.

"Fuzzy navel?"

"Hairy back," Ellen retorted, giggling.

Michael could not help but laugh. He pulled out his cigarettes as the barmaid asked him for his order. "Brandy, please."

"Brandy?" Ellen asked.

"I'm frozen. My fingers are numb. I spent fifteen minutes scraping snow and ice off the windows. Then the heater in the car finally starts working just now as I pull into the parking lot. A brandy sounds like it will warm me," Michael said.

"How was work?"

"It was slow last night. More quiet than it's been the last two nights," Michael said, lighting a cigarette. Tantalo's allowed smoking at the bar, because it was an isolated room with a separate ventilation system. There were a few tables for people to sit and eat while they drank and smoked. Those tables were hard to get. Reservations in advance were helpful. Ellen did not smoke. Michael knew she would have reserved a table in the non-smoking section of the restaurant.

"I don't mean at the dive. I mean at the paper," Ellen said.

Michael shrugged. "It was dull. I typed out some obituaries and did some leg work for one of the journalists."

"That sounds exciting," Ellen said, flatly.

"Writing obituaries, or doing research for a journalist who plans on taking all the credit for the article he's writing?" Michael asked. He thanked the barmaid for his drink and took a good long sip. The brandy was strong and definitely seemed to burn going down his throat. He felt it burn in his belly and longed for a beer. It was too late to order a beer. He had already made an ordeal out of having a brandy. Even the barmaid had flashed him an odd look when he ordered.

"You only just started with them, Michael," Ellen said, placing a hand on his shoulder.

It should have felt comforting having her words and her hand reaching out to touch him, but it didn't. He took another sip of brandy. "I graduated from college with a three point seven G.P.A. I was editor of the school's paper. I covered news breaking stories on campus . . . some that were even recognized by the City Chronicle."

"And those things are what got you a job at the paper," Ellen was quick to point out. It was also easy for her to say. Everything came easy for her. She graduated at the top of her class and landed a job with a medium-sized, Rochester based, law firm three weeks after graduation. "Honey, this is a different world . . . completely different from the one you knew in college. Competition is fierce in school, but quadruple that, and you'll see what it's like outside of school. I've got to think that reporter jobs on the City Chronicle don't open up very often. Those writers are part of the union."

"And so am I," Michael said. He knew he sounded like a baby. He felt like he was whining, but he did not bring up the topic. "Can we talk about something else?"

"Sure, how about the menu? I really am hungry."

After the hostess led them to their table, the waitress appeared to take their orders. "Can I get the Surf-n-Turf, only with twin tails? And another one of these?" Ellen asked, pointing to the full Fuzzy Navel she had brought over from the bar.

Michael cringed at her order. The last time they went Dutch treat, Michael was still in school earning his degree in journalism. He wondered what would possess her to order such an expensive item from the menu. Sure, he was working at the paper, and the second job was extra income, but he had rent to pay, and student loans rolling in. Also, she seemed a little gone already. Michael knew this could not be her second drink. He wondered if the alcohol was clouding her judgment. He wondered how she planned to get her car home. Maybe she would get drunk enough and pay for the entire meal.

"And for you?" the waitress asked Michael.

"Actually, Linguini and clams in a red sauce sounds wonderful," Michael said.

"And to drink?"

He wanted a glass of wine, but thought better of it after the brandy fiasco. "A beer. Whatever you have on tap will be fine."

After the waitress took their orders, then Michael apologized. "I'm sorry I snapped at you over at the bar. I'm a little stressed out."

"It's no wonder, working two jobs like you are," Ellen said. "I'm surprised you're not too tired for dinner with me this evening."

"Well, I am tired," Michael admitted. "My body just needs time to adjust. I only started at Jack's on Friday. It'll get easier. And, hey, you know what happened on Saturday night?"

Ellen smiled. The facial expression looked odd. Michael thought she might be drunk. She did not look happy. "No. Why don't you tell me?"

"You feeling all right?" Michael asked. Ellen picked up her drink and swallowed away half of its contents. "Ellen?"

"I'm fine Michael."

"Did you have a bad day?"

"You might say that, thank you for asking," Ellen said.

"I'm sorry. That was very inconsiderate of me. What happened?" Michael asked, sincerely. He leaned forward to show Ellen he was giving her his complete attention. She stared at him, and he stared back. He felt uneasy meeting her eyes. He looked away.

"Is something wrong, Michael?"

"No. You're just making me uncomfortable."

She drank the rest of her drink, just as the waitress returned with their bar orders and a basket of warm bread.

Michael peeled back the layers of cloth napkin that covered the pre-sliced, intimate-sized loaf of fresh baked bread. "Want a piece?" Michael asked, handing over a thick slice to Ellen, and putting one for him on a plate. "Butter, too?" He gave her a pad.

While he buttered his slice, Michael asked her again about her day.

"I'd rather not get into it, yet. Tell me about Saturday night," Ellen said, suddenly cheerful. She spread butter on her bread, then took a sip from her new drink.

Michael told Ellen about the attempted robbery. She listened intently. By the end of the story, she looked scared to death. "My God, Michael. That man that knocked the gun out of the crook's hand, do you know who he was?"

Michael leaned back in his chair. "No. I wish I did," he said, lying about Marcus, even to Ellen.

"This doesn't sound like the right job for you. Is that all that happened?"

"Is that all? Isn't that enough?"

"It sure is. I want you to quit, Michael. It's not safe there. No good can come of you having this job."

"Ellen, if I'm going to prove my worth to the people at the paper, I've got to show them I can find an interesting story. This place is full of stories. You know the prostitute that was murdered back before the holidays, how she used to stand at the corner there? Yeah, well, these people knew her," Michael said.

"I don't like you hanging around whores. I have to tell you, I don't like the idea of you being around a killer, either."

"Who says I'm around the killer?" Michael asked.

"You just did," Ellen said. "I don't like it."

The waitress set their food down in front of them, asked if they needed anything else, and then left them alone with their conversation. "I can't quit. I won't quit. I need this job. It's an experience. As a writer, as a journalist, I feel like I've tapped into a entirely new world of stimulation."

Ellen started to cry. She placed her elbows on the table and rubbed the heels of her hands against her eyes. "I don't want to see you again, Michael. I don't want to ever see you again."

Michael felt as if he had been punched in the stomach. This had to be a joke—an elaborate, cruel joke. "Ellen?"

"I want to tell you about my bad day," she said. She was drawing attention with her tears, her sobs and with how loud she was talking. She bordered hysteria. "This morning I got a phone call in my office from one of the senior partners in the firm. He says he didn't know if he was doing the right thing, but he knew he couldn't just hide the truth from me. Any idea what he might have been talking about, Michael?"

Michael shrugged. He felt confused. "No."

"No? Well, let me continue. Fast forward. I came here tonight and had a few drinks. When you showed up, I planned to wait. I wanted to give you every opportunity," she said. Now she seemed to have the attention of everyone in the restaurant. A show for their dining pleasure.

"Me?" Michael said, barely audible.

"Yes, you. You. I wanted to give you every opportunity to tell me that you were out with another girl on Saturday night," Ellen screamed, losing control. "And I did give you every opportunity!"

Felicia. Their sandwiches. He could get out of it. "It was a friend from Jack's. We went for something to eat after the robbery," he said. It sounded so melodramatic, going for something to eat after a robbery.

"I don't know a thing about what you ate. All I know about is the two of you in the parking lot, standing in front of your car . . . all over each other," Ellen said. Michael sensed, without even looking around, that she had the patrons of Tantalo's on her side.

She stood up, taking her coat in her arm, and picked up his beer. Michael knew what was coming. She threw it in his face, then slapped him hard. She stood there, looking unsatisfied, then slapped him again and stormed out.

Everything in Michael's vision moved in slow motion. As he watched Ellen leave the restaurant, his legs felt more frozen and numb than his hands had ever felt. He wanted to get up and leave, but found himself unable to do so.

Without being asked, the waitress brought his check. "I appreciate that." He did not feel good about himself. He felt like a jerk, and not just because everyone in the place was staring at him. "Can I get these meals to go?"

Chapter 18

None of it made any sense. Knowing he needed to stop and assess things in his life, Michael sat in his car with the motor running. The car had not had time to cool down. The engine was still warm. Heat came out hot from the vents. With the radio off, he sat in silence and tried to concentrate.

Nothing between him and Ellen had been wrong. Everything between them had been right. They got along, and enjoyed the same things—mostly. The biggest difference between them had been the fact that he smoked and she did not. Where did it go wrong? What caused it all to change? Michael knew he felt crushed. His heart ached. He and Ellen had been together for nearly two years. After she graduated from college, Ellen had landed a nice job with a large law firm as a junior staff attorney. Though they never talked marriage, Michael had been certain that one day the two of them would marry.

What confused Michael even more was the one thought that kept flip-flopping in his mind, waiting for his attention. Why don't you try to fix things?

As though a dangerous enemy, Michael almost refused to go near the question. If he wanted, he could race to Ellen's place—he had the dinners with him. He knew if they talked things over, everything could be worked out. In a way it would be like starting over. She would not trust him for a long time, and rightly so. He would need to prove to her that he was worthy of being trusted again.

He put the car in reverse. Because the dinners were getting cold, the night was still young, and he imagined lobster tails reheated in a microwave oven tasting awful. Michael pulled out of Tantalo's and back onto Ridge Road in a hurry.

* * *

Michael pulled into the parking lot of Ellen's apartment complex, saw her car, and stopped. She would be waiting for him. She would be expecting him to come here and beg for forgiveness. A part of him knew this entire mess was his fault alone, and apologizing would be the right thing to do. The other part of him, the part less concerned with doing the right thing, posed a serious question. Is this what you really want?

It was a far cry from a yes or no answer. At the moment, however, yes was not the answer registering. For reasons unbeknownst to him, being with Felicia struck cords inside him. It had been hell resisting her urges Saturday night, and right now Michael was not sure he wanted to resist those urges any longer.

Where would a relationship with a prostitute lead him? Pulling out of Ellen's parking lot, and driving toward Felicia's Cape-Cod, Michael knew there would be only one way to find out an answer. A lot of his thoughts made little sense. Most men would not entertain the thought of being with a hooker. Michael did not want to be with a hooker, but thought he might want to be with Felicia. Anyone would think he was acting ludicrous. What did he have to gain by pursuing such a unique woman? What consequences could he expect if anything did take form between the two of them? Was he ready for any of this—the unexpected?

The drive to Felicia's went quickly. For the most part, Michael could not remember operating the car. His mind, trapped in a whirlwind of emotions, did it's best to stay focused.

Stopping in front of Felicia's house, Michael saw the silhouette of a woman through closed curtains. As best he could,

Michael searched his memory trying to remember why he was here. At no point in time did Felicia say, “Hey big boy, why don’t you come over and see me some time.” If she had, he would have remembered that quite clearly.

They had a couple of kisses in a parking lot. Nothing more. She kissed a lot of guys. She had sex with a lot of guys. Michael was sure a kiss did not normally amount to an open invitation to drop by anytime, uninvited. “I got twin lobster tails,” he said to himself. “But nothing to drink,” he said. How could he stop by her house and not bring something to drink? “But I have lobster.”

He found the courage to pull out of the street and up her driveway, switching off his headlights as he did so.

He saw the figure in the house standing by the window as if staring through the curtains, trying to figure out who might have pulled up in her driveway, perhaps wondering if she should go to the door, or wait and see if the car would back out again.

Michael sat in the driveway for a long minute before switching off his car.

When the front door opened, and Michael saw Felicia standing in the doorway in jeans and a long-sleeved white turtleneck, he thought his heart might stop beating. She looked stunning. With her burgundy-colored hair pulled back tight and wrapped in a ponytail, Michael knew he needed to get closer—to see Felicia’s face up close without the hair blocking her features. He opened his door and, baring the cold, stood in the triangle space between his door and car.

“Who is that?” Felicia called out.

“It’s Michael, from Jack’s,” Michael said. Presumptuously, he held the foam cartons containing the quickly cooling dinners from Tantalo’s.

“Yeah? And what do you want?”

“To eat. I’m hungry. I brought some dinner from Tantalo’s, if you’re interested?” Michael realized he was holding his breath. He wanted Felicia to invite him. The way the conversation seemed to be headed, he was not at all sure of how this might turn out. A part of him regretted pulling into her driveway.

“Like what did you bring?”

"Lobster tails and Linguini with clams . . . in a red sauce."

"Get the hell out of here," she said. "Lobster tails?"

"No, I'm serious. Does that mean you're hungry?"

"That means I might be hungry," she said. She waved him in and disappeared back into her home.

Michael locked up his car and ran to her front step. He felt funny just walking in, but did so anyway. He closed and locked her house door behind him. He saw her in the next room, the kitchen, setting the table. From where he stood, in the family room, he saw that she had a lonely evening planned. The TV guide was opened on the sofa with the remote holding the place in the booklet.

He kicked off his shoes, set the dinners down, and took off his coat. Felicia placed two wineglasses on the table. "You know, I forgot to pick up wine," Michael admitted, weakly.

"I have some. It's a red homemade wine. My uncle makes it in his basement. He's always giving me a few bottles," Felicia said. She emerged from the kitchen with a bottle against her chest, the neck resting between her breasts. "It's the fruitiest wine I've ever had."

"Sounds good," Michael said.

* * *

Felicia took the dinners out of the microwave, stuck a bowl with a stick of butter into the microwave, and set the timer long enough to melt the entire stick. She picked up the dinner plates and brought them to the table. Michael scooped linguini and clams into each plate, then gave Felicia the larger of the two tails.

"Umm," he said. "Nuked lobster tails."

"It's still lobster, right? I don't care if it was prepared in an Easy-Bake Oven," Felicia said. She poured two glasses of wine and handed one to Michael. She watched him taste it.

"That *is* fruity," he said. "I like it."

"I'm telling you, it's the best wine out there. I told him he should get his own label and market the stuff." She set the bottle down in the center of the table, and sat down.

Michael waited for the timer to go off. “I’m so starving.”

“I wasn’t, but I am now,” Felicia said. The timer went off. Michael removed the bowl of melted butter and set it on the table just as the telephone rang. Giving Michael an apologetic look, she stood up and answered it. “Hello?”

Michael tried not to appear as if he were eavesdropping. However, watching Felicia’s face change expressions from somewhat happy to grim, told Michael that something was terribly wrong. “Okay, okay. I’m on my way.”

When she hung up the telephone, Felicia looked like she might cry.

“Felicia, what’s wrong?”

“That was my sister. She says my father just had a heart attack.”

Chapter 19

Felicia was in no condition to drive. They took Michael's car. He drove as fast as he could to Park Ridge Hospital. Felicia sat silently beside him. She did not cry, but she looked deeply troubled.

"What will I do if my father dies?" She asked.

She was staring out the window when Michael turned to look at her. He was not sure how to respond. His parents were both alive and, at the moment, healthy. "Let's not worry about that just yet. All right? Let's get to the hospital and see what's going on."

Felicia reached over and placed her hand on Michael's leg. She squeezed his thigh. "Thank you for driving me."

"Forget about it," he said, turning onto Long Pond Road. The hospital was less than a mile away. Michael drove a little faster, figuring if a police officer pulled him over, he would be able to provide a reasonable excuse for his excessive speed. "How old is your sister?"

"Thirteen. Her name's Marcia."

Michael never actually pictured Felicia having a family—an uncle that made wine, a mom and a dad, and a sister named Marcia who was only thirteen. It seemed unnatural, like being six and seeing your first grade teacher shopping in a grocery store. He wanted to hear more about Felicia's family, and obviously knew now was not the time to ask questions.

Following the hospital signs, Michael pulled off Long Pond and drove toward the Emergency entrance. He pulled the car up in the ambulance loop. “You take care, all right? Let me know how things turn out,” Michael said. He wanted to go in with her, but did not want to get in the way.

“You’re not coming in?” Felicia asked. Tears brimmed around her eyes.

“Do you want me to come in with you?”

“Please.”

“I’ll go park.”

“I’ll ride with you. I don’t want to walk in there alone,” Felicia said.

Michael pulled out of the loop and found a spot in Visitor Parking. Then he and Felicia walked toward the Emergency entrance. She wrapped her arm around his, and rested her head on his shoulder as they walked. “I’m so scared,” she said. “I’ve never felt this scared before.”

Inside, Michael immediately recognized Marcia. She looked identical to her older sister. They had matching long burgundy-colored hair, milky-complexioned skin, and the largest, most unique, gray-blue eyes he had ever seen. Marcia and Felicia even looked about the same height—five-eight. The only visible difference was their weight. Though Felicia was fit and slim, she might weigh close to one-twenty. Marcia would be lucky to weigh more than one hundred pounds.

As the sisters embraced, Michael stayed in the background. Marcia watched him, while hugging Felicia, and did not look happy about his presence.

“Marcia, how’s dad?”

Looking away from Michael, Marcia swallowed hard. “Not good. Mom’s with him now. They won’t let me in there,” she said, tears rolling down her cheeks. “I just want to be in there with him.”

Felicia went to the nurses’ station. “Excuse me. Why can’t my sister be in the room with our father? He was just brought in . . .”

“I understand the situation, ma’am. Your father’s condition is not stable. As soon as he is, we will let you know. I promise," said a stern-faced nurse.

Felicia, too, was crying. "But if my father doesn't stabilize . . . if he dies . . . then you've prevented my sister and me from saying good-bye."

Felicia's words caused Marcia to cry even harder. Michael wanted to help. He wanted to comfort the young girl. She looked so much like Felicia it was amazing. He moved closer and held out his arms. Marcia regarded him as if he might be a serial killer. She turned away and walked to a row of seats, then sat and buried her head in her hands and sobbed.

Michael strolled down to the end of the hall. Felicia was sitting with Marcia, and the two seemed to be comforting each other. Michael studied the art on the wall—lighthouses in pencil sketches—then flipped through a magazine that had been left sitting on a windowsill beside the vending machines.

When he looked down the hall, Felicia was staring at him. She motioned with her head for him to come back and sit with them. Hesitant, Michael bought two sodas. When he walked back, he handed Felicia a can and offered the other to Marcia.

"No thank you," she said.

Michael set the can down on the armrest of her chair. "For later, then." When the awkward silence lingered, Michael asked, "Any news?"

"Nothing. I wish my mom would come out. I want to know what's happening," Felicia said. She had an arm around her sister and, while she spoke, she hugged the young girl tightly.

By midnight, Michael thought he might fall asleep. No one was talking. Marcia remained distant toward him. Twice she got up to take sips from the water fountain, choosing to completely ignore the soda he had purchased for her.

Felicia stood up and stretched. She ran her palms down her thighs, past her knees, and arched her back. When she stood up, she said, "Why don't you go home? I didn't mean to make you stay this long."

Michael figured that Felicia did not know he had a day job with the City Chronicle, and would need to be up in five hours for work. He tenderly placed his hands on her shoulders. "I'd rather leave after we hear something," Michael said. The paper gave him two weeks paid vacation. He had his supervisor's number in his wallet. If the night looked like it might not end, he would call and request the day off.

And at one, Michael called in for vacation.

At two, Felicia and Marcia's mother came through a set of automated doors. The woman did not look like her daughters. Her hair was dark, almost black, and she wore it short and straight. She had a tissue balled up in her hand and her hand near her mouth. The woman's eyes looked bloodshot-red from crying.

Felicia and Marcia stood up when they saw their mother. Michael could not get a handle on the situation. He could not read the mother, could not guess the prognosis. When the mother spread out her arms, and the girls rushed into them, longing to be held, Michael thought for sure the father has passed away.

"He's all right. Thank God, he's all right," the mother was saying.

The three of them cried. Michael stepped outside for a cigarette. It was five minutes later, as he took the last drag, that the sliding doors opened. Michael expected to see Felicia. He was more than surprised to have Marcia standing next to him. She took a sip from the can of soda he had bought for her. "They say my dad's going to be okay," she said, finally.

Michael just nodded. "I heard. I'm glad." He did not know why, but he felt choked up. A combination of events that had taken place this evening—all of it brewing inside him—seemed like it wanted to spew forth.

"Thanks for the drink," Marcia said.

Holding it in, Michael nodded and watched as Marcia went back inside.

"I got to get out of here," he said out loud. Instead, he crossed the ambulance drop-off loop and walked toward a picnic table in the snow. He used his arm to brush snow of the top of the table. When he sat down, the cold wood almost instantly stung his rump through his jeans. Ignoring the burning cold, Michael smoked a second cigarette, appreciating the moment alone with his thoughts.

Chapter 20

Wednesday, January 16

It was after five. Mostly everyone at the City Chronicle had gone home for the day. Michael stayed in his cubicle and worked on his computer. He sat reviewing a file he had named OBITS. He kept the folder right on the computer desktop. He knew by naming it something boring and work related, no one would be tempted to read through it. Inside, however, Michael kept the drafts on the pieces he was writing about the people at the diner. He also had amassed information related to Casey Hawthorne, the prostitute savagely murdered.

The Rochester City Chronicle was located in an entire high rise downtown. It towered on the west bank of the Genesee River. The structure, designed and built in the early 1900's had a gothic look to it, so much so, a unique gargoyle manned each of the four corners around the twentieth floor.

Crime journalist, Matthew Sinopoli, had been with the City Chronicle, seemingly, since its inception. Though the old man could still write, he was protected by the union, and clearly had lost his vigor, at least to Michael, anyway. He would watch Sinopoli sit at his desk and work on an entire story without ever leaving the office. Sure, computers made things easier. Fax this. E-mail that. Though Michael respected Sinopoli and the man's many achievements, it was hard not to feel resentful toward the ancient journalist at the same time. If Sinopoli wanted a job that tied him to a desk all day, they should switch places. Let Sinopoli write the obituary column while Michael dove headfirst into his passion and fulfilled his dream of becoming a crime reporter.

Sinopoli was famous for his coverage of the Arthur Shawcross case. Shawcross was notorious in Rochester. He had killed many prostitutes, and prior to that, some children. Sinopoli did an amazingly competent job at it. Over the holidays, Michael spent several hours reading the old electronic clippings. What he noted right off was the fact that after Shawcross lost his "Front Page" marketability, Sinopoli's byline stopped appearing on most of the articles. Many of the smaller pieces just had a byline lending credit to the generic Staff Writer.

Michael did some background checking on Jason Cocuzzi, the homicide detective assigned to both the Shawcross case and the one involving Hawthorne. Cocuzzi came with some impressive background information. Since rising to the level of detective, the officer had solved more cases than any other Rochester homicide detective had. The cop modestly explained during an interview that most cases solved themselves. He liked to point out that public involvement made a world of difference. He appreciated neighbors calling in to report a suspicious car parked on the street, or if they spotted someone in someone's backyard.

Michael Buzzelli spent time shadowing Sinopoli. He thought for sure, by demonstrating his interest, the seasoned veteran would throw him a bone, perhaps put in a good word with the editor. His efforts, however, had the exact opposite effect. At the end of the year, just after Christmas, the chief editor had called him into the office. To sum up the conversation in as few words as possible, Michael was ordered to stay away from Sinopoli.

It was this kind of treatment that got Michael thinking. If he was going to make waves, and he so desperately wanted to do so, he would have to find a way on his own. It made more sense to him now. Following around Sinopoli could never have worked. He would have remained in the man's shadow. He needed to find his own angle on the story and write about it. A well-written and unique take on the story would attract the editor's attention. Might he ruffle Sinopoli's feathers? Sure. Did he care? Not at all. Sinopoli had thrown the first literary punch when he had talked to the chief editor.

It was right after the New Year that Michael got the idea to apply for a job at Jack's Joint. He had driven by the place a few times and had taken some photographs. The prostitutes hung out on the corners and people sat inside. There was a story around Jack's. Michael had no doubt about it. The story would be a killer, too. Now he understood, maybe working at Jack's wouldn't help him solve any murder, but the personal pieces he planned to write could lead him down an entirely new career path. Either way, whether he solved the crime, or wrote astounding personal pieces, he would be writing, reporting, and not just typing up obituaries.

Chapter 21

Friday, January 18

Jason Cocuzzi did not hate winter. He hated shoveling. Though only forty-eight, and in top physical shape, he found the laborious act devastating to his back. Tonight, eight-fifteen, the snow was wet and heavy. Hunched forward and over the handle of the shovel, his back relentlessly begged him to stop. All the muscles in his lower back constricted painfully. Each time he scooped up the snow and tossed it onto his snow-covered lawn, the muscles in his back burned as if on fire. With every scraping pass he made across the driveway he thought he might not ever be able to stand up straight again.

It resembled a blizzard, but the news reports on the television had claimed only a winter advisory. The temperatures had dropped ten degrees in the last two hours. Jason, bundled to the hilt in a heavy down winter jacket, gloves and a wool hat, was sweating. Dropping his shovel, he walked to his front step and removed his jacket. Wearing a heavy cotton sweatshirt and a T-shirt underneath that, Jason went back to the chore of clearing his driveway, until three minutes later when a police car turned onto his street.

Leaning on the shovel, Jason watched with curiosity as the squad car drove slowly down the street, shining a beam of light on houses as it made its way, perhaps searching for house numbers.

When at last the path of light played over him, and then his house, the police car stopped. Jason noticed immediately that it was an Irondequoit car, and not a town of Greece car. Irondequoit was on the opposite side of the Genesee River.

Jason groaned inwardly. He did not have to wonder why a police car was at his house. He knew, though he found an Irondequoit car odd. Tempted as he was to turn and run, he remained steadfast and stood his ground. When the officer in the passenger seat rolled his window down and stuck out his head, Jason Cocuzzi asked, “Can I help you, officer?”

“Are you Jason Cocuzzi, sir?”

“I am.”

“Detective Cocuzzi, there’s been a body found in Durand, up at the top of White Lady’s Castle,” the officer explained. “The investigating detective at the scene has been trying to get a hold of you, sir, but no one’s been answering your phone.”

“I left the thing inside while I was shoveling,” Jason said. He tossed the shovel toward his yard. Like a sharp knife into a woodblock, the shovel’s blade landed in the snow and the thing stood erect. Walking to the car, Jason tried to nonchalantly massage his lower back in front of the younger officers. “If the body was found in Durand, why is Irondequoit Police calling me?”

“I’m not sure, sir. We were just told to locate you and give you a ride to the scene if you required one.”

“I won’t need a ride. But if you want to hang on, I’ll change real quick and follow you guys? Want to come in for a quick cup of coffee while I change?” Jason asked. As a policeman since the age of twenty-four, he was in uniform for nearly seven years before moving into plain clothes as a homicide detective. On nights like tonight, a hot cup of coffee always hit the spot and made the rest of the long cold night a little more bearable at times.

“That would be great, sir, if it’s not a bother.”

“None at all. I need a cup myself,” Jason said. He stepped aside so the squad car could pull into the snow-free half of his shoveled driveway.

* * *

Homicide Detective, Jason Cocuzzi, of the Rochester Police Department, found investigating murders to be a hideous task. Most nights, when on a case, sleep came with a price. His dreams were anything but pleasant. In his seven years as a detective he had been exposed to more graphic sights than one might imagine. The horrors of seeing murdered victims were always gruesome, despite the circumstances of the actual killing.

People were cruel to other people. How someone could use a hammer to bludgeon to death a girlfriend was beyond him. The thought of someone poisoning their own child made him sick. In the city of Rochester, it seemed the weapon of choice was the gun. Based on his personal numbers, last year eighty-seven people were murdered. Sixty-nine of them had been killed with a gun. Fifty of those sixty-nine dead were between the ages of sixteen and twenty-five. All but three of the fifty were black, inner city people. Most of the killings took place out on the streets. And in Jason's mind, all of the violent deaths could have been avoided.

Having several unsolved murders going at once, Jason racked his brain trying to figure out which case this new body might be linked with. Since the first month of the New Year was not even over, most people might suspect that the body in Durand would be the first homicide for the year. It was not. This body would make the seventh. The numbers, the victims, the crimes—it was disgusting.

Jason knew of only one reason why he kept at his job with relentless enthusiasm and vigor. He was one of the best at it. He was passionate about his work. To be a detective you needed to be passionate. You had to believe in the cause, if you were going to be of any value on the force and in serving the community.

There were others in the departments who were good at their jobs. Jason did not think "good" cut it. "Good" is okay for some vocations, but not for a police officer—at any rank. More often than not, the work of a police officer is thankless. The people got mad and upset when someone was shot and killed by a police officer, especially if the suspect was black and the shooting officer was white. Never mind the fact that the person was in a crack house during a raid, and had pulled a gun on the police officer.

The road that led to what was falsely known as White Lady's Castle had Lake Ontario to its left. There was no such thing as White Lady's Castle. Even in the dark, with only a crescent of a moon in the sky, Jason could see the white-capped rough waves rolling toward the shore. To his right was Durand Eastman Park—acres of ideal land for summer time picnicking, parties, and family reunions.

Just past the park, and past a large frozen pond, was a shoulder of the road large enough to park a few cars. Jason parked on the main road, switched on his hazard lights, and walked toward the gathering of official cars. There were several Irondequoit squad cars, an ambulance, the medical examiner's station wagon, a mobile forensic unit, and an undercover police car that, except for it being black, matched Jason's white company car identically.

Somehow, a legend spawned a legend. The Lady in White, the original legend, became known as White Lady's Castle because of the decrepit structure Jason Cocuzzi now stood in front of. The Lady in White was the urban legend of a young girl who was raped and murdered by unknown assailants. Years later, the ghost of the girl's mother was said to be roaming the park woods at night with two large dogs, no less, looking to reek revenge on any boys not treating girls . . . respectfully.

The castle part of the myth was tacked on years later because of a wall that resembled something that might be part of a castle. Actually, the wall was part of a walkway and diner that surrounded the old Durand Eastman Park, built back in 1912. The place sold soda pop and ice cream to beach goers. Then there was a devastating fire in 1970 that burned down the roof and first floor. All that remained was the wall and a terrace.

It was not until the 1980's and 90's that the place really became known as White Lady's Castle, when witch covens met in the area and desecrated the wall with spray-painted satanic symbolism. Eventually, a local ordinance forbade people to be in the area after dusk.

Bright lights, the ones professional photographers used, stood like lighthouse beacons at the top of the castle wall. Extension cords ran down the face of the wall and into the forensic mobile unit. A police officer stood at the bottom of the stairs and held up a hand to stop Jason Cocuzzi from going any further.

"I'm Detective Cocuzzi, Rochester Police Department," Jason said.

The officer stepped aside. "Just up this slope, detective. There are rock stairs buried under the snow, and they are covered with ice, so it's slippery. They didn't want us to shovel a path until the area been combed over more closely. With all this new falling snow, you never know what's under it?"

"Footprints?"

"These are all fresh. All made by our guys. We know the killer dragged the victim up to the top from the other side. So you can walk a little easy," the officer said.

"Thank you," Jason said. He walked up the slope, felt the icy stone steps beneath his shoes, and slowed his ascent considerably. He did not want to slip, fall, and roll down the hill.

Once at the top, it looked like a photo-shoot for a pornographic magazine layout. The naked black woman lying on her back in the snow, however, did not look very erotic covered in stab wounds and frozen blood.

* * *

The Irondequoit detective, Peter Cage, stood with Jason Cocuzzi a few yards away from the body, and just out of range from the pool of lights. "We couldn't find I.D. Could be her purse is buried under a blanket of fresh snow and we haven't come across it. We're going to handle it like an archeological dig and explore the area in portions."

"What made you call me?"

"When forensics arrived, they took a finger print, ran it through their computer and came up with a name . . . Vanessa Vorhees. She has an arrest sheet . . . a couple of misdemeanors."

"Soliciting?" Jason asked.

"Yep. Her regular office is the same as the Casey Hawthorne case you're working," Peter Cage said, crossing his arms. "M.O.

looks the same. A knife was used. He cut this one up pretty bad. I didn't see the other victim's corpse, but I've no doubt that a link between the two exists. So once I realized this, we tried getting a hold of you."

"Had the phone off. I was shoveling the driveway," Jason said, patting the phone clipped to his belt. "Can I look more closely at the body?"

The two detectives walked over to the crime scene. The forensic team had already bagged Vanessa Vorhees' hands to protect foreign substances from contaminating possible evidence trapped under the woman's fingernails.

"Murder didn't take place here?"

"We don't believe so. Not enough blood. Of course, all the blood could be in the old snow underneath, but if you look at the snow you can see, she was dragged up the embankment. Doesn't mean she was dead, though."

"Time of death?" Jason asked, looking at the wounds on the victim's body. Though not identical to the ones found on Casey Hawthorne, they appeared similar enough. The vaginal area looked bad, covered in lacerations. Both women practically had their breasts sliced off. Each woman also shared a long cut from between the breasts down to the pubic area. Definitely, the wounds were similar.

One disturbing thing about the Hawthorne case was the fact, before dumping the body, the killer washed the victim's body using a powerful hose and abrasive soap. He scrubbed down her skin with a sponge and flushed out every orifice by inserting the hose, as if trying to fill a water balloon. The act washed away any evidence that may have been left behind.

"The forensics tech took a temperature. The M.E.'s here, but wanted to wait until he had the body on his table before he commented. Can't blame him. With how cold it is, he's going to need the liver to give us a better idea," Cage noted.

"Any witnesses . . . anything?"

"Nothing like a witness. An old man walking his dog without a leash found the body. The dog took off, ran up here, and started sniffing around. Guy came up for his dog, saw the body, and puked."

Jason stood up straight. "When was this?"

"Two hours ago."

It had been snowing all day. "How exposed was the body?"

"Wasn't. The dog did a little digging. When the first police car arrived, he secured the area. No one was really around. The man and his dog were waiting for him at the bottom of the slope. By the time I got here, everything was still preserved, minus the mutt's digging," Peter Cage explained. "The victim's toes were sticking out of the snow, but her legs, belly, and arms were buried. The dog had done his digging around the head."

"What would you guess . . . four inches of snow on top of her?"

"Sounds close, for a guess," Cage said.

"Let's contact the weather bureau, find out the accumulation and times, and see if we can't better determine how long ago the body was dumped." Jason walked back toward the snow-hidden staircase. He wanted to get his own camera out of the car.

"So you think it's the same killer, too?"

Without looking back, Jason said, "It sure as hell looks that way."

Chapter 22

Never married, Jason did not feel the pang of guilt many police officers felt when they needed to work long grueling hours. Most women he dated understood this going into the relationship, but seemed to forget their "understanding" after a few weeks. He could not blame them. Relationships were difficult and trying enough without adding the variable of a time-absorbing-homicide-detective to the list of seemingly never-ending compromises. Not that compromise is bad. It is not. It is good, at least when it is two-sided. Women wanted Jason to compromise his life's work to attend a friend's party, or a wedding, or a funeral. His schedule was not a nine-to-five day. Day or night, if someone was murdered, Jason needed to be available.

The first forty-eight hours after a homicide are the most critical. For two days he would not see, or even call, a girlfriend. All his girlfriends hated that part of the relationship. What they continually failed to realize was, if a murderer was not caught within those two days, the chances of catching the killer grew less and less likely with each passing minute.

Most murderers kill a person they know, so police spend hours around the clock investigating, by interviewing friends and family of the victim. More times than not, this task-intensive method produced several suspect leads. It is rare, although it does happen, when a person is killed by a stranger.

The serial killer is more unique. Though only two victims had shown up, there was a pattern that Jason was all too familiar with. The definition of a serial killer is when a person kills more than three people at different times, when the killing methods are similar, and the killer does many things to protect his identity and avoid being apprehended.

Jason Cocuzzi knew he was dealing with a serial killer, regardless of the low body count, and serial killings were nothing new to the Rochester area. One of the most renowned serial killers was Arthur Shawcross, who moved from Watertown, New York to Rochester. In 1972, Shawcross was convicted and served only fifteen years of a twenty-five year sentence. His crime? Shawcross brutally murdered two children—a young ten-year-old boy and an eight-year-old girl.

When Shawcross arrived in Rochester, and got married, few people knew about the murderer's horrid past. Not owning a car, Shawcross would often be seen riding a "girl's" bicycle to go fishing along the banks of the murky waters of the Genesee. However, in 1988, a killing spree started. Bodies of murdered and mutilated prostitutes began showing up all over the place.

Within two years, and five bodies later, the police knew for certain that they were dealing with a serial killer. The name donned for the maniac? The Genesee River Killer.

As luck would have it, a police helicopter spotted a body in Salmon Creek and a man on the bridge with his car, urinating into a bottle. A squad car was dispatched and followed the driver to a nursing home. Shawcross had borrowed his mistress' car. The police eventually let him go, but picked him up the following day when, upon further exploration of the impounded vehicle, they found an earring to match that of one of the dead prostitutes. After four hours of interrogation, Arthur Shawcross confessed to being the Genesee River Killer.

One of the gruesome details from the case that struck a chord with Jason was the fact that Shawcross often times cut out the vaginas of his victims, and then ate them. The killer Jason was dealing with now seemed to be using his blade like a penis. If

Shawcross had not been sentenced to consecutive life terms, he would swear the bastard had escaped from prison and was back to terrorizing his old stomping grounds.

Though the police and the FBI did fantastic work combining talent, resources, and technology to find and convict Shawcross, Jason did not want to risk waiting for another three bodies to show up before catching this new Rochester nightmare.

At his trunk, Jason Cocuzzi retrieved his own crime scene bag. With experience teaching him what to pack, Jason felt confident that he would be ready for most situations. The bag was stuffed full with boxes of Latex gloves, brown paper bags in a variety of sizes, Kodak one-time-use cameras, a tape recorder, flashlights, batteries, a knife, tape, a rope, paper, pens, and just about anything else he might need or want at a crime scene.

When he closed the trunk lid, Peter Cage was standing at the front of Jason's car with his hands in his pockets. "Hey, detective."

"You can call me, Jason."

"I just got off the horn with my chief. He wants me to offer my assistance to you. He doesn't like the idea of the body being dumped in his neck of the woods," Peter said hesitantly.

"I don't have a problem with that," Jason replied. The department was always short warm bodies. He would welcome the help of an experienced detective.

"Yeah, great. I'm sure there's some PR bullshit tied up in there someplace, too," Peter Cage added, thoughtfully.

"Usually is. How many homicide cases have you worked?" Jason asked.

"Including this one?" Cage said, disdainfully. "One."

The body of Casey Hawthorne had been discovered at the base of the Charlotte Lighthouse by a couple taking photographs of the historic landmark. To get to the lighthouse, you needed to drive down Stutson Street. Stutson Street also led you over the river into Irondequoit. So, in retrospect, both of the victims were dumped in a generic central location.

While the detectives walked back up to the scene, Jason began to brief Peter on some of the facts of the Hawthorne case. "Casey was twenty-three, pretty—or was—until the killer used a blade to slice up her skin. She had a distinct hair color—blond with black streaks in it. Like Vanessa Vorhees, Casey had been a prostitute, too. She had a short arrest record, but little else. A case like this was more difficult to investigate because the chances were much better that a john—a total stranger—killed them."

"Where'd you start digging?" Detective Cage asked.

"The corner they hang out on has a small restaurant . . . a diner, really . . . a place called Jack's Joint. The hole's filled with all the types of city riff-raff. Believe it or not, we rarely get calls to dispatch units. It's kind of like a place for the crooks and prostitutes to hang out while they wait for their next . . . I don't know what you'd call it . . . thing," Jason said. "I went there, talked with the owner, talked with some of the other girls, talked with a couple of regulars, but turned up nothing. It took me forever to have everyone relax. They were all so worried about getting arrested themselves, that they only half-heard everything I was saying to them. The girls I talked to were helpful. They knew Casey and were genuinely distraught by the news of her death."

"So now we have to stand out here freezing our asses off because another two-bit whore gets herself killed?" Peter Cage said. "This is great . . . just wonderful."

Jason closed his mouth and stared intently at the unseasoned detective. "You got a problem, detective?"

"No. Yeah, I guess I do. I can't see why . . ."

"I didn't ask you what that problem was, and I don't want to hear about your problem again. For your information, the two-bit whores being murdered are women. They are people . . . human beings. Believe it or not, I'll bet my pension that neither one of these unfortunate victims went out and 'got themselves killed.' Someone brutally murdered them . . . vicious, disgusting, and just brutal murders," Jason said more loudly than he had planned. His voice attracted the unwanted attention of those working the scene. His purpose was not to humiliate the Irondequoit detective, just to sternly reprimand him.

"You're right, detective. And I'm sorry," Peter Cage said.

Satisfied, Jason nodded.

"From now on, I'll keep my problems to myself," Cage said

spitefully, and walked away.

Shaking his head, Jason nearly jumped when someone tapped his shoulder.

"Sorry, I didn't mean to startle you," the man said. Except for dark brown eyes and wrinkled skin around them, Jason saw little of the man's face. He was sure a person was somewhere buried under the layers of winter clothing.

"Detective Jason Cocuzzi. Can I help you?"

"It's Dr. Green," the man replied.

The M.E. "Alex is that you under all that clothing?"

"I been out here two hours. I'm damn glad I wore all this."

"They call you away from home, too?" Jason asked, figuring Monroe County would want to use the same medical examiner for this victim as was used for Hawthorne.

"They would have, I'm sure, but no, tonight was my night on call," Dr. Green pointed out. "Get a chance to look at the body? Is it all right if we wrap it up and head back to the morgue?"

"I just want to snap off a few photos. I'll be quick about it," Jason explained.

"That's fine. Hey, I heard that exchange between you and the other detective."

"Young and inexperienced," Jason commented.

"You could say that," Dr. Green said. "I just think he's a prick."

Chapter 23

Fatso and Michael Buzzelli had been arguing about the Super Bowl all night. "You're not seeing it, kid. The Giants are a more powerful team. The Dolphins look good on paper, but they only win games by the skin of their teeth," Fatso said. The sports section of the paper was laid out in front of him on the counter. "Most of the games they won, they only won by three points."

"Did they win the games though, Fatso? Huh? They won them, right? From what I hear, you only need to win by one point. Unless the rules have changed," Michael said sarcastically. "The quarterback is young, has a strong arm, and his line gives him enough time . . . more than enough time . . . to get rid of the ball."

"He's no Dan Marino," Fatso commented. Marino had been critically acclaimed as the Dolphins best quarterback ever, but many thought he may have been the best quarter back in NFL history—despite never winning a Super Bowl.

Growing increasingly annoyed with Fatso, Michael silently noted that Marcus had not been in yet. He wondered if the man would show. He could not help but think the reason behind the absence was based on the altercation that had taken place last Saturday night.

The wind picked up outside, sounding like a giant rabid werewolf howling at a full moon. In truth, the moon was hidden behind thick snow clouds which loomed over Rochester all day and had been relentlessly hammering the city with inch-after-inch of the annoying white stuff.

When Sandy came in, her cheeks were so red she looked like a Raggedy Ann doll. "Do you know how cold it is out, Michael?" she asked, sitting at a counter stool. "I'm wearing a mini skirt, these stupid cowboy boots . . . with no traction on the bottom . . . and the fake fur coat. I'm frozen. Look at my hands," she said, holding her fingers out for Michael's expression.

"They are red," he said. "Why don't you wear gloves?"

"Too much clothing isn't good in my line of work." Sandy lit a cigarette, smiling.

"A sexy pair of thin black leather gloves. Sounds kind of erotic to me," Michael said.

"You think?"

"Sure."

"Maybe I'll have Speed pick me up a pair tomorrow," Sandy said, nonchalantly. "Fatso, you seen Felicia? She hasn't been around all week. I've tried calling her, but nothing. Between her and Vanessa, you'd think I'm the last prostitute on earth. Hey . . . there's a good title for a book. The Last Prostitute on Earth."

"Yeah, great title, Sandy. Why don't you write it," Fatso said.

Michael was thinking it was a great title for a book and stored the name away in his memory. "Felicia's father had a pretty bad heart attack last week."

"He did? Oh, the poor thing." Sandy looked around the place. "Should I try calling her again?"

"How do you know this?" Fatso asked Michael.

Smiling, Michael shrugged. It was answer enough as far as Fatso would be concerned. Michael thought he noted a look of disapproval on Fatso's face before the large man lifted the sports page and buried himself in an article.

"Michael? Should I try calling her?" Sandy asked a second time.

Michael shrugged. His attention focused on the window. A part of him felt elated. A larger part of him was disappointed. "I don't think you'll need to."

The door opened and Felicia walked in. Her eyes darted around the diner, and settled on Michael. She rewarded him with a small timid smile. She looked stunning. Michael could not believe how taken he was by her beauty. He loved that hair, those eyes. Today, unlike Saturday night, she wore her hair down. The long loose curls bounced as she walked over to the counter and, when she sat down, she needed to brush the hair away from her eyes, but did not. The dangling curl made her look exotic.

Sandy placed a hand on Felicia's arm. "I'm sorry to hear about your dad."

Felicia threw a dagger-look at Michael. Those gray-blue eyes looked hard as steel and cold as ice. It was a quick fling of her expression that hit its mark. Michael knew instantly that he had done something wrong. He knew instinctively what it was, too.

"Thank you," Felicia said to Sandy. "He's doing much better now, thank you." The words came out short and abrupt. It seemed evident that Felicia preferred not to talk about her father, wanting to keep her personal life private.

"So, working tonight?" Michael tried to ask casually. His words caught Fatso's attention. He saw the man peering at him from over the edge of his paper. Even Sandy gave him an odd look.

Felicia looked uncomfortable. "No," she said. "I'm here for your cooking."

Sandy laughed. Michael just smiled.

"It's slow out there tonight," Sandy said. "You'd think when it's cold more people would want to get warmed up."

"You'd think," Felicia said. "Maybe I will eat before I go out. Can I get a tuna-melt, with chips? It's the closest thing to Lobster tails."

Michael, continuing to smile, went in back to the cooler. He picked out the small tub of tuna, added extra mayonnaise, mixed it up, and made her sandwich on the counter in back. He added some pre-sliced cheese to the bread, then put away the cheese and tuna. He set the sandwich on a plate and went out front to grill the order.

Two men stood in the doorway. They had everyone's attention. One guy resembled a cop in his long tan overcoat. The other man was wearing a heavy winter coat, but did not look like a cop. He looked like a punk.

"Do you know where Jack Murphy is?" The man wearing the heavy winter coat asked. "I'm Detective Jason Cocuzzi, with the Rochester Police Department. This is Detective Peter Cage, from Irondequoit."

Setting the plate down, Michael walked the length of the counter and extended his hand to both. "I'm Michael Buzzelli. I started here about two weeks ago so Murphy could have his nights off. Is there anything I can help you with? Is this about the attempted robbery from last week?"

Michael recognized Detective Jason Cocuzzi immediately. He had seen enough about the police officer in the articles written by Sinopoli at the City Chronicle. Michael wanted to keep things cool. If he let on that he knew who Cocuzzi was, people might begin to wonder. It would ruin his angle on the story he planned to write.

Detective Cage shook his head. "Afraid not, son."

Michael clearly saw the distressed look on Sandy and Felicia's face. He wondered if they were about to be busted for soliciting. That did not feel right. He thought the police needed to catch a prostitute in the act of trying to sell her body for money before an arrest could be made, but he could be wrong. The women obviously knew the one policeman. They kept watching the detective in the heavy coat, Detective Cocuzzi, expectantly.

"Well," Michael said, tentatively, "is there something I can do?"

Detective Cocuzzi stepped forward, closer to the counter, but when he spoke he was addressing all of the diners. "Did any of you know of a woman by the name of Vanessa Vorhees?"

"Ah God, I knew it," Felicia said. All at once her body began to tremble. She and Sandy were crying. "Please, no."

Detective Cage leaned on the counter. Michael did not like the look on the young cop's face as he addressed the women. "Then you both knew the prostitute?"

Michael felt his pulse rate increase. There must have been another killing. It was the only thing that made sense. Where he thought he would be excited and anxious to be this close to the news, Michael felt his stomach muscles tightening. Could Venus have been murdered?

Felicia, as if she had been slapped, turned to look at Cage. Cocuzzi put a hand on the cop's shoulder. Cage stood up. "I spoke with you ladies a few months ago," Cocuzzi said, softly. "Before the holidays, when your friend Casey Hawthorne had been found."

Michael liked the way Cocuzzi proceeded. Tactfully. Gently. The careful reference to Casey Hawthorne spoke volumes. Everything Michael had read about the detective suggested a warm personality. It made all the difference, though, to see the man in action.

"Of course I remember talking with you," Felicia said. "Vanessa's dead?"

"Her body was discovered a little earlier today," Cocuzzi explained. "When was the last time you saw her? Can you remember?"

Felicia had tears that continued to roll down her cheeks, but she was not sobbing. She chewed on her thumbnail while she thought. "It feels like yesterday."

"Could it have been?" Cage asked.

"No. No, it couldn't have been. I haven't been around . . . not since last Saturday," Felicia said.

"On a vacation, were you?" Cage asked.

Sandy said, "I've been calling Vanessa at home since Saturday. The last time I saw her was Friday night."

"Do you remember where you saw her last?" Cocuzzi asked.

"It was here. We were all here," Sandy said. She had her eyes closed as if she might be trying to materialize an image in her mind. When she opened them, she was looking directly at Michael. "It was your first night. Vanessa was telling you to call her Venus."

"I remember," Michael said, somberly. A pang of guilt gripped him. He knew why he was here, working at Jack's Joint. However, the thought of why he was here had not troubled him before. He felt his chest constricting suddenly, while his breathing became irregular. The two police detectives, Felicia, and Sandy watched him. Michael was not aware of what was going on around him. At the moment, he did not care.

"Everything all right, Mr. Buzzelli?" Cage asked. He held onto a six-by-nine spiral notebook and stopped taking notes long enough to ask his question. "Sir?"

"With me? Yes. I'm sorry. I'm just a little overwhelmed."

"How so?" Cocuzzi asked.

"I mean, I didn't know Vanessa or anything, but to think that now she's dead . . . that's a little . . . I don't know . . . unnerving."

"Vanessa Vorhees was murdered, Mr. Buzzelli. Would you happen to know anything about the crime?" Cage asked, effectively accusing Michael of murder without making any accusations. Michael stood up straight. From his peripheral vision, he knew everyone's attention was focused on him. He desperately wanted a cigarette, but refrained. He did not want the police to interpret his actions as quirky and nervous.

To Michael, this felt like the times when he would be driving down a road and a police car would pull up behind him. Though he had not been speeding, and was actually following all traffic laws, he would think for sure the police officer was just waiting for him to screw up so he could pull him over. At that instant, driving would become an extremely difficult challenge. He would feel drunk. Keeping the car straight and between the lines would seem impossible. And when the police car made a turn onto another road, leaving Michael alone, he would sigh with relief and wonder why he had become nervous in the first place.

"I don't know a thing about it. She was here, just like Sandy said. The three of them," Michael said. He wanted to be sure to answer the questions, but not to over do it. He craved a cigarette now more than at any other time in his life.

"Do you remember if Ms. Vorhees was working that night?" Cocuzzi asked again, using care and grace in his wording. Michael knew the older detective was studying him. He wanted to tell them what was going on—about why he was there. Now was not the time to do so.

"She was," Sandy answered. Michael was thankful for the break in attention, though Detective Cocuzzi continued to watch him a full ten, intense, seconds longer.

"Did the three of you go out to work together?" Cage asked. He managed not to call the ladies whores, and he managed not to use any other insulting words in his question. Still, his tone clearly voiced his prejudices.

While Sandy and Felicia seemed to wrestle with their memories, Michael remembered the night clearly. It had been his first night working, so everything was more vibrant—an overdose to his senses. Then afterward, he had logged into his journal the accounts of the day. He did not want to bring up his journal. The police would confiscate the electronic file as evidence. Hell, they might take the entire computer.

"She went out alone. It was cold that night . . . windy. Sandy and Felicia stayed inside for a while," Michael said. As much as he did not want to forfeit his journal, neither did he want to withhold information which might prove helpful in the murder investigation.

Once again, he had everyone's full attention. He hated seeing Detective Cage writing notes so vehemently. Surely the man was capturing every word he had spoken with dead-accuracy. A journalist stuck inside a homicide detective's body. The thought almost made Michael smile. The seriousness of the current situation kept him from doing so.

"Know a time?" Detective Cocuzzi asked.

"Three-thirty. No later." Michael Buzzelli thought at that instant he might be in trouble. He seemed to have more answers than anyone else did. He felt uncomfortable talking. It felt like his tongue was drying out in his mouth and swelling.

"You saw her go outside?"

"Yes."

"Would you be able to see Vanessa if you looked through that window?" Cocuzzi asked, pointing to the window in front of the first booth which provided a picturesque view of the street corner.

"I suppose I could. Yes," Michael said. His mind chewed on the question, beginning its search for a memory of Vanessa standing outside. He was sure he had watched her, even if for a moment. It fascinated him to think of a woman hopping into a car with a strange man, ready to perform such intimate acts.

"Can you remember seeing her standing out there?" Cage asked.

"I can, I think."

"What's she doing?"

"She looks cold. She's hugging herself. She's rocking from side-to-side."

Both detectives moved a little closer to Michael. Cage asked the inevitable. "Did you see anyone stop to pick her up?"

Michael prided himself on being observant. Details were part of his professional training, yes, but also a part of his person. Perhaps if he did not love writing as much as he did, he would have considered a job in law enforcement. Racking his brain for even the hint of a recollection became almost painful. Michael realized that his eyes had been squeezed shut. "I can't remember."

"But you're suggesting that you might have seen her get in a car?" Cocuzzi asked.

Again, he tried to recall seeing a car stop and Vanessa climb in, but still nothing. "I don't know. I can't remember."

"Well you sure did do an excellent job remembering a lot of other specific details," Detective Cage was quick to point out, only he seemed to be talking to Cocuzzi when he made the statement. "What time do you get off work, Mr. Buzzelli?"

"Like . . . seven."

"Are you familiar with the police precinct down on Lake and Ridgeway?" Detective Cocuzzi asked.

"I was just there on Sunday," Michael said.

"Ah . . . yeah . . . right . . . the attempted robbery. Detective Cocuzzi filled me in on that incident," Cage said. "How about you meet us down there at seven? We have a few more questions we'd like to ask you."

Michael shrugged. "If you think it's necessary."

"We do. We think it's necessary," Cage said while Cocuzzi began handing out his business card.

"Please, call any of those numbers if you can think of anything . . . anything at all . . . that might be helpful to us in solving this murder. Maybe you remember seeing Vanessa at the mall on Monday, or at the grocery store on Wednesday. Anything, no matter how unimportant it may seem to you . . . it could be the exact piece of information we've been searching for. All right?" Detective Cocuzzi asked. Most of the people shrugged, nodding their heads.

Fatso, studying the business card, raised his hand as if he were in school. "Detectives, are we to assume that the same person who killed Casey might have killed Vanessa, too?"

"No one is supposed to assume anything," Cage said in a harsh tone.

"But you think the deaths are linked in some way?" Fatso persisted.

"What are you, a freaking reporter?" Cage said.

Cocuzzi put a silencing hand on Cage's shoulder and said, "It is far too early in this investigation to determine if the murders are linked. We know that someone killed Casey Hawthorne, and we know that someone killed Vanessa Vorhees. Right now, that's about all we know."

When the detectives looked like they might be ready to leave, Fatso asked, "So let me ask you this, then. Are more working girls missing, and you just don't know about it yet?"

"That's always a possibility," Cocuzzi said. "It's a possibility because most working girls do not work set hours, do they? A lot of working girls don't have a lot of close family that might become anxious if they haven't talked to each other in a while, right? It is unfortunate, but without a report, there is not much the police can do. More people need to get involved and let the police handle things. What is even more unfortunate, are situations like this, where it's too late to file a missing persons report."

Cocuzzi waited a while before turning to leave.

"One more question," Fatso said.

"Who's he think he is? Freaking Columbo?" Cage asked.

"Like you say, since most of these working girls do not have close family ties, if someone called you and told you a prostitute hasn't been around in a while, would you take that call serious?"

Point well made, Michael thought. *Bravo, Fatso.*

Unhappy with Fatso's question, Cage looked like he needed to vent. He pointed an unwavering finger at Michael. "We'll see you at seven?"

"I'll be there," Michael said, stuffing Detective Cocuzzi's business card into his back pocket.

* * *

Jack's Joint remained silent, long after the policemen left. Felicia and Sandy sat side by side on stools, with their backs to the counter. They held hands, but neither cried. Michael lit that cigarette. A sudden sense of relief filled him as he inhaled the smoke. Fatso ignored his paper and stared at the window in front of the first booth.

Michael knew the moment he met her that Vanessa was high energy, wild, and untamable. Her attitude, like an obscenely strong perfume, preceded her into any room she entered.

"So what the hell was that all about?" Fatso asked, finally. He stared at Michael. "Why you think the cops want to talk to you?"

"Do you have a lawyer?" Sandy asked, spinning around on her stool.

"A lawyer? No," Michael said. He felt touched. These people he had known a few days appeared genuinely concerned for his well-being. "Look, they liked the way I answered questions. They think maybe I might know more than I told them . . . like there's more in my memory, and if they spend a little more time with me, they might be able to piece something together. That's all."

Felicia faced Michael on her stool. She reached across the counter and placed her hand over his. "It didn't sound that way. I think that Cage cop is mean. I wouldn't want to answer questions for him. He's the kind of cop who's good at twisting words around for his benefit. You go in there to answer questions, next thing you know, and that cop has you confessing to something you didn't do. I don't like him, Michael."

"Me either," Sandy said.

"Michael, maybe you should call a lawyer. We know one, Sandy and I, and he's good."

"And affordable," Sandy added.

Michael loved the feel of Felicia's hand on his. He wanted to turn his hand palm-up and envelop her long slender fingers in his own. Because the others were watching, he did not. "I appreciate this . . . your concern . . . I do. Trust me, I'm not in any trouble here. I was here with you guys when we all saw Vanessa last. There is no way I am a suspect," Michael said trying to convince himself as much as the others.

Chapter 24

Saturday, January 19

The detectives were both drinking coffee out of Styrofoam cups, and offered Michael Buzzelli some. When Michael passed, Detective Cocuzzi led him down a hallway, a file in his hand, talking all the while. "We reserved a room so we could talk more privately. When we talk, we're going to record the conversation, just to make sure we get everything you say, and that also gives Detective Cage's hands a break. He's been scribbling away like a fiend. Do you have a problem with us recording the conversation?"

Michael looked at Detective Cage, who flashed a crooked smile. Michael enjoyed the fact that they were calling it a conversation instead of an interrogation. It made the entire ordeal a little more informal and relaxed. Michael shrugged. "No. I don't have any problem with that."

They led Michael into a ten-by-ten room with bare pale-blue walls. The room's only furniture was a slate gray steel table, with four matching chairs. Detective Cocuzzi placed the file on the table and removed a sheet of paper from it. "If you'll sign here. It's a form saying you understand we'll be taping the conversation," Cocuzzi explained after seeing the questioning expression on Michael's face.

"Am I going to need an attorney present?"

"Why would you?" Cage asked. "We haven't placed you under arrest. We just want to talk with you . . . ask you some more questions. It was hard concentrating at that diner . . . too many people and distractions. In this environment, we are free of those distracting elements, don't you think?"

"But if you decide you want an attorney present, you can stop the conversation at any given point and request one. I don't see why you would. You're not trying to hide anything, right?"

"Of course not. I'm just . . . this is new to me. It's odd, you know? You guys do stuff like this all the time," Michael said, taking the pen from Cocuzzi and signing the form. Suddenly unnerved by the turn of events, he did not feel safe, despite all the police officers in the building. He felt open and vulnerable. Truthfully, he wanted to leave. If he was not a suspect, then he did not have to be here. If anything, he knew he should have an attorney present to protect his rights. Cocuzzi made it sound like it would be an admission of guilt if he requested to have an attorney present for the laid-back and casual conversation. Though Ellen was not a criminal attorney, just listening to her talk about violated rights, Michael knew differently.

"Have a seat?" Cocuzzi offered, motioning with his hand while he sat down on one side of the table. Michael sat down, feeling moderately equal with Cocuzzi, but intimidated by Cage who remained standing.

"Not much of a file," Cocuzzi said, pushing the manila folder toward the center of the table. "No priors . . . nothing. You've been a good kid. Graduated from Gates-Chili High School with slightly above average grades. You went to SUNY Brockport and earned a degree in journalism. Worked for the college paper all four years, but made it as the editor for the last two. Impressive."

"Thank you," Michael said, uneasily. It was odd having someone sum up your achievements. It was also odd knowing that they had done a check on him. He could not help feeling violated and vulnerable—it was an inescapable feeling.

"Graduated slightly above average than the rest of your class and landed a nice entry level position on The Rochester City Chronicle," Cocuzzi said, wrapping up the information. "Like it at the paper?"

"Yes. For the most part."

"See, I wouldn't think you'd like it at all," Cage said. "You went from being an editor at the college paper, to working as the obits columnist. That must suck."

"Got to start somewhere," Michael said evenly. The job at the paper did suck. Everyone in the room knew it sucked. He knew Cage had to be shrewd. He planned to pace himself and think before he spoke.

"But writing obits?"

"Some friends of mine, that I graduated with, can't even get a job on a paper," Michael said. It was true. More than half the people at Brockport who graduated with a degree in journalism were without a job. Some were landing jobs as assistants to copy editors.

"I see they pay you pretty good," Cocuzzi said. "Nice starting salary, benefits, vacation."

"I can't complain there."

"What would you complain about?" Cage asked.

"Nothing."

"There's got to be something," Cage said. "No job is perfect. With my job, I hate all the paperwork. It doesn't end. When I was in uniform, I hated writing a speeding ticket. It didn't seem worth the effort. I just would warn everyone. I'd say, 'Don't let me catch you speeding again.'" Cage wiggled his finger at an imaginary person. Smiling, he looked at Michael and crossed his arms. "Worst part of the job . . . paperwork."

"Well, I would like to be an actual journalist and work on a real story," Michael said, stating an obvious truth. He hoped by giving a little that they would be happy.

"Of course you would," Cocuzzi said.

"I know if I stick at it, I'll get my shot," Michael added. He inwardly cursed himself. He knew he should keep his replies short. Whether they knew of his ambitions or not, he should never volunteer more than what is asked. Still, the silence lingered. He felt compelled to talk.

"Ever think, 'Hey, if I can get an exclusive on a story they'll have to move me into a better position with the paper?'" Cage asked.

"Only all the time," Michael said. He knew now why he had been called down to the police station. They did not want more information about Vanessa. Everything he told the police the other night had been written down. They did not seem to have any questions about Vanessa. This preamble of questions was about him. "Can I explain something here?"

"By all means," Detective Cocuzzi said.

"I took the second job at Jack's so I could hopefully find an exclusive. You saw that place . . . the people in it. It's a story bubbling to be noticed. A piece waiting to be written. I could do several articles on the variety of people I've met in just the last few weeks.

"It's no accident that I picked Jack's, either. I followed the article in the paper about Casey Hawthorne. I knew that was her hang out. I don't want to say I was hoping for another murder . . . that's sick . . . but I was hoping to find out more about her, about what happened. In a way, I think I was hoping to solve the crime," Michael said. "But that was not the purpose." He hated having to reveal his "secret identity." He also knew how he must sound. *I was hoping to solve the crim*e. He felt as if he had just lodged his foot in his mouth.

Cage smiled. "And that's why you gave up your weekends, to try to get some inside tracks to stories dealing with real peoples lives. Let me ask you this. The people at Jack's . . . they know you're a reporter?"

Michael lowered his head. "Not really."

"Why didn't you tell them?" Cage asked. "I'll tell you why, because not a single person in there would talk to you if they knew the truth, isn't that so? So here you are befriending people under false pretenses . . . why? So you can write stories about their poor, pathetic lives. How wonderful for you. What a wonderful opportunity you've come across."

"That's enough Cage," Cocuzzi interjected.

"I think most reporters are scum. Heartless people. Meeting you, fresh out of school, has done nothing to restore my faith in your kind. You know what? You people are almost as bad as attorneys," Cage said with conviction.

"I said, that's enough," Cocuzzi yelled.

Cage raised his eyebrows. "You worked Friday night until Saturday morning, seven in the morning, right?"

Back to the business at hand. "That's right."

"At seven, Saturday morning, were there many people in Jack's Joint?" Detective Cocuzzi asked.

"A few." Speed was having breakfast, he remembered.

"Were Felicia or Sandy around?" Cocuzzi asked.

"No."

"Were any of the 'working girls' around?" Cage asked.

"No."

"After you left Jack's, where did you go?"

"Home."

"Directly?"

"Yes," Michael said. "And no, I didn't stop anywhere along the way. And no, I don't have an alibi."

"So is it safe to say that you might have been the last person to see Vanessa Vorhees alive?" Detective Cage asked as smoothly as a man with his crass personality would allow.

"If Friday night is the actual night someone killed her, then yes. I guess you might say I was the last one to see her."

"How long did you know Vanessa?"

"I'd just met her," Michael said. He felt tense. He did not like how this was playing out. The police were doing a wonderful job of making him feel insecure. He wondered how his answers sounded to the police. Inside he felt jittery, shaky.

"Did you ever sleep with her?" Cage asked, crass back in full swing.

"No. I had just met her."

"So then you were attracted to her?"

"I never said that, either. She offered to let me . . . what she called . . . test-drive her for free." Michael regretted even bringing that up. It sounded irrelevant.

"And when did you test-drive her?" Detective Cocuzzi asked.

"I didn't. I wouldn't."

"Wouldn't? Why not?"

"I didn't find her attractive. Besides, I have . . . had a girlfriend." Feeling more and more trapped by the moment, Michael wanted to scream. He knew a mistake when he saw one. With every question he answered, he was subjecting himself to more and more questions. Each question seemed to travel further and further from Vanessa's murder, and deeper and deeper into his personal life, and somehow linking the two together.

"Had?" Cocuzzi asked.

"We recently separated."

"Because of Vanessa?" Cage asked.

"Not because of Vanessa," Michael said. *Because of Felicia*, he thought.

* * *

Michael Buzzelli felt whipped. The questions kept coming at him. He did the best he could. He answered everything honestly. It made it easy to keep the facts straight, despite the variety of ways Cage worded his line of questioning.

When finally the "conversation" seemed about to end, Cocuzzi sat down in a chair next to Michael and stared into his eyes. "You know Michael, it might be true, what you said about trying to find a story. You might be this noble reporter out to catch himself a killer, but listen to me. All right? Don't let me find out you've jeopardized an official police investigation. You can write as many articles as you want about the people who hang out at that dump on Lake Avenue, but don't . . . got me? Don't screw with my investigation."

Cage was grinning. Michael stood up. "Are we through now?"

"One more thing," Cocuzzi said. He remained sitting, leaned back in the chair, crossed his legs at the ankles, and hooked his thumbs into his gun belt. "By some fluke of nature, should you stumble across the killer, you better have it set in your head to contact the police as soon as possible. This is not some Lawrence Block novel. You let the police handle it."

Michael thought about this. If he found the killer and contacted the police with the information, he wanted an exclusive. At this point, saying so would be moot. "I can go now?"

"You can go," Cocuzzi said.

Chapter 25

Martin Wringer did not understand his feelings. Before losing his job, he considered himself a focused man. His wife even thought he suffered from Obsessive Compulsive Disorder. He always hated when his former wife would do that—label him. If anyone had a disorder, it was her. He never met anyone like her. She would start something and not finish it. She would do something, but not with her whole heart behind the task. Sometimes she called him anal-retentive. Between that and saying he suffered from OCD, Wringer knew she had not been complimenting him. When he started something, he put all he had into the task, and by God, he finished it. It could take him twenty-four hours straight, but he would not stop until everything was done, and done correctly.

Screw her!

Now, with everything changing in his life, these new feelings felt confusing. For all intents and purposes, he should not feel the way he did. He lost his job, but felt wonderful. He lost his wife, and was elated. He had nowhere to live, but in his van, and he felt free.

Free. For once, no rules bound him. No responsibilities controlled him. He had thought he had been happy before. He had thought his life was near perfect. Why wouldn't he? Wife, kids, house. Why wouldn't he be happy? Because the wife and the kids and the house—God the house—they were like chains holding him back, tying him down. What more could he have been responsible for, that carried as great a weight as the ones he only so recently freed himself from?

So maybe he did not understand his feelings because they were entirely new to him. Freedom, in the past, was little more than a word he thought he understood. He, of course, knew the definition. Of course he did, but the meaning of the word? No. He knew now—right at this very moment—that he had never known the meaning of the word "free."

With a clear mind, the clearest his mind had ever before been, Martin Wringer pulled into a do-it-yourself car wash, and directly into an empty end stall. The stalls resembled house garages. Because it was still snowing out, and not at all a nice day, Wringer's was the only vehicle at the place.

He shut off the van's engine and climbed out with a pail and sponge in his hand. He pulled a small wad of cash out of his pocket. He had used his credit card at an ATM for a cash advance. He inserted one of the bills into a machine and removed the extendable spray hose from the wall. The water was automatically mixed with car soap. He filled the pail with this concoction and dropped the sponge into the water. He sprayed down his van. On the passenger side of the van, he pulled open the large sliding door. Ignoring the blood on the paneling, and in the carpeting, he took the bundle of rolled-up bloodied sheets and dropped them into the metal garbage barrel. He used the van's cigarette lighter to ignite a fast food take-out bag. He tossed the bag into the barrel after the sheets. While the items burned, he went back to washing the van.

Taking his time, sure to do a thorough, anal, job, Martin Wringer scrubbed his wheels and white walls. He washed his windows, inside and out. He went to the sliding door with the pail and sponge, climbed into the van, and worked on removing the dried blood from the paneling which seemed to come out a lot easier than he had anticipated.

The carpeting, on the other hand, was an entirely different ordeal.

Working up a sweat, on hands and knees, Wringer scrubbed the van's carpet until the sponge gradually, at first, disintegrated, and finally became literally useless.

Chapter 26

When Michael finally made it home, he felt physically and mentally whipped. There did not seem to be a joint, or bone, or muscle in his body that did not ache. He had smoked so much that a constant and steady throb beat in the front of his skull making even his eyes hurt.

In the kitchen he downed three aspirin with a cold glass of tap water. With only the thought of sleep on his mind, he half-considered not answering the door when someone rang the bell. It was not a security complex. Anyone could walk into the individual buildings and up to any apartment door. This made his rent cheaper. Living on a shoestring budget, Michael was thankful for any savings he could accumulate. Besides, he was a single male. He was not worried about thieves crouched, hiding in the hallways.

Checking the door's security peephole, Michael quickly thanked God that he did not ignore the doorbell. He unlocked the deadbolt and opened the door. "What are you doing here, Felicia?"

"I brought pizza."

"Come on in," he said, pushing open the door. He did not ask her how she found his address. He was in the book. Taking the pizza box from her, he let her into the apartment. In the kitchenette, he set the box on the counter. "What are you doing out here?"

"I've been calling. I figured you'd have to be home by now." Felicia removed her coat and placed it over the kitchen chair. "Have wine?"

"Did, but don't. I have beer?"

"Beer's better, especially with pizza," Felicia said, helping herself to Michael's refrigerator. She twisted the tops off two long neck bottles of Genny Light. "So what happened? How'd it go?"

Taking an offered bottle, Michael took a long swallow. "I'm not sure." He opened a cupboard door, took out two plates, and set them on the counter near the pizza box. "I have a bad feeling though."

"Bad, how?" Felicia asked, leaning against the kitchenette wall, near the wall-mounted telephone. Michael watched as her lips wrapped around the bottle as she took a sip of beer.

"I think you guys were right. I think the police might suspect me of something."

"You've got to be kidding me. That's crazy," Felicia said.

"I know it is," Michael said. "But listen, if you want to leave . . ."

"Leave?"

"If the thought of me possibly being some kind of deranged killer makes you uncomfortable," Michael explained, "then I won't hold it against you if you want to leave."

She set her bottle down. She moved closer to him, and put her fingers on his hips. She ran those fingers up his sides. "I don't want to leave."

Michael, putting his arms around her slim waist, pulled her in close. He enjoyed the feel of her body pressed against his. It was from the opposite end of the rainbow, that part of Michael felt apprehensive. His body responded to Felicia's, but his mind was more aware. There could be no denying Felicia's history. She was a prostitute. How could he proceed and not fear contamination? Diseases thrived and flourished in her profession. He knew going forward without protection could be detrimentally dangerous.

"What about your girlfriend? Do you want me to go?" Felicia asked. She moved her hands all over his back, her fingers massaging all of his aching joints and muscles. "You don't want me to go, do you?"

"There is no more girlfriend." He kissed her lower lip only, gently. "I want you to stay."

She kissed his lower lip. "Then I'll stay."

* * *

When they finally finished making love, never having made it to Michael's bedroom, they were under a blanket on the floor in the parlor. Winded, neither Michael nor Felicia could control their breathing. Though some questions of inadequacy and feelings of insecurity crept into Michael's mind, he did his best to ignore them. His experience with other women was not extensive. In his life, he had had sexual relations with thirteen women. Felicia was a far more experienced lover, and proof of that had been offered for him to sample tonight.

"Hungry?" Michael asked, removing his condom.

"Like you're reading my mind," Felicia said. "I'll get it."

"You will not," Michael said, standing up. Naked he walked to the kitchenette. "Want me to warm it up?"

"I actually like it better cold," Felicia confessed.

"Same here," Michael called out. As he picked out two slices of pizza, his breath nearly caught in his throat. Standing in the kitchenette threshold was Felicia. During all of their lovemaking he had not been given the opportunity to view and study her body.

"I was going to ask for a glass, for my beer, so I could add some ice-cubes," she said, smiling seductively. She knew exactly what she was doing. She was posed in the small passageway, hands on her hips, one hip tilted, one knee jetted outward. Starting at her feet, Michael took in the small dainty-looking toes and the thinness of her legs around her ankles. Her calf and thigh muscles were perfectly shaped, solid, and covered in the silkiest and softest skin Michael had ever seen or touched. She had a flat belly, slightly creased, revealing muscular tone. His eyes rested on perky round small breasts. They were the perfect size and shape for her body. He loved her neck—her throat. He wanted her again and felt his body respond accordingly.

Mutually decided, the pizza and iced beer would have to wait a little longer.

Chapter 27

At two o'clock in the afternoon, Jason Cocuzzi knew his energy was fading. He was operating on no sleep, after being up all night. Talking with Michael Buzzelli proved intriguing, and he and Detective Peter Cage spent the rest of the morning filling out paperwork and outlining a course of action. One minute Jason was staring at Buzzelli's closed file on his desk, the next his eyes were closed.

"Sleeping on the job, detective?" Peter Cage said, slamming his hands onto his Cocuzzi's desk.

Startled, Cocuzzi's eyes opened wide as he lunged forward in his chair. He banged his stomach into the desk.

"Scare you?" Cage asked.

"Prick. Look, I'm shot. We've been at this all night, all morning, and right now I don't have the energy to go at it another minute. The food around here is crap. Let's get out of here, get a good meal, and rejuvenate some. How's that sound?"

Cage shrugged. "Perfect. I'm starved, myself."

"After we eat, I think we should do like you said," Jason Cocuzzi said. He stood up and began turning off his computer.

"What? About seeing Buzzelli's old girlfriend?" Cage took his winter coat off the back of a chair and put it on. "I figure if she and Buzzelli were together long, she'd know him better than most. I also want to go to the City Chronicle . . . talk with his boss and some of his fellow employees. You work with a guy, you get to know a guy. Am I right?"

"I'm with you," Cocuzzi said.

"But what? You have this tone to your voice that tells me you're not convinced." Cage slid his hands into gray wool gloves. "You don't think maybe Buzzelli is the killer?"

"I'm not saying I think he's innocent, but I'm just not convinced he's the one we want. I do want to follow-up on these leads. That's important, but I don't want to be so closed-minded as to miss something even more important," Cocuzzi said.

"The way I see it, it looks like crap, it smells like crap, then maybe it's crap."

"True enough. I just want us to keep an open mind," Cocuzzi said.

"I just keep thinking of this kid, right? He's ambitious, fresh out of college with a degree in his hand, okay? He was all high and mighty on campus, editor of the school paper . . . even getting some regional recognition . . . not too shabby," Cage said.

"I know where you're going with this. It just doesn't feel right to me," Cocuzzi said.

"Doesn't feel right? Look at it this way. Buzzelli applies to newspapers all over the country."

"Do we know he did that?"

"I have someone contacting his career counselor at Brockport. We'll be able to assess just how broad a job hunt was conducted," Cage explained. "So he gets an offer from the City Chronicle to write obituaries. Is he crushed? Sure he is. He's like a rookie policeman, ready to take on the world, to stop crime . . . to save people. That dream fades quickly. Just like Buzzelli's dream. He envisioned a newspaper begging him to take a job with them. He envisioned an office, the editor asking his advice. Buzzelli expected the world when he graduated. How do you think he felt with his first assignment? I said it before. I'll say it again. Crushed. That's how he felt. I'll bet advancement at the paper isn't easy, or often, either. Of course, I'm just speculating here. I don't look much at the bylines . . . accept your Dave Berry and Ann Landers types."

"I'm sure the writers would be thrilled to hear that confession," Cocuzzi said. He locked his desk drawers and put on his coat.

"All I'm saying is the guy has a reason for killing these girls. Let's just hypothesize for a minute, all right?"

"Can we do it while we walk? I've got to eat something," Cocuzzi said, making his way out of the precinct to the back parking lot, listening to Cage, on his heels, hammering out Cage's theory.

"Buzzelli wants to make a splash . . . wants to be a star again . . . right? Of course right. Being a journalist is like being an actor. These kinds of people need to be in the limelight. They need that byline the way a junkie . . ."

"Quit using the metaphors. All right? They suck."

"Whatever. My point is simple," Cage said.

"I know your point. Your point was clear the minute you started talking. You think Buzzelli killed a prostitute . . . and why not a prostitute? Who's gonna miss one? So that he could cover the story, right?"

"Bingo."

They stood by the trunk of Cocuzzi's car. For once the sun was out and shining brightly. Though it was still cold, without the wind blowing, the temperature was tolerable.

With his hands in his pockets, Jason Cocuzzi asked, "Did he kill Hawthorne and Vorhees, or did he just kill Vorhees . . . to get in on the action?"

"Good question."

"If he killed them both, and he starts covering the story, where is the resolution if no killer is caught?" Cocuzzi cocked his head to the side. "If he read about Hawthorne's murder, took the job at Jack's Joint, hoping to get a story . . . then decided to kill Vorhees to keep up the action . . ."

"Now you see where I'm going? Either way, he'd have motive," Cage said.

"But it's weak," Cocuzzi said. "It still doesn't sit right with me. Suppose most of that entire scenario is true, right down to the profiling you did. What makes him a killer, instead of an ambitious journalist working two jobs, trying to get a story break?"

"Like the way Buzzelli explained it?" Cage asked in disbelief. "No way. Too simple."

"But like you said, if it looks like crap and smells like crap, right?"

"So you think Buzzelli was telling the truth? That he took the job hoping to get some stories to impress his editor? And that's it?"

Cocuzzi nodded. "It's just as possible, and as plausible as the conspiracy theories you've been spinning. My point? Let's just keep an open mind, all right?"

Cage shook his head. "Want to make a bet on this?"

Cocuzzi thought he had been doing pretty well. He had all but ignored his inner instincts, and had been friendly to Peter Cage all night and all day. He had let the man's insistent babble and prejudices go in one ear and out the other. Every man reaches a point, however, where holding in feelings serves no useful purpose. "*This*, Cage, is not a game. *This* is not a horse race. I will not wager bets on who is right. If you're right, then I will be thrilled when we nail the suspect. If you're wrong, I will not try collecting money from you. What the hell do you think is going on here?"

"Look. I was just trying to add some excitement . . ."

"Don't we have enough? We have two bodies . . . and only a paper-thin lead."

"I don't think it's paper-thin."

"Good. I hope you're right and we can wrap this sloppy mess up before the weekend's over," Cocuzzi said. The two stood staring at each other. Detective Cocuzzi had seniority. They were investigating the murders on his playing field. Everything must feel awkward to Detective Cage, coming across the river to work the cases with him. Cocuzzi knew a crap load of police officers. Many of them thought and behaved similarly to Cage when they started out. After a few years on the job, they lost the "hot dog" attitude. "Want me to drive? I thought we'd go to this barbeque place."

"Dragon's?" Cage smiled.

"Know it?" Cocuzzi returned the smile. They were going to fight, he knew, and disagree. Together, he also knew, they would solve these murders. Cage had enthusiasm, drive, and desire. A fire, that only dedicated police officers ever experience, must burn in his belly.

"Know it? I'm there so much, I rent a booth."

Chapter 28

By five o'clock, Michael knew he was in trouble. "You know how long it's been since I've slept?" They were in Michael's bed. It looked as if a tornado had passed through, shaping the sheets and covers into a pretzel twist at the foot of the bed. "I've got to be in to work in a few hours."

"Call in sick," Felicia said, her head resting on Michael's chest, playing with his hairs, and using her fingers like a fork twirling spaghetti onto tines. "We can rent a movie and hang out all night together."

It sounded wonderful. A perfect plan. "I can't."

Propping herself up onto an elbow, Felicia gave Michael a puppy-dog look. "Why not?"

Why not? "Because, that's why. For one thing, Murphy is depending on me to be there. I can't mess this job a few weeks into it."

"No, I guess you can't," Felicia said. She slid out of bed. "Where are my clothes?"

"The parlor. You don't have to leave."

"You need your sleep for work. I don't want you to be too tired to cook tonight," Felicia said, leaving the room.

Michael got out of bed. He took his bathrobe off a hook on the back of his door, it on, and tied the rope around his waist as he walked into the parlor. "I don't want you to go, Felicia. I don't."

She looked as if she might begin to cry. "This sucks, you know."

"What does?"

She looked around the room, extending her arms, panties in one hand, shirt in the other. "This. All of this. You. You suck," she said. Now she was crying. Black mascara teardrops rolled down her cheeks.

Michael almost laughed. "I don't get it. I thought we had a great afternoon. I mean, I could still go for some pizza . . ."

She pushed his stomach with both hands and smiled, but did not stop crying. "I don't want to see you anymore."

Michael laughed.

"I'm not joking, Michael." She put on her underwear, her shirt. She bent over and picked up her socks and pants.

"What?"

She sat at the kitchen table, put on her socks and pants. "I had a good time today. But that's all it was. A good time. It's nice not to have to do that for work. To just do it because I wanted to do it."

"That's all this was? All you wanted was to get screwed . . . on your terms?"

His words had the effect of a face-slap. She looked stung. She did not deny a thing. She stood up and went to the door. She kneeled down and put on her shoes, tying the laces. "You can keep the pizza."

Michael grabbed her arms and pulled her up. He spun her around so that she stood facing him. "Do I look dumb?"

She did not answer.

"I'm not dumb," he said.

"Oh no?"

"No. You're pulling, like, a psychology one-oh-one here. The first time I ever saw it performed was in that movie with Ricky Schrodder and John Voight, The Champ. It's a classic scene. Ever seen it? Voight's a single parent, a washed-up boxer. The boy's mother, Faye Dunnaway, is rich . . . but wants nothing to do with the child, until she sees him at the horse races eight, nine years later. So it's the part where they're in the stadium bleachers and Voight tells his son to get lost . . . see, he's not doing it to be mean, he's doing it because he can't take care of him as well as the mother can. And even in the movie, the little boy knows what his father's doing, until the father's standing there with a hysterical child, who is begging to stay. So he slaps the boy, calls him a pain in the ass," Michael explained. "And at that point, still knowing what his father's up to, the boy says fine. He'll go with his mother."

"I saw the movie, Michael."

"So why didn't you stop me?"

"Because you're a pain in the ass," Felicia said. "Fine. You want to be right, you're right, Champ. I want you to get lost, all right. I'm tired of you hanging around." She slapped him hard across the face. "Take it any way you want. I don't want to see you again."

She opened the door and left quietly. Rubbing his face, Michael cursed. "Damn. That hurt."

* * *

Marcus was back in town. Michael noticed him as soon as he walked in from the back room. Murphy was behind the counter, cooking up some burgers. Michael said hello to Fatso.

"See the paper today?" Fatso asked. He took a moment to shake out the creases so the paper could fold naturally.

Michael took the paper and stared at the front-page headlines: JOHNNY THE BLADE STRIKES AGAIN. *Catchy and cute*, Michael thought. *Matthew Sinopoli may be old and he may be lazy, but he still knows how to work well with words*. Giving the killer a nickname, especially one like Johnny the Blade, would sell papers. It could also send people into a panic. "Says police have some leads, but are not releasing any names at this time." He pointed to himself. "What? Am I one of the leads?"

Fatso, smiling, shrugged. "I like the name, Johnny Blade. Menacing, isn't it?"

Murphy was standing next to Michael with his hands on his

hips. “Police giving you a hard time?”

“They were. I think things were squared away. I had to go down there. They didn’t like the fact that I remembered so much about last Friday night,” Michael said, casually aware that he had Marcus’ attention. “It’s nothing to worry about, Murphy.”

“You may not think so. This place is no gold-mine, but if my customers think Johnny Blade is slinging hash, they aren’t going to be too happy,” Murphy said.

“Nothing to worry about,” Michael said, again.

“Not exactly denying anything with that statement,” Murphy said. “Are you?”

“It’s not me. I’m not him,” Michael said pointing at the newspaper headlines. “The police are just digging. That’s all.”

Murphy clapped Michael on the back using both hands. “I hope so.”

When Murphy walked away, Michael lit up a cigarette. “You know, Fatso, this is nuts. Can I help it if I remember things that happened last week? I have that kind of mind, you know. I pay attention to the details. The police think I know too much so I have to go down for questioning, only they referred to it as ‘having a conversation’.”

“How’d that go, anyway?” Fatso asked. Michael gave him an edited version. “See how they do that, playing with your words, twisting them to make them out to be something they’re not?”

“That’s exactly what they tried to do, too,” Michael said. Leaving out the part about him working at the paper had made most of the “conversation” seem weak and less important. “I’m not worried. I’m more annoyed than anything.”

As if on cue, Detectives Cocuzzi and Cage entered Jack’s. Neither looked happy, yet they both looked relieved to see Michael Buzzelli once their roaming eyes settled on him. “Ah, shit,” Michael murmured. He was innocent. He knew he was innocent. He did not experience blackouts. No dogs spoke to him, telling him to kill people. He did not worship the devil. “Are you guys looking for me?”

“Mr. Buzzelli,” Detective Cage said with a sneer. He spoke loud to ensure everyone in the diner could hear him clearly.

"How's our little writer, friend?"

Michael cringed, wondering who might have caught on to what cage had said.

Murphy stood next to him. "What can I do for you guys?"

"We were wondering if Michael wouldn't mind helping us out some?" Cage asked, talking to Murphy, but staring directly at Michael Buzzelli.

Michael turned to look at Murphy, who shrugged indecisively. "What do you have in mind?" Michael asked the detectives, acutely aware of the people watching and listening to his conversation.

Cage puckered his lips and shook his head. "How about you come with us for a little ride? That sound all right?"

Michael looked at Murphy, again, who said, "Take the night off. I'll handle things here. If you finish with the police and want to come back, fine. If after they're done, you just feel like going home, then fine."

Chapter 29

"Long day for you guys," Michael said as he voluntarily climbed into the back seat of a white unmarked police car. Jason Cocuzzi sat in the driver's seat. Cage sat in back, next to Michael.

"We have a demanding job," Cage said. Michael sensed the detective did not like him. He wondered why. Was he despised simply because he was "suspected" to be a murderer? They had no proof to tie him to any crime. No proof. None whatsoever.

"We have some evidence, Mr. Buzzelli, that was recovered from the second victim. After the killer murdered the first woman, he took careful precautions to protect himself. Deranged serial killers will do that, you know," Detective Cocuzzi announced.

"Yeah, you know you have a lot against you," Cage said. "You're white. You are in your mid-twenties. I don't think you're insane."

"Well thank you for the back-handed compliment," Michael said.

Jason smiled. "When you profile a serial killer, you'll find more often than not the person committing the crime is a white male, between the age of twenty-two and fifty. Rarely are serial killers crazy. In fact, they are often times the exact opposite."

"I doubt very much you're a genius," Cage said to Michael.

"Ah, thank you," Michael said, pretending to sound

emotionally stung by the detective's comment.

"We saw your ex-girlfriend today," Cage said, with heavy emphasis on the "ex" part of ex-girlfriend. "You never got around to telling us the reason why the two of you broke up."

"I didn't see how it could be any of your business," Michael said. He had had enough. No way could the police have evidence against him. How could he be implicated for a murder he knew he did not commit?

"How about we believe you've been screwing that prostitute with the red hair," Cage said, yelling. His face was less than an inch away from Michael's.

"Cool it," Cocuzzi said. "Look, Michael, you may not think this is any of our business . . ."

"You're right," Michael said.

"You're wrong," Cage interjected.

"Let me tell you this Michael, we are not arresting you. Notice, we are not reading you the Miranda rights, okay? However, we want you to submit a semen sample, a pubic hair sample, and give us a set of prints," Cocuzzi said calmly, making a left hand turn. They were headed south down Lake Avenue, heading in the general direction of the police station as the car bounced on the pitted road.

Cage had a drunk-looking smile as he bounced with the worn shocks. His eyes were open wide with anticipation, making him look crazy. If this were a movie, Michael thought, he would know exactly who the killer was. Crazy Cage. Yet, a fisted knot formed in his belly. He could not help but begin to wonder why the police were so intent on fingering him as the murderer. There were innocent people in jail. Things like that did happen. People have been railroaded by the police, prosecuted, convicted and sentenced. Was this how something like that could happen? He knew DNA testing was accurate and the results presentable in trials. Providing a sample of his semen suddenly made him apprehensive. How in the world could his semen match the semen found on Vanessa's body? It could not . . . could it? Why did the police keep coming back to him?

"You got a little sloppy this time," Cage said.

"Excuse me?" Michael was quick to object.

"I apologize," Cage said with mock-sincerity, holding his hands up and backing away from Michael. "The killer got sloppy this time. First whore he sliced up, he did a good job of cleaning the body before dumping it."

"The M.E. was pretty sure a condom had been used, both for oral sex and vaginal sex," Detective Cocuzzi said. "However, aside from the knife wounds, and traces of metal from the blade on her rib bones and on skin tissue, the assailant was careful to wash away any fingerprints, hair. Nothing."

"But Vanessa had semen, pubic hair, and finger prints?" Michael asked, the reporter in him stepping up to the plate. He had been blinded by fear. Cage seemed like a force to fear. Talking to Cocuzzi, though, made all the difference. He realized at this very moment that he could be an asset to this investigation, and not a liability.

"Did the detective say that?" Cage asked.

"No. I'm just gathering here. If you want my semen, a pubic hair, and my prints . . . what else should I think? Let me ask you this," Michael said, quickly. He did not want to be cut off. "What makes you think it's a serial killer? Why do you think the same man killed both women?"

Cage and Cocuzzi exchanged knowing glances. "You tell us?" Cage said.

"How would I know?" Michael asked. He knew what Cage was up to. They wanted to see if he would reveal anything about the crimes that had not been revealed on the news or in the papers. The police were notorious for holding back specific details of a crime. It helped them distinguish the real killer from all the insane people who called, claiming to be the killer. *That would make for a wonderful, other story, a story in and of itself,* Michael thought and mentally noted to research the topic later.

Cocuzzi stopped the car for a red light. He turned around and looked at Michael. "On Ms. Vorhees we found semen and a few coarse pubic hairs. We are printing you to have a record of your prints on file."

"So no prints were recovered at the scene," Michael said. The killer took time to quickly . . . what . . . wash away the prints, but not his body fluids and hair samples? How could he do that? Maybe he just wiped her down with a towel, or paper towels?

"They were wiped away. We found some points of some prints, but you need eight points to lift a print. We were lucky to find two or three points at any given spot. Not very helpful," Cocuzzi said.

Why was Detective Cocuzzi volunteering so much information? Good cop? Bad cop? "Is it possible that the second killing was an accident?" Michael asked. He wished he could take out his own notebook and jot down information. He was under a little duress, locked in the back seat of a police car with an angry looking detective. He hoped the conversation would remain fresh in his mind by the time he got home, if they let him go home.

"Not likely," Cocuzzi said. "The women were victimized in a nearly identical pattern."

"So how about it?" Cage asked as Cocuzzi pulled into the police parking lot. "Feel like masturbating into a little cup for us?" Michael said, smiling, "Feel like lending me a hand?"

He did not feel comfortable, and thought now might be the best time to call in an attorney. The police made everything to date seem informal and casual. He knew they were, hour by hour, attempting to build a case against him. Though he knew he was innocent, he did not want to act foolishly. "I think before we do anything, I want to talk to my lawyer."

Chapter 30

Michael saw it in her face right away and inwardly cringed while trying to display a warm happy smile. He stood up when she had entered the room, and now, like a fool, just stood there, smiling stupidly. He did not know if he should approach her and attempt hugging, or if he should put out his hand and settle on a friendly, if not, cordial shake. Instead, he ran his palms nervously on the front of his jeans. "Ellen, I'm glad you came. For a while there, I thought for sure you'd ignored my message."

Ellen turned to face the detectives that had escorted her into the room. "Could you excuse me and my client for a few minutes," Ellen said, accentuating the word *client* with as strong a repulsed tone as she could.

Michael watched Cocuzzi and Cage look at each other with puzzled expressions. He was sure they did not anticipate seeing Ellen enter the precinct as Michael's attorney. When the police left, Ellen set a briefcase down on the steel table and stared long and hard at her ex-boyfriend in a powerfully intimidating silence. "I wasn't going to come," was what she finally said. "In fact, give me one good reason why I should stay. The entire drive down, I kept asking myself . . . and I mean out loud . . . I'm driving and talking to myself . . . why am I doing this? You know what? I didn't come up with one reason why I should be here right now."

"I'm glad you came."

"I didn't say I was staying. What's going on? These guys came to see me a few hours ago. They wouldn't tell me a thing. They wanted to know why we'd broken up, what kind of a guy you were. I told them the truth . . . basically. I didn't go off and tell them I thought of you as a complete shit-head. Michael, what's going on? Did you call me to help?"

"You're an attorney," Michael said.

Ellen snapped open the locks on her hard-shell briefcase, and flung open the top. She took out a ream of papers. "I do paperwork, real estate closings, contracts . . . Michael, I handle contracts. I don't go in front of judges. I don't handle criminal cases. I'm not a trial lawyer."

"Trial? Slow down, Ellen. There's no trial. There isn't going to be a trial. I haven't even been arrested. The police want to have me give them some specimen samples. I just want an attorney present to make sure this is how things are done, that my rights haven't been violated, or aren't being violated. That's what I need. Guidance." Michael sat down in the chair, crossing his arms over his chest.

Ellen's temper faded quickly. She sat down across from him. "Michael, what's going on? Does this have to do with that robbery?"

"I wish." Michael brought his ex-lover up to date. He explained to her everything. Of course she knew about his ulterior motives for taking the night job at Jack's. Unlike the police, she believed him. "Now they want semen, a pubic hair, finger prints . . . Ellen, what the hell is going on? I was so sure once they heard I was a reporter trying to advance my career, they'd realize I wasn't a sick serial killer." He laughed. "It looks like the exact opposite of that is true."

Compassionately, Ellen reached out and touched his hand. "There was a journalist who logged onto a kiddie-porn site. He was writing an article on how easy it was to access this kind of thing on the net. One of the sites he hit was an FBI site. They arrested the journalist. They didn't care that he had more than half his research article written at the time either. He didn't go to jail, but he went to trial and was sentenced to, I don't know, a few years on probation. That journalist now has a pretty sick criminal record."

"Great story, Ellen. A real confidence builder."

Ellen was not smiling. She wore one of the most serious facial expressions he had ever seen on her before. "Michael, if you give them these samples, what will the police find out?"

"They'll find out that I'm innocent," he said.

She seemed to study him, was perhaps waiting for a tell-all reaction. When Michael Buzzelli remained somber looking, she sighed. "Let's give them what they need then and get this over with. All right?"

They both stood up. He hugged her. "I'm sorry about what happened between you and me," Michael said in her ear.

"I wish it could have been different," she said. When Michael did not reply, she added, "I still hate your rotten guts."

They kissed, on the lips, the way two friends might.

* * *

While waiting for Buzzelli and his attorney to finish talking, Detective Jason Cocuzzi heard the phone on his desk ring from across the room. He made his way around desks and picked up the receiver before the end of the third ring. "Detective Cocuzzi."

"Hey Jason, it's Harvey."

The forensics tech. "What have you got Harvey?"

"We finished a run down on the soap used to wash Casey Hawthorne. The soap was easily identified as a product made by Tortoise. It's used all over the country. However, I talked with the representative for the region. He told me that his biggest customer was a company known as Car-U-Wash. That's the letter 'u,'" Harvey explained.

"I know of the place," Cocuzzi said. There were many of them around the city. Like a giant six-car garage. People pull their vehicles into independent stalls. They deposit money into a time-limited washing machine where they can use the water and soap to clean their cars.

"Well, it turns out there are seven locations in Rochester." Harvey rattled off the locations. Jason Cocuzzi jotted down the addresses. "The soap supplied comes in a big tank. When the water is turned on for a customer, pumps proportionately distribute the water with the soap and it sprays out the end of the hose."

"Thanks for the mechanical lesson," Jason said. "What about other places the soap is used?"

"Well, the representative explained that those are his steady customers, but the Tortoise product is found on supermarket shelves, at car part stores, and your K-Mart and Wal-Mart's carry the stuff. It comes in liquid and a concentrate formula. When the soap is mixed with water, it's not easy to differentiate which type was used," Harvey said.

"It's not easy, but you can do it?" Jason asked.

"Or course, and I have. From samples taken, I would say that, almost ninety-nine percent positive, the soap used on Casey Hawthorne came from one of the Car-U-Wash facilities."

"Why didn't you just say so in the first place?"

"Because, detective, there is always that one percent chance that I'm wrong, and I want you to have all the information so you can make an educated decision," the tech said, as if tacking on mild sarcasm was for good measure.

Hanging up, Detective Cocuzzi wondered how he could effectively respond to this information. With several Car-U-Wash locations, he would need to enlist help from surrounding police departments. This could work to his advantage. Rather than gather a handful of men from the department and post them at each site, a combined effort could prove a more resourceful use of manpower.

Chapter 31

Sunday, January 20

Michael called in sick to Jack's. He hated doing so. He had been at the part-time job for less than a month. There seemed little else he could do. His mind was in shambles. Too much was going on. He could not think straight. He could not remember a time when he had ever felt more confused or scared.

Though he showered, Michael dressed only in a clean pair of boxer shorts, socks, and bathrobe, then lounged around the apartment all day. The pizza from Felicia was still wrapped in foil in his refrigerator, so he ate some slices for lunch, and finished the rest up at dinner. Sipping a beer and smoking a cigarette, Michael sat on the sofa with his feet propped up on the coffee table.

Ellen had been great yesterday. He knew it killed her coming down to the police station on his behalf. He was glad she had. In a way, he knew they had begun to patch things up. They might never be good friends, or friends, but he knew she would no longer hate him, or hate him too much. There would perhaps come a day when he could call her as a friend, when the two of them could go out, have some beers, play some pool, and shoot some darts. It might never happen, but then again, it might.

The hardest thing about calling in sick to work this night was the fact that Michael would not get to see Felicia. They were on some unstable ground. One could not even say they were in a relationship. He knew they were not. He wanted more from her. She was an amazing lover, but it was more than that. So much more, and it intrigued him. He wanted to find out as much about her as he could, but she wanted nothing to do with him. Whether she meant it or not, he could not go against her wishes or reasons.

Or could he? Or should he? Or would he?

He did not know what to do. Nagging at the back of his mind, more and more lately, was the fact that if Felicia did not change careers, he could not be positive how the "relationship" would progress. It had nothing to do with wearing a condom. He had always done so, even with Ellen. Wearing a condom when making love to Ellen was for obviously different reasons. With Ellen, Michael did not want to get her pregnant. With Felicia, yes, Michael did not want her pregnant, but neither did he wish to contract any type of Venereal Disease.

He finished his beer, put out his cigarette, and went to his bedroom. He closed his eyes. It was not even seven o'clock, but Michael was ready just to sleep away the rest of the worthless day. When the telephone rang, he let it. He did not feel up to running to the living room to answer it. He waited for his answering machine to pick up the call. He heard someone talking, but softly. He could not tell who it was. It could be Ellen. It could be Felicia. He jumped out of bed and ran down the hall. He got to the phone just as he heard Felicia say "good-bye." He picked up the telephone. "Hello? Felicia?"

Dial tone. "Damn," he muttered. He saw that a number one was flashing on his machine. He pressed "Play."

"Hi Michael. It's Felicia. I just wondered if you were planning to attend Vanessa's funeral. It's on Tuesday, at St. Theodore's Church, on Spencerport Road, in Gates. Bye."

Of course he knew about it. His task at the paper had been to write the obituary. There would be a service, but no calling hours. Michael had not planned on attending the services. Now he saw no way to get out of going. He did not like funerals, which would be a stupid excuse, because who did?

* * *

Martin Wringer felt itchy. The insides of his fingers and wrists itched. Inside his ears and throat itched. He kept rolling his fingers and scratching at the surface of the skin, but to no avail. He kept rolling his tongue, and running its tip along the roof of his mouth, but relief continued to allude him. So instead, Wringer drove with a white-knuckle grip. The cold steering wheel, if nothing at all, at least numbed the skin some.

He had an unopened bottle of Jack in a brown bag under his seat. He wanted to find a secluded spot, drink as much as he could and pass out. Drunk and passed out seemed like a reasonable solution to cure the nagging itch that persistently kept at him. Drunk and passed out would also take up more of his time on this godforsaken planet.

What he wanted, though, was not to be alone. When he parked the van a block away from Jack's Joint, anticipation swelled within him. Never taking his eyes off the corner, he reached under his seat for the bag. Smiling anxiously, he opened the bottle and took a long swallow. At first the coffee-colored fluid burned going down his throat. He thought he might start drooling. He wiped his mouth across the sleeve of his coat. For the next fifteen minutes, his mood changed drastically. It was close to midnight, and not one girl had stood out on the corner. Wringer wondered, *Where in the hell are all the whores*?

Now, continually looking from the time displayed on the dash, to the corner, he thought he should find loving somewhere else. He did not owe the hookers at this location any kind of loyalty. In fact, he could not even figure out why he kept coming back to this same location. The last two he had picked up had been major disappointments. It was not often that a man like him required this kind of attention, but when he did, he should be satisfied with the product received, right? He was not made of money. He could not just go throwing money away, right? *Damn straight that's right*!

Twisting the cap onto the bottle, and placing it in the bag and under his seat, Wringer pulled away from the curb. He threw the diner the finger and honked his horn as he drove by. Rochester was not a huge city—far from it. However, the city streets were loaded with women of the night. As he turned right onto Lyell Avenue, Wringer slowed the van to twenty-five miles an hour and began prowling the streets.

It seemed a shame that nearly all of the storefront windows of small local businesses were imprisoned behind wrought iron bars. Wicked graffiti colorfully, and often obscenely, marked the sides of most of those same buildings, while many of the businesses without bars had graffiti-free walls. Was it a message to the owners? Was there a trust issue there?

Wringer found it sad the way people desecrated their own neighborhoods. He understood those who lived in the city were poorer than the rest of the people in the area, but why did they chose to deface property? Why was the crime rate so high? Why did they insist on killing each other? Hell, if he lived in the city and was poor, he would be in towns like Pittsford and Perington, the rich suburbs on the East Side of the tracks. He would be desecrating and defacing their property and homes, not those found in his own backyard. Wringer knew he would never understand people. Sometimes people acted the way they did with no reasonable explanation.

Though it had not snowed in a while, the street, houses, and buildings along Lyell Avenue looked like something out of an arctic ghost town. The wind was picking up, rocking the van with its massive powerful gusts. The heavy streetlights dangling over the road swayed continually, as if threatening to fall onto an unsuspecting car. Each time Wringer drove under one, he sped up some. He had heard of people dying when those things fell. They weighed enough to crush the hood of a car, and then some.

Not many people were out around here, either. *The wintry weather must have them all holed up inside tonight*, Wringer thought. *But maybe Sunday nights are not big money making nights, anyway.* Wringer had no intention of giving up, though. The bottle under his seat, still mostly full, would keep until he found suitable company.

He knew if he headed back the other way, deeper into the city—into the poor projects in the area—he would have better luck. Yet, most of the women in that section of town had severe drug problems, and they were more than just drug users. Their arms and legs and bellies were riddled with needle marks. Their skin looked bruised. They looked dumb, unable to stand up straight, and barely able to walk or talk. He had been down there before, and there was little that appealed to him. He doubted he would find any jewel, but as a last resort he could cruise around and see if any diamonds stood out from the rest of the ruff.

Just when he was about ready to turn and head deeper into the city, he saw a lone woman standing outside on the side of a small bar. The place was open, but looked dead. The woman was smoking, leaning against the building, trying to keep out of reach from the harshness and relentless fury of the bitter wind.

Wringer drove by the bar, slowly. He looked out his window at her. She knew he was looking at her, and looked right back at him. She stopped leaning on the wall and, instead, stood in a provocative pose, one thumb hooked through the front belt loop of her jeans, then exhaled a plume of smoke that the wind sent into a crazy dance before blowing away.

He passed the bar and turned around at the next light. He approached the bar again, pulled up to the curb, and stopped a few feet past the establishment. She was still outside, still smoking, but had gone back to leaning against the wall—until she saw him.

Hesitantly, she came forward. Wringer lowered his window. "What are you doing outside on a night this cold?" he asked. He wanted to sound charming. He could not tell for certain who this woman was. She might be a whore. She might not. Either way, he found her cute.

"Got tired of the losers in there," she said, nodding her head back toward the bar.

Wringer produced his bottle of Jack. "Interested?"

Her eyes lit up. Her tongue wet her lips, as though she were thirsty—lost for days in the middle of a desert—and oh, so thirsty. She took a puff on her cigarette. While she exhaled, she looked away from him as if checking out traffic down the road. "I ain't no whore, you know?"

"Did I say you were?" Wringer said, smiling, as if stunned by her testimony. "I'm either going to find a place to park and drink this alone, or . . ."

She bit on her lip. "Will you give me a ride home later?"

"I'm going to have to be honest here. When I'm done drinking this bottle, I won't be fit to drive. Better still, I may not be awake. I can give you a ride in the morning."

She smiled. "That was a real honest answer." She walked closer to the van. She was looking at him. Her eyes seemed to say, *Yeah, you look okay to me*. "Where do I hop in?"

He unlocked the doors. "Right in front."

She climbed into the van. "Where we going to drink this?"

"I know a cool place," she said.

"My name is Martin. Martin Wringer," he said, handing over the bottle.

"Donna. Call me Donna." As she twisted off the cap, he watched her. She was an alcoholic in a bad way. Wringer knew immediately that this woman was not a prostitute. She wanted the bottle from him, nothing else. He would wager that she had no money and that was why she was no longer in the bar. Can't drink without cash. This was all right with Wringer. It had been a while since having sex with a woman who did not expect him to pay for his pleasure. She had long dark hair. It looked like she might be growing out the remains of a perm. Bright lipstick, heavy eye shadow, cheeks a little too rosy on pale white skin. Wringer found Donna cute, in a trashy sexy way.

Chapter 32

Donna had Wringer drive north down Long Pond Road. “Ever been to Sawyer Park?” she asked. And he had, but not in years. He remembered picnicking with his wife and daughters. There had not been much by way of playground equipment. Of course there were swings, a slide, and one of those constructed contraptions that kids liked climbing on, running through tunnels and climbing across monkey bars. It was more than that which made the place beautiful. There were tall trees, a footbridge running over a brook, and a mile or so of trails that led through shallow woods and along the water bank.

Turning right, onto the unpaved roadway near the YMCA, Wringer remembered his visits with the family well. Taking the bottle from Donna, and after having a long drink as he steered the van toward the park, a few hundred yards away from the main road, Wringer felt anger welling up inside him.

“I love it here,” Donna said. She lit a cigarette. In the fifteen-minute drive, she had consumed a large amount of the Jack Daniels. She did not look drunk, but the whites of her eyes had been ensnared in a web of red streaks. She was not slurring her words, but neither was she talking articulately.

Wringer handed back the bottle. He parked in the last available spot, near the bridge, and shut off the van’s lights. He kept the motor running, the heater on high.

While she smoked, Wringer and she passed the bottle back and forth. "This is a cool van," Donna complimented. She kicked off her shoes and put her feet up on the dashboard. She cracked the window open some, and flicked the ash off the end of her cigarette out it. "What do you do for a living?"

Wringer did not feel like talking. He was pissed off at his wife. Who was she to throw him out of the house? He was the one who had paid the freaking mortgage. He paid the bills. Was she mad at him for losing his job, or for catching a disease from some two-bit whore? Couldn't she see he didn't mean anything by it? He had been distraught at the time. He had just lost his job and was confused, upset, and lonely. She was up on some high-and-mighty horse, riding around like a queen—living in his castle—and judging him? Who in the hell did she think she was?

"Martin, you all right?" Donna asked. She took her feet down. She sat facing him, leaning against her door. "You look sad."

"I am sad, Donna. I'm terribly sad. I lost my job. I lost my wife and kids and house. In just a few months, I've lost everything that was once important to me, Donna. I lost it all. The American dream? I had it, had it all, and then lost it. I lost every freaking thing in the world that I once had. Lost it . . . it all," Martin said, and was surprised to find himself crying.

Donna reached out tentatively, and quickly ran her fingers through his hair. "You poor baby," she said. She drank some more whiskey. She dropped her cigarette out the window. "Want to talk about it?"

Wringer did not want to talk about it. He considered himself a private person. He was upset with himself for crying. He could not believe he was that out of control over his emotions. He blamed the alcohol. He held out his hand. Donna passed over the bottle. Wringer took a long swig. "No, Donna, no, I don't really want to talk about it."

Everything seemed to move in slow motion for Wringer. It was the feeling he desired. He was not drunk, but he planned on becoming so. Whiskey had a different effect than beer. With beer, as with wine, people got that shit-faced smile, an unflattering grin that just did not go away. Whiskey effected people on a deeper level. It went to the heart of emotions and pummeled the crap out of senses. You did not giggle when you drank whiskey. You pondered life and tried to figure out what had gone wrong in the world.

"Yeah, well, I know what you mean, you know," Donna said. She put both her feet up on her seat. She spread her knees wide. She held the bottle between her thighs and had both hands wrapped around the bottle's neck. "I was with this guy for, I don't know, maybe six months. I was talking marriage, kids . . . and you know what the bastard tells me? One day we're talking on-line, you know, and he says I'm scaring the hell out of him."

Wringer laughed. Donna looked like she might start crying. "What's so funny? I didn't laugh at you when you told your story," Donna said. She was drunk. Now, Wringer could tell. However, drunk or not, Wringer did not appreciate the tone she used to address him.

With his smile instantaneously vanishing, Wringer gripped the steering wheel with both hands. When he spoke, it was between clenched teeth. "What's so funny is the fact that I'm talking about losing my life, Donna. I lost a job I'd held for decades. I lost a wife I'd had for just as long. I have two young daughters, Donna, and when I call home to talk to them, they say they aren't ready to talk to me. What did I do to them? Nothing. So why are they giving me the cold shoulder? This, Donna, this is why my life sucks. You, on the other hand, are upset with a guy for dumping you. Men, my dear, are frightened at the thought of commitment. If you bring it up, and they talk about it . . . marriage, kids . . . so what? Yeah. Maybe one day they do want to get married and have children, and hey, what do you know, that's what you want, too. But then you keep at them. You show them engagement rings that you think would look great on your finger, and you show them gowns that you think would be perfect to wear for the ceremony . . . and guess what? That guy is freaked out. He thinks of you, not as a girlfriend any longer, no, he thinks of you as a stalker. And you're mad at the guy for being honest when he tells you that you're scaring the hell out of him?"

Donna stared at Wringer with the most hateful look he had ever seen. He reached for the bottle nestled against her crotch and, as he curled his fingers around hers, around the neck of the bottle, he let his fingertips brush across the fabric of her jeans.

She stirred, held tightly to the bottle, and continued to stare. He yanked on the bottle and, while staring back and taking a sip, noticed the change in her expression. "You want me, don't you?" she said.

He shrugged. It did not matter. He was feeling pretty drunk himself. Drunk and tired. He would screw if she wanted to. He would sleep if she did not. At this point it did not matter.

Wringer thought she seemed turned on by his lack of response and interest. He posed to her a challenge. He was also single, and she wanted desperately to get married, so who knew what ulterior motives lurked behind her own deranged skull.

When she got on her knees and spun his captain's chair around to face her, he became immediately aroused. She moved into the back of the van, taking him by the hand. He followed her, closing the drapes to the front of the cab. In the dark, they spent the next hour and a half getting to know each other more intimately, on an animal instinct level.

And when they were done, when Wringer switched on the lamp, he saw the expression on Donna's face change in the soft glowing light. "What are you doing with the knife?" It sounded like such a stupid question. It was also the last thing she said before, once again excited, Wringer pounced on her.

Chapter 33

Monday, January 21

By noon, Michael found it impossible to work. His little cubicle felt more like a prison cell than an office. Though he had never felt claustrophobic before, he certainly was experiencing the phobia at a heightened level now. Breathing seemed painfully difficult. He sucked in each breath as though a plug was in his throat preventing the air from reaching his lungs. Loosening his tie did nothing to eliminate the sense of suffocating.

Everything seemed to be getting more and more complicated in his life. He knew a lot of people who were on medication to prevent panic attacks. He always used to wonder why. Why can't these people just control their emotions? Why do they need medication to help them remain calm?

Well, he suddenly understood why, and would give anything for a pill to curb the strength of his sudden attack. As he got to his feet, ready to leave his cubicle, the telephone rang. He stared at it, reluctantly. He remembered Felicia calling him at home. What if it was Felicia on the line, again?

"Rochester City Chronicle, Buzzelli speaking," Michael said, hopefully. His wishful thinking was quickly doused.

"Mr. Buzzelli? It's Detective Jason Cocuzzi, Rochester Police Department?"

"Yes, detective. What can I do for you?" Michael wanted to just hang up. A part of him could guess why the detective was calling him at work. Most of him did not want to know a thing. Deal with my attorney, he wanted to say.

"We got back the results from all the samples you supplied."

"That was quick."

"You're right, it was," Cocuzzi said. "At this point, we are not actively considering you as a suspect in either murder."

Michael, for an instant, felt immediately relieved. A man of words, his relief stopped short of jubilation. "What does that mean, not actively considering me?"

"Just as it sounds. Look, everyone in the city of Rochester at this point is a suspect. You should feel pretty good. Right now, we're not looking at you anymore. We're going to be concentrating our efforts elsewhere. That's the bottom line. Anyway, I called your ex-girlfriend, the attorney, and told her the same. I wanted to call you, as well. We appreciate how helpful you've been," Cocuzzi said.

An opportunity. "Is there anything I can do to help?" His spirits felt lighter. They were lifting.

"It depends. Can you remember anything else about the night Vorhees disappeared?"

"Nothing more than I've already told you."

"Then I'm afraid right now we won't require any assistance." Cocuzzi hung up.

Michael hung up his phone and continued to stand in his cubicle. He had been cleared of the murders. The murderer was still out there. The police had wasted a lot of time and effort on him. The real killer could be long gone by now. Michael did not think so.

Sitting back at his computer, Michael opened up a fresh page on his software application and began writing. He wanted to document the conversation he had just had with the detective.

He felt the anxiety he had been experiencing, slowly drain away. A lot of the pressure he had felt had been lifted off his shoulders. Not being the police's prime suspect in a serial killing could do a lot to a person's emotions. It was no wonder he had felt depressed lately. Even though he had known he was innocent, he feared wrongful prosecution.

Michael found his supervisor and explained how he needed time off tomorrow for a funeral. He went back to work and concentrated on finishing his assigned work tasks. He did not have to work at Jack's tonight, but planned to stop by. He wanted to fill Murphy in on all that had been happening, and apologize for missing work the other night. He also wanted to see Felicia. They needed to talk. Her call the other night proved she cared about him. She was not fooling anyone, even herself, but was just being stubborn.

* * *

Peter Cage wanted to go out for a beer after work. It was eight when they left the office. "We can have a drink and a meal. I don't know about you, but I got crap in the fridge at home. If you don't want to, I can always hit the drive-thru at a Mickey D's or something."

Though Jason Cocuzzi was tired, he also felt hungry. It proved to be a rather long and unproductive day. Although it took some coordinating, they did manage to obtain permission from the bordering police departments to have uniformed officers stake out the Car-U-Wash locations. With Buzzelli eliminated as a suspect, the moral of the team working on the murders was taken down a few notches. They were now at square one as far as suspects went. Square zero made more sense, since they had not one suspect, and leads were non-existent. "I don't see why not."

After a few beers and a filling meal, Jason drove home in a drab mood. The seriousness of time weighed heavy on his thoughts. Though months had passed since the first murder, only little more than a week had gone by since the second body had been found. Something about the case bothered Cocuzzi. He was almost certain it was the same person who killed both prostitutes. He wondered why the killer had been less careful with the second victim. Why had the killer gone to such extreme measures to clean and scrub, inside and out, the first corpse, and basically just wipe down the second?

The killer could be getting careless, growing less concerned with the aftermath of his actions and only concentrating on the "here and now," a kind of the-world-revolving-around-him mentality. This would be bad. A serial killer is a unique kind of killer. One thing proves true. The killings generally become more frequent and the killings themselves become more grotesque.

With close to two months between the killings, Jason Cocuzzi knew it would not be long before another woman was turned into a victim. And then it came to him. Chasing the killer might be too complicated in this situation. As he had explained earlier on the telephone to Michael Buzzelli, everyone in the city was a suspect. What they needed was a sting operation, a way for the killer to come to them.

Chapter 34

Tuesday, January 22

Michael decided to take the entire day off from the paper, and after clearing this with his boss, felt better for having done so. When he had stopped to talk with Jack Murphy the previous night, he had hoped to see Felicia. Fatso had told him she had not been in. In a way, that news made Michael feel good. As best he could tell, she had not worked since they had been together. Maybe their lovemaking had been as special to her as it had been to him. Her not being to work was a hopeful sign, anyway.

Murphy understood what was going on and had not minded Michael missing a few days of work until things were sorted through. He had been more relieved to hear everything was straightened out between his cook and the police. Michael, before leaving, promised he would be to work as early as possible on Friday to give Murphy some extra time away from the diner.

Now, after getting off the expressway, Michael drove west down Spencerport Road. He passed a large grocery store and a fast food place. On his right was St. Theodore's Church. Michael found it unusual that Vanessa Vorhees was a Catholic. He thought most African American people were Baptist. Though he was no theologian, he did not think there was a big difference between the two beliefs.

At one point in time, at St. Theodore's, there had been a parochial elementary school. Tuition rates kept going higher and higher, while enrollment kept decreasing. Eventually the school part of the church closed, but the church itself thrived, regularly undergoing major cosmetic updates.

Michael parked in the mostly empty lot. A large white hearse sat in the loop by the church doors. Michael saw Sandy's car and hoped Felicia was with her. He approached the church, noting the statue of the Virgin Mary struggling to keep her head above the snowdrift. Michael entered the vestibule and, through the next set of glass doors, could see the altar.

No longer did the church resemble the standard two columns of pews. Instead, there were six rows of pews in a semicircle around the altar. The vaulted ceilings and the circular shape of the altar made you feel as if you were in an immensely round room. In actuality, the room was still rectangular-shaped.

Michael stepped onto the marble floors, stopped at the large marble fountain. He dipped his fingers into the Holy Water and made the sign of the Cross, touching warm, wet fingertips to his forehead, sternum, left shoulder and right.

The casket was down this center aisle. A plain dark wooden casket. People sat in pews on both sides of the casket. Michael heard people crying. Choosing to remain discreet, he sat in the last row, with Mass beginning almost on that cue. He followed along, saying the prayers, singing the songs.

It had not been hard to see Felicia, her hair worn up under a hat, with only wisps of that trademark burgundy hair dangling across her neck and down her back. Sandy stood at Felicia's side. It was when the priest asked that everyone greet the person next to him or her, in a sign of peace, that Felicia saw him.

He knew he must look pathetic, sitting alone at the back of the church. They made eye contact—she was crying. He showed her a somber smile. She returned it before slowly turning her attention back to the priest and his gracious words.

Michael noticed an older white man sitting next to a young black woman. The woman was dressed in a black hat with a black veil and matching business suit. The woman had to be Vanessa's mother, the way she was crying and holding the white handkerchief to her mouth through the entire service. The man had a comforting arm around her shoulder. Periodically, she had reached up and held his hand, her nervous twitching fingers seeking to touch . . . what? A lover's hand?

It was after the church service, and after Vanessa Vorhees was lowered into the ground, that Felicia finally approached him. While they stood on the cemetery road, near the gravesite, she walked swiftly up to him, wrapped her arms around his neck, and buried her face into his chest. Her tears soaked through his shirt and felt cold on his skin.

Michael had no trouble hugging her, holding her while she cried. He wished he could take away her pain, to stop her suffering. He knew he could not. He remained silent, and while she continued to cry, he just rubbed her back.

He watched over Felicia's head as the people disassembled. Then Felicia and Sandy hugged and kissed each other before Sandy walked away. Many of them looked at Michael and Felicia, but showed little interest. Aside from the man who had his arm around the woman in black, they were the only white people in attendance.

The white man led the woman in black toward Felicia and Michael. The woman was still crying under her veil, that handkerchief wadded into a ball in her fist and remaining near her mouth. The man held out his hand, and Michael shook it.

"We're Vanessa's parents. We, unfortunately, did not know many of her friends, but it means a lot to us to see she had some close ones. We want to thank you for showing up today. If you'd like, some people are coming back to our house. So many people have brought over food that it will go to waste if we don't share it," Mr. Vorhees offered, graciously.

Felicia had stopped crying, and had positioned herself in Michael's arms so that she could see the couple in front of them. "Thank you, Mr. Vorhees," Michael said. He had no intentions of attending, but saw no reason to say so.

Mrs. Vorhees held out her hand, then slowly placed it on Felicia's shoulder. "Don't go back to doing what you do," she said in a voice not much louder than a whisper. “Look at what happened to my baby. Please, dear God, let this serve as some kind of lesson. Don’t go back to doing what you do.”

Sobs overtook Mrs. Vorhees. Mr. Vorhees turned her around and led her toward the waiting limousine.

Michael heard Felicia say, “Do you have to work?”

“I’m off,” Michael answered

“Feel like coming with me for a drink?”

Chapter 35

They were both drinking beers, sitting in a back corner booth in a small city bar known as The Bent Elbow. With it not being more than ten minutes past eleven, aside from the newspaper-reading, chain-smoking bartender, they were the only patrons. Michael shook two cigarettes out of his pack and lit them. He handed one over to Felicia, who took it hungrily. "Mr. Vorhees," she said. "What an asshole he is."

Michael waited. He knew Felicia would tell him why she thought Vanessa's father was an asshole.

She leaned back against the maroon vinyl seat and said, "Vanessa was the story book whore, you know?" Her gray-blue eyes were brimmed with tears. Felicia brushed them away before they had a chance to slide down her cheeks. "Classic storybook."

"Her father . . ."

"Her father? Ha!" She took a long drag on the cigarette. She leaned in close, and spoke while she exhaled. "Vanessa never knew her real father. This guy was the divorce attorney. You saw Vanessa's mother. She's a nice looking lady. She was also poor. She couldn't afford to pay for the divorce, but Mr. Asshole found different ways of accepting payment. So who knows what happened, right? They fell in love, or lust, or whatever, and wind up getting married. Vanessa was maybe five at the time. Then

Vorhees legally adopts her when she's like, ten. Sounds like a fairy tale, huh? Well it is like a fairy tale; like one you might read by those Grimm Brothers, because that bastard was molesting her from the time she was ten until she was a young teenager. By the time she was sixteen, he was raping her."

"Didn't her mother know?" Michael asked in disbelief.

"She had to know. They only lived in a raised ranch in Gates, not some mansion with twenty rooms. Vanessa's bedroom was two doors down from her parents' room. No way her mother couldn't know what was going on. Except, I remember Vanessa telling me once that her mother got heavy into sleeping pills. No kidding. The old bag wanted to block everything out, keep herself hidden in the dark."

Felicia drank down her beer.

Michael reached for her hands. She pulled away. "Why the hell do you like me?"

The question stopped Michael cold. "Why?" he asked.

"I'm a prostitute, Michael. I sleep with guys for money. Is that what you want in a girl friend? You want to bring someone like me home to meet your parents? Why do you want to be with me?" Felicia asked.

Michael stared into her angry eyes, and beyond the fire in them, he saw the need to be accepted. However, words escaped him. He knew they were not *in love* yet. It was far too soon for an emotion as strong as love. Though the possibility for love was strong, how did one convey those feelings appropriately?

"Am I some kind of novelty, Michael? You screwed a whore without paying, and now it's like a game, a conquest?"

"Why are you doing this? Do you think that's fair?"

"Fair? What do you know about fair? I'll bet your parents put you through school, bought you cars, paid for your clothing, took you to movies. I'll bet you've hardly ever had to go without. Buzzelli. Nice Italian name. Big Italian family, right? Lots of support, hugs, and kisses?" Felicia seethed. Both her hands were balled into dangerous looking fists. Michael let her keep talking, even though most of her "facts" were incorrect.

"I had a mom and dad, but you know what? I meant nothing to

them. Not a thing," Felicia said.

Felicia seemed to throw herself back in the booth. She stopped her emotions as if it had been an easy thing to do. Michael knew already that opening up was something Felicia had difficulty with. She was used to keeping her feelings in. This could be the closest she had ever come to revealing a part of her life to someone. Michael had the distinct feeling that no one knew Felicia's "story."

There was a technique that psychologists used. They would tell the patient something about themselves, in hopes of building trust—a relationship—so that the patient would not feel awkward in return. Often times, psychologists took the first part of this practice a step too far. They opened up *too* much, inadvertently pulling the focus off the patient and placing it on themselves. Michael had no skill at this kind of thing, but letting Felicia sit and sulk was not the answer.

"I guess I have been lucky," he finally said. "I do have a large and supportive family."

Felicia made a humph sound. Michael waved at the bartender. Once he got the man's attention, he signaled for another round. The guy looked annoyed, but brought over fresh drafts while Michael lit up two more cigarettes. When he handed Felicia hers, he asked, "What did your family do wrong?"

She cupped both hands around the frosted mug and seemed to concentrate on staring into the white foamy head. "I had a brother," she said, tentatively. Her lips trembled. "He was almost two years older than me. Wouldn't you know his name was Mike . . . Mikey." Again tears brimmed, and again she wiped them away on her sleeve. "I was five, he was six, almost seven. We were out front playing with a ball. I kicked the ball and it rolled toward the street. My mother was sleeping on a folding chair on the lawn, taking in some sunrays. She wasn't watching us. She never did. And I can . . . I can still see everything so clearly, so clear in my mind. The image is so vivid at times. It comes into my head sometimes when I'm awake, like a nightmare," she said, then stopped talking. She pressed the web between her thumb and first finger across her forehead and shook while she cried.

Michael again reached over the table and touched her other

hand. This time, her fingers wrapped around his. They were cold and wet from holding the mug.

"He, Mikey, ran across the street to get the ball. He picked it up, and stood at the curb. A car was coming. He was playing catch with the ball, just throwing it a little in the air while he waited for the car to pass by. But he missed it, and as he leaned forward to snatch the ball out of the road again, to keep it from getting run over . . . the front grill of the passing car smashed into his head."

Felicia took back her hand. She hugged herself while she cried. Michael stood up and moved to sit beside her in the booth. First he touched her shoulder. Then he ran his hand down her arm. She fell into his arms. Michael knew he had just experienced an amazing breakthrough.

"The car was going too fast, Michael, way too fast. And my mother blamed me for the accident. She jumped out of that chair . . . the driver didn't even honk his horn, but he slammed on his brakes. He slammed on those brakes, and the sound the car made as it skidded to a stop was worse than a million fingernails scratching their way down a blackboard. I'll never forget that sound," Felicia said.

She seemed to have brought herself under control. She had one hand on his thigh. Her fingers squeezed him every once in a while. Her other hand, she used while she talked. It moved like a flag, waving back and forth, up and down. "When my mother talked to my father, she had to have told him she blamed me, so he blamed me, too. Then they just seemed to stop talking to me. My house was like a mime's house. No one said a word. That year, when I turned six, there was no party. No party and no presents.

"By the time I was in junior high I'd become used to the silent treatment. I wasn't at all surprised, nor did I care, when my parents got separated. They never discussed it with me. One day I got home from school and my dad was just gone. His stuff was all cleaned out of the garage and from his den. I remember asking my mom, and all she said was he was leaving for a while. It was years later when they finally worked things out between each other. That was a real shocker, too. I got home one night and my father's on the sofa with my mother. They're sitting real close, you know?

They tell me they're getting back together, that they've worked all this crap out. They want me to forgive them and just forget the past," Felicia explained. She let out a laugh as if the thought of forgiving her parents was part of a joke. "So when they get together what do they do? My father gets my mother pregnant. Marcia's on the way, right? My brother's dead. I've been ignored. My parents split, get back together . . . and the first thing they do is have another baby. Where do I fit in with those plans? Even if I accepted their apologies, even if I forgot the past, don't you think they'd be too busy for me? Wouldn't the upcoming arrival of the new baby keep them from spending any quality time with me? What about all the birthdays where I got nothing or all the Christmas mornings where Santa didn't bother coming. Why would he? After my brother died, we never got another tree. What about me?"

"Did you give them a chance?" Michael asked.

Felicia shot him a desperate look. It said, *Don't.*

"But before they get back together, before the baby's on the way, I'm hitting puberty, right? At this point, raw toxic emotions are surging through me. I'm a mess. I wear mostly black make-up and teachers can't stand me. I have no friends that are girls . . . because all the boys are attracted to me. It isn't long before I find out why, either. I had sex for the first time when I was twelve, and despite my distorted past, I enjoyed it. Having sex made me feel like I counted . . . All the guys at school paid so much attention to me, it was amazing." Felicia retold the story with a thin smile.

"I know what you're thinking, I had low self-esteem. I have low self-esteem. But that's not it. That wasn't it. Maybe I did have low self-esteem, but so what? Having sex felt wonderful. Having people wanting to talk to me felt wonderful. Not since before my brother's death had I ever felt so . . . so necessary. And when I was sixteen, I dropped out of school and left home. I started working as a hostess at a strip club on Lyell Avenue. The owner didn't care that I was sixteen. He paid me under the table. He had enough mob ties that he didn't have to worry about the police showing up unexpectedly. There were enough hiding places in that place. If he needed me to be invisible, I could easily become invisible.

"It wasn't long before I was dancing for him, too. I drew in a crowd. I did some stag parties, making more money than I thought could be possible. And then I learned how to make some extra money at those parties. I did this to one guy, let another guy do something to me, and they practically threw money at me," Felicia said without emotion.

Michael was again at a loss for words. In her short life, she had experienced worlds that he would never know or understand. He could not even begin to comprehend some of the things she must have felt. One question kept flashing in his mind, over and over again. What was their next step together?

When Michael drove her home, they sat silently in his car for several long, uncomfortable minutes. "You know," Felicia said, "I've never told anyone that much about me before." Michael stayed quiet. "Don't even ask me why I told you any of it," she said, throwing her hands in the air. They landed on her lap, and immediately after, her fingers began fidgeting with each other. She had lowered her head, and Michael knew she was crying, again.

"Felicia," Michael said.

She held up a hand. "Stop. Stop it right now, Michael. I don't want to hear whatever it is you think you have to say to me. I don't want to hear. You know what I want? I want some time alone. I want to go into my home, have a beer, and fall asleep on the couch. No radio, no television, nothing." She looked over at Michael.

He loved her eyes. It was a shame that they looked even more beautiful when wet with tears, because he hated to see her hurting so much. "Then good night, sleep tight."

"I hate that saying. What does it mean?" Felicia said, trying to smile as if trying to make it look as if everything was going to be all right. Maybe she wanted Michael and the entire world to know just how strong she was—a high school drop out, orphan, and loner, but tough and determined.

"These old mattresses, back in the time of Shakespeare, were literally tied to the bed posts with rope. You had to pull the ropes every night and get them good and tight if you wanted a firm mattress. So goodnight, sleep tight is derived from that," Michael said, casually.

"You sound like Fatso," Felicia said.

"He's the one who told me."

Felicia reached out and caressed Michael's face with the back of her hand. "You really are a special person, aren't you?" She kept her eyes open only a little as she leaned forward and pressed her lips gently against his. The kiss was brief, tender, and loving. "I'll see you around."

She got out of the car and ran up to her door. Michael waited in the driveway until she was inside. His heart was hammering inside his chest. His mind was all mixed up. He knew there could be no denying his feelings. He was falling in love with Felicia, and though she was denying it, fighting it, he knew she felt the same way.

Chapter 36

Wednesday, January 23

Bob Wendell, the local high school football star at Greece Athena enjoyed smoking a little pot now and then. He knew he did not have a problem with the drug because he never bought the stuff, and during the season he never touched drugs or alcohol. Well, sometimes he drank a few beers at a party, but he had to. Peer pressure took on an entirely new meaning when you were captain of the football team.

His parents talked to him many times about being a leader and not a follower. He knew they loved him, and he respected their well-meaning talks. He even loved them more for it, despite the fact they were getting on his nerves.

They were always explaining to him the power. He had to make a difference because of who he was. Everyone knew that he, Bob "Gunshot" Wendell, was a school leader. The other players on the team looked up to him. The other students admired him because of his accomplishments and notoriety. His touchdown pass throwing abilities made him a local star. He had taken his varsity team all the way this year, bringing home a grand regional trophy. Wendell had even appeared in a television commercial for a used car dealer.

What his parents failed to realize was the fact that being a leader made him feel even more like a loner. Having people idolizing and worshiping him felt more stressful than most people could imagine. At many times, feeling untouchable made him feel ostracized. The guys on the team never seemed to have trouble saying hello, but they always treated him differently from how they treated each other. Wendell's father, a supervisor with Kodak, tried one time to put it into some kind of perspective, by making the comparison that Wendell was like a supervisor. His people, the players, would respect him, but not necessarily like him—and that, according to Wendell's father, was a good thing.

How could he not smoke a little pot at a party where everyone was smoking?

He remembered his first time. The paranoia he had felt after finishing a joint. He thought for sure that he would get caught. His parents would kill him, but not before the coach made sure he would never play another high school sport. He would never get an athletic scholarship to a decent college and would wind up trapped in Rochester for the rest of his life, maybe working at Kodak like his father.

After that night, and after not getting caught, and not getting killed by his parents, the paranoia slowly faded away with his increased usage. He swore—he made a pledge—if his grades ever suffered because of his pot smoking, he would quit. Aside from his political science, chemistry, and English classes—where he had only dropped a single grade level—his grades had not suffered at all.

When Kenny, the team's wide receiver, stuffed the small bag of weed into Wendell's knapsack at school this afternoon, he had said, "Keep it. I'm giving it up."

When Wendell got home from school, he studied the bag. There was just enough in it to roll a single joint. Not wanting to risk having his mother or father find the baggie, he decided he had better get rid of the stuff.

Wendell tore a piece of paper out of his history notebook, folded it, and tucked it and the bag of weed into his front pocket. Leaving his knapsack in his room, and putting his winter coat back on, Wendell ran out the garage door. His house backed up to the woods outlining Sawyer Park. Growing up, he and neighborhood friends practically lived in the woods and at the park.

Now, he sought solace. He felt as if all the neighbors backing up to the park were standing at windows watching him knowingly as he made tracks toward the woods. It took every bit of strength he possessed, not to turn and check out the houses around him. If someone were watching him, they would find it suspicious if he kept nervously glancing over his shoulders. Instead, he stared at a tree directly ahead of him and focused all of his concentration on it, until he walked past it and into the refuge of the trees.

The water seemed to be running fast and hard as if despite the cold, the snow was melting, and the creek was filling with more water than it could handle. The sound it made felt exhilarating. Bob Wendell knew right where to go, to keep hidden, but to be close enough to the water to enjoy the natural surroundings while he rolled and smoked his reefer.

The rock was covered with snow. He did not care. He brushed away the snow with the sleeve of his coat. He removed the paper and baggie from his pocket and sat down. He unfolded the paper and ripped it into quarters. He stuck three of the quarters into his coat pocket, and set the fourth onto his lap. He poured out the herb, rolled the paper, and twisted off the ends.

"You're a lot fatter than I thought you'd be," Wendell said to the joint. He put one end in his mouth and lit it. He sucked in, filling his lungs with smoke, and kept it in his lungs for twenty seconds before exhaling slowly. The notebook paper was burning too quickly, wasting the drug. He smoked faster, taking many drags on the joint.

When the last of it was gone, he was laughing. He could not believe how fast he had smoked that thing. Tears rolled down his face, he was laughing so hard. How could he have smoked a joint, all by himself, that quickly? It was unheard of. Not just an amazingly quick football player, he was also an amazingly quick pot smoker.

He jumped to his feet, arms raised in the air in victory as if he had just sent another pass into the arms of a touchdown-bound receiver. He pivoted his body to the left and right, looking at the woods and over the water as if a crowd of elated fans had gathered and witnessed his speed-pot-smoking ability.

He stopped in mid-pivot when his eyes happened upon a purple foot protruding out of the water. "What the hell is that?" Wendell still had his arms in the air as he tried walking toward a spot on the bank, closer to the foot in the water.

He slipped once. His own shoe went into the frigid water. He ignored the fact that his sock was soaked and his foot immediately felt frozen. He walked along the bank toward the thing in the water, the more sure he was that he was hallucinating.

"Freaking Kenny! The stuff was laced," Wendell said, suddenly crying. He lowered his arms and clamped the palms of his hands to the sides of his face. His fingernails dug into his temples. "What am I supposed to do now?"

He spun around. The woods seemed to mock him. He knew someone had to be watching him, laughing. "This isn't funny," he shouted toward no one. "It's not funny!"

He looked at the water again, expecting not to see the foot. But the foot remained. Tentatively he walked closer. When he was across from the foot, he no longer thought he was hallucinating. He could not be. He had lost his mind, and it was that simple.

"I'm not going in the water," he said to the invisible taunting people hiding in the woods. "I'm not! I know she's not real. That's not real!" He was pointing at the naked woman apparently trapped by tree roots on the opposite bank.

Wendell closed his eyes. He shook his head. His hands had not left his face. He wanted to scream, because he knew he was screwed. When he opened his eyes, if the body of the woman was still submerged in the water, then he definitely was not hallucinating, and might not be losing his mind. When he opened his eyes, if she was gone, he'd freakin' kill Kenny!

When he opened his eyes, the naked body of woman was still there. Wendell screamed for help with all of his might and then walked into the creek. The jolt from the cold water shocked his system. Always the tough football player, Wendell pushed on and waded across the thigh-deep creek. He stood over the naked woman, who was just a few inches under water. She was staring at him. Her eyes and mouth were open wide. It looked like her arm and head were wedged between some rocks and tree roots. The roots had erupted from the bank and continued to grow and spread in the creek.

Wendell thought he should pull her free and get her up onto the embankment. He knelt down in the water, then stood up. “Screw that, naked or not, I’m not touching some dead chick!”

The effect from the weed was gone, completely gone. He was not high at all. Though the realization presented itself like a flash of lightening in his mind, Wendell was not disappointed. Mostly, he felt relieved.

He took a cell phone out of his coat pocket and dialed 911.

Chapter 37

The police cars and other emergency vehicles were parked outside of Sawyer Park. Only one set of tire tracks was in the snow in the lot and no one wanted to risk contaminating the scene.

Detectives Jason Cocuzzi and Peter Cage stood side by side with their hands stuffed into their pockets. The temperature had continued to drop all day long, though finally stabilizing at thirteen degrees. However, the winds had picked up bringing the wind-chill down to four below.

A black tarp had been placed on the snow while paramedics lifted the body out of the water and set the victim down on the tarp. Alex Green, the Monroe County M.E., was present and giving the body a preliminary examination.

"Robert Wendell lives just on the other side of the park's woods," Cocuzzi said to an officer. "Once we establish a time of death, I want a door-to-door done on that residential street. The usual. Did anyone see anything out the back windows? Did they hear anything? Go with those types of questions. Let's see if we can come up with anything."

When the officer took off, Cage shrugged. "Even though the trees are bare, those woods look pretty dense."

"Never know," Cocuzzi replied. At this point, with their third suspected victim lying on a tarp in front of them, they could not afford to speculate. They needed to move fast on every possible technique that might assist them in producing a solid lead.

Walking away from the body, with Cage following, Cocuzzi backtracked in his own imprints in the snow toward the parking lot. A lab technician knelt, casting the tire tracks into a mold. "Anything?"

The tech looked up. "Snow's powdery, I'm having a hard time. We've taken a lot of photographs. Used your camera, too. Your equipment is back on your front seat."

"Thank you," Cocuzzi said.

"No problem. Thing is, the driver of this vehicle had bald tires, mostly. The few tracks made are not very good. The wind's been blowing, and well, I can't guarantee a thing here," the tech said.

"Well, let us know if you come up with anything," Cage said, trying to sound authoritative.

"Of course," the technician said, and went back to the difficult task before him.

Cocuzzi had his shoulders raised, hunched forward, in a vain attempt to block his face from the brutal lashing of the wind.

When Dr. Green stood up, he looked around the scene, saw the detectives, and waved them over. Cocuzzi took this as a hopeful sign. When they were huddled together, the M.E. shrugged. "This sucks, Cocuzzi. Sucks. I've done pretty much all I can out here. I want to get the victim back to the morgue. I'm going to do my best to lift prints, but if she spent any considerable amount of time in the water . . . with the creek raging the way it is, I don't know what type of evidence will be recoverable."

"Got enough pictures?"

"Plenty."

"The M.O.?" Cage asked.

"A large knife was used again. Markings are pretty consistent to those found on the other victims. He's slicing them up pretty good, then cuts . . . not deeply . . . but cuts from between their breasts down the center of their bellies to the pubic area. Once in that domain, he hacks them up something awful," Dr. Green said. "I'd say, ninety-nine percent positively, that this is the same killer."

Jason Cocuzzi felt like exploding. The city did not need a serial killer on the loose. No city did. “Let me know the minute you I.D. the victim.”

“Yeah, sure.” Green looked down at the woman on the tarp. Cocuzzi followed his gaze. The woman’s bloated body was an awfully vibrant shade of blue and purple. Where the killer used his knife, her skin puckered like a sliced-open baked potato. Only, instead of revealing tantalizingly white potato inside, Cocuzzi was staring at dark-red human meat.

Chapter 38

Friday, January 25

Michael could not wait for the day to end. He had been in his cubicle slaving away at the computer since eight and had worked through lunch, munching away at a sandwich between keystrokes. His eyes burned and he had suffered from a dull-throbbing headache ever since just before lunch. He had swallowed down some aspirin tablets, but the pain never even attempted to subside. He wondered if he might need glasses.

Part of the reason he stayed busy was because the office was busy. Johnny the Blade had done it again. Though the City Chronicle had two designated crime reporters, every journalist on the payroll wanted a piece of the action. Articles showed up in the latest edition in a variety of topics, written by a number of people. Of course the front-page headlines deserved the coverage. The serial killer diversified his predatory actions, adding to his victim-list a woman who was not a whore. The local section pounced on this latest revelation by assigning reporters to poll Rochesterians, as if trying to start a citywide panicked frenzy. The business section of the paper showcased a piece on shop owners in and around the area, focusing on the ones open around the clock. The article touched on security, employee safety, and the need to work together and watch out for each other. Many of the places on Lake and on Lyell had contracted security guards to watch buildings and escort employees to cars. It was the article in the sport section that seemed unbelievable. One sports writer managed to work the Johnny Blade reference as a metaphor when talking about the kind of season the Rochester Amerks hockey team was having.

Everyone was getting in on it. Johnny Blade was a hot topic. Hot topics sold papers. When papers sold, the bosses at the City Chronicle smiled happily. When the bosses were happy, employees were happy. All around, everyone came out a winner. Except, Michael Buzzelli did not feel happy. Aside from writing the obituaries for the victims, Michael was the most removed journalist from the sensationalism of the moment.

Donna Pappalardo. She was the third known victim murdered by Johnny Blade. Michael entered the information he had been given the other day. Donna Pappalardo, only twenty-seven years old, still had living parents. A middle child sandwiched between two brothers. A healthy list of names included living grandparents, aunts, uncles, and cousins.

Michael watched Matthew Sinopoli closely. The aged crime reporter spent the afternoon at his desk talking on the telephone. It was not hard to notice since the man had a huge office with floor to ceiling windows. Sinopoli always kept his door closed, but his curtains kept open. Sometimes it surprised Michael to see the veteran using a computer. A word processor or even a typewriter would look more appropriate on the man's desk. Inside Michael, an insatiable itch grew. It felt fierce, the burning in his belly. He was closer to the story than any of the writers at this paper. He wanted the chance to prove himself.

Sinopoli had covered many of the bases. He had interviewed the families of the victims. He had talked with the ones unfortunate enough to find the victims bodies. Sinopoli knew how to work closely with the police, too. Most of the information Sinopoli wrote about came directly from Detective Jason Cocuzzi. To the casual onlooker, or chief editor, Matthew Sinopoli appeared all over his assignment. He knew he was mentally beating a dead horse, but it drove Michael nuts that Sinopoli conducted ninety percent of his business over the phone.

As Sinopoli switched off his monitor, Michael filled a cup at the water cooler. He shook his head as the star reporter pulled a dangling chain to shut off his desk light. Michael sipped his water as Sinopoli snapped closed his briefcase. As Michael slowly made his way toward his own cubicle, Sinopoli slipped his second arm into the sleeve of his long down jacket. Peering over the top of his cubicle, Michael watched as Sinopoli closed the curtains.

Michael sat at his desk and stared at the monitor. Tonight he would be working at Jack's. He knew he needed more discipline. He was letting the people he had met at the diner influence his decisions. Though he had sketched out articles on his home computer, he'd done very little digging to find Johnny Blade. Where could he find the time?

It was possible the killer was a regular at Jack's. Most killers knew their victims. Michael did not think Fatso was a possibility. He remembered when the two of them first met. They had shaken hands. He had introduced himself as Fat Joe. He did not give Michael a last name. Neither had Speed, for that matter. In fact, he did not even know a first name for Speed. There were other regulars at the diner. Michael thought of the two teenagers who had recently attempted robbing the place. Though they had been unsuccessful, they could be suspects. They had tempers and clearly displayed a violent disposition.

Michael picked up the telephone. He dialed Detective Cocuzzi's direct line. Smiling, he waited for someone to answer.

"Detective Cocuzzi's desk," a man said.

"Hi. I was hoping to speak to the detective," Michael said.

"He's kind of busy right now, can I take a message?"

"Is this detective Cage?" Michael asked, knowing that it was Peter Cage on the phone. He recognized the sound of the man's voice. The young cop sounded overly cocksure of himself. It annoyed the hell out of Michael.

"It is. And who is this?"

Michael knew he had succeeded at unnerving the man. "Michael Buzzelli. Remember me? I was thinking. Remember the robbery, the attempted robbery at Jack's Joint? There were the two guys in Halloween masks?"

"Yeah, and?"

Michael knew he had the detective's undivided attention, despite the tone of boredom in the policeman's voice. "Well they were picked up that night, right? I mean the police caught them, right?"

"They did and I know where you're going with this. Cocuzzi spent time with each of them separately. He questioned them for hours. We thought the same way you're thinking," Detective Cage said.

A long silence ensued. Michael could no longer hear any background noise, where before he had heard other telephones ringing and the murmur of people talking. He wondered if the officer had hung up on him, completely unappreciative of his phone call. "Detective?"

"Mr. Buzzelli?" Phones must have changed hands. Michael knew Cage was no longer on the line. "This is Detective Cocuzzi. I appreciate your call."

At least someone did. "It was bugging me. I keep thinking the killer has to be someone close to the victims. The closest people to the girls are probably the regulars at the diner. Wouldn't you agree?"

"It's a solid theory," Detective Cocuzzi said. "Those two that tried to rob the place have alibis for the night of Vanessa's killing. We even cross-checked them for the latest victim. They are basketball players at the high school. Not only were they at the games, they scored enough points between them to be covered by your sports writer, whatever his name is."

"Daniels," Michael said absently.

"What's that?" Cocuzzi asked.

"The sports writer, his name is Gray Daniels." Michael held his mouse and wiggled it back and forth, watching the pointer on his monitor dance across the screen. "I got a question for you, Detective Cocuzzi. You ever look into Marcus? I don't know a last name on the guy. He looks like he's a lone-mobster or something."

"Marcus Bovenzi?"

Michael typed the name into his computer. "Yeah, him."

"Listen," Cocuzzi said, "Cage and I appreciate your call. We really do. Do us a favor though, all right? Leave the investigation to us. If you have a lead, if you have a suspect, do exactly what you did today and call us. You know how to get a hold of us."

"If I bring you information, will you guarantee me an exclusive?" Michael asked.

"Where would that leave Matt Sinopoli, huh? I don't know that it would be fair to him. I'm a fair man. He's been covering the case since the beginning. I've worked with Matt for years," Detective Cocuzzi said, though he did not sound firm in his stance.

"If you're a fair man, and I bring you information that leads to the capture of Johnny the Blade, then wouldn't it only be fair to give me an exclusive?" Michael said. While he spoke, he logged onto the newspaper's database. He entered a password when prompted to do so. "Well?"

"How about, we'll see?"

"My parents used to say that, detective. You know what 'we'll see' meant to me as a kid? It meant 'no.' Are you giving me a political 'no?'" Michael asked. The database opened up. Michael typed, "Bovenzi, Marcus." He hit the "enter" key and waited.

"You bring me information that leads to the capture of the serial killer, Mr. Buzzelli, and I will give you an exclusive. You have my word."

"That's what I like to hear, because I get the feeling that after I solve this case, you and I will be working together on future assignments." Michael watched as an empty rectangle appeared on the monitor. Slowly the bar began to fill in with blue and white stripes. The system timed how long it would take to complete a search through the electronic archives for documents containing the words Marcus and/or Bovenzi.

"Well, if anything, I wish you luck, Mr. Buzzelli."

Michael hung up. He smiled when he read that one hundred and thirteen articles had been retrieved. He did not need to be to work at the diner for another few hours. Michael leaned back in his chair, closed his eyes, and massaged his temples with his fingertips. He stretched and yawned before settling down to work.

He opened the first document and started reading.

Chapter 39

Michael pulled into the back parking lot at Jack's Joint. Sandy and Felicia stood by the Dumpster smoking cigarettes. They both had on an angry face and both seemed to be talking at the same time. Neither paid much attention to Michael as he parked alongside Murphy's car. When he shut the engine and stepped out of his car, he was immediately assaulted by a harsh and bitter wind. Zipping up his coat, Michael walked toward the women, instead of toward the refuge of the diner.

They were almost arguing, Michael noted as he rounded the rear of his car. "What's going on?"

Felicia turned on him. "Cops are all over the place."

Cocking his eyebrows, Michael looked from Felicia to Sandy.

"They think we're too stupid to realize it," said Felicia. "How dumb do they think we are?"

"I don't get it," Michael admitted.

"They have a sting set up," Felicia explained. Her cheeks and nose looked rosy and matched the shade of her lipstick. "I'm freezing."

"Why are you back here?" Michael asked. He hoped he sounded concerned and civilized. "Why don't you two at least go inside and stay warm?" He wanted to ask why Felicia was back at all. He did not expect to see her here. He did not expect to see her working. A knot formed in his belly as a mixture of emotions flooded through him. Jealousy and anger were in the forefront and remained the most prominent. He felt sad and cheated. He wanted answers, but did not want to ask her any of the questions spinning around in a whirlwind in his mind. *Why are you here? How can you still want to do this? Why? How?*

"Screw this, I'm just going home. There ain't going to be any money made tonight," Sandy said. "How about you Felicia?"

Felicia looked at Michael. "I might go in for some coffee first. Warm up some."

* * *

Fatso looked like a man watching a movie. He had positioned himself on the stool so he could face the front window. He waved to Michael and Felicia as they walked around the front of the building, before they entered the diner. Michael waved back, absently. His attention was immediately drawn to the prostitute standing at the corner.

"Who's that?" he asked. He had never seen this working girl before. She had long blonde curly hair. Michael felt certain the hair was a wig. She wore a thigh length fur coat. The woman's legs were shielded from the elements in red nylon stockings and knee-high leather boats. She stood by the street sign with her hips cocked, all her weight on one leg.

"'What's that?' might be a better question," Felicia said loud enough to get the attention of the woman working the street traffic as she linked an arm around Michael's. "She's a cop. Part of that sting. There are a few more inside posing as customers. There are cops in some parked cars along the street, too."

Michael looked up and down the road. Traffic was thin. Cars whipped by, coming from both directions. Michael noticed a man sitting in a black Lincoln a block away. He also noticed the cream-colored van with tinted windows across the street, parked in front of a fire hydrant. "Cops, huh?"

He knew what was going on. The police wanted to catch Johnny Blade. It seemed a little risky, but valiant. It stood to reason the Blade might come back to Jack's Joint. He had killed two women from here before. But his third victim, who was not a known prostitute, had been picked up on Lyell Avenue. Johnny Blade must realize that establishing a pattern would only wind up getting him caught. Still, what else did the police have to go on? Jack's Joint was a logical starting point. He would not doubt if the police had units staking out the bar on Lyell, too. "Let's get inside. I'm frozen!"

Upon entering, Michael initially expected to see Detectives Cocuzzi and Cage. That would not make sense though, not if the police suspected a Jack's Joint customer. Having shown their faces before, they would risk being identified. Michael thought he could pick out the undercover officers easily. Though he did not recognize everyone, picking out the police seemed a piece of cake. The man at the counter with sandy blonde hair, maybe in his mid-twenties, dressed in a long black trench coat, had to be a cop. The man in the trench coat sat sideways on the stool. He had a copy of the newspaper open, and though he appeared to be reading, Michael felt himself being sized-up and assessed.

The man sitting in the second booth closest to the front window was an undercover police officer. A plate with a half-eaten hamburger and a few fries sat on the tabletop. The man was maybe thirty-five, forty at the oldest. He had a horseshoe head of hair and a dry-looking scalp. This man was heavy, out of shape. As he held a coffee cup to his lips, Michael noted the unusually thick fingers. The man's wedding band was nearly swallowed by the swollen-looking flesh on either side of the ring.

Two cops for sure, and a third working the corner. It might prove to be an interesting night. Michael smiled at Felicia. "Coffee?"

She smiled back. "Please."

Chapter 40

Detective Jason Cocuzzi sat in an old Subaru along the street, on the adjacent corner. He watched Michael Buzzelli skeptically. Though he did not believe Buzzelli to be the killer, he still had reserved feelings about the overly ambitious young journalist. Though he often times did not agree with Detective Cage's mannerisms and obnoxious outbursts, he did side with the Irondequoit cop when it came to comparing most journalists to attorneys.

The plan did not sound desperate at the design stages. However, it felt desperate now that it was actually being carried out. There were many factors calculated into the equation. The one obvious point made was the fact that the killer, Johnny Blade, was striking more frequently. Donna Pappalardo bothered Cocuzzi and the others assigned to the task force. She did not blend into the mix. Serial killers were known to work consistently. They worked a pattern; used a plan. All three victims had been killed with the same kind, or the exact same knife. The first two victims were prostitutes. The first two victims worked the same street corner. These two facts showed a pattern. One of the prostitutes was white; one was black. This, in a way, deviated from the pattern. All of the bodies were dumped out in the open. Pattern. Pappalardo, however, was not a prostitute. She worked in a factory. She was picked up on Lyell Avenue, and not from outside of Jack's Joint.

Cocuzzi and the newly assigned task force were scrambling. The FBI had contacted the chief of police. Two agents were being sent over. They planned to profile the serial killer and lead the task force. Cocuzzi resented this. He appreciated the FBI's wanting to help. He could handle the case, though. When the chief explained the news to Cocuzzi, the homicide detective held his tongue. Foolish pride would be the only reason to complain. Foolish pride. If the FBI could help catch the killer, then he agreed to welcome the agents with—mostly—open arms.

Detective Cage, on the other hand, had flown off the handle. The chief quickly put Cage in his place. "Who in the hell are you to complain, detective? You aren't even with this department. I'm letting you work the case with Detective Cocuzzi as a favor to your chief!"

Cocuzzi's radio crackled with static and came to life. "See Buzzelli? Asshole."

Cocuzzi closed his eyes. "I saw Buzzelli, Cage. Let's keep comments like 'asshole' to ourselves so we don't needlessly tie up the airwaves. Out." Cage was in the van across the street from the diner. The truck, loaded with video and audio equipment, monitored Christine Wrzos. She looked like a stereotypical whore. Cage said she should be smoking, too. Smoking, Cage explained, was a sexual turn on. Men found women more attractive when they smoked. He told Cocuzzi and the others that a cigarette was a phallic symbol and represented a man's penis.

Christine absolutely refused to smoke. "I quit five years ago. It was one of the toughest things I've ever had to do. If you think I'm going to risk getting hooked on that crap again . . . you're out of your wacked-out mind, detective."

Cocuzzi laughed at Christine's brazen statements, and respected the young detective immediately and immensely. It amazed him that she'd be willing to risk her life posing as a prostitute to catch a knife-wielding killer, but refused to risk getting re-addicted to nicotine.

The undercover cops inside Jack's Joint had it made. They

were in a building, drinking coffee and staying warm. Jason Cocuzzi had a thermos of coffee, but it was not the same thing. He kept the car running with the heat on high and still felt a chill in his bones. He had set the radio down on the seat beside him and intently concentrated on the surroundings.

One of the flaws in this sting set-up was painfully apparent. More than likely, unsuspecting johns would stop and solicit Christine for sex, or sexual favors, in exchange for money. The johns would have to be arrested. However, this process would require Christine to place herself in some dangerous situations, mainly because the task force did not want to make busts in front of the diner.

Christine readily agreed to the assignment, knowing the risks involved. The task force did not try to dissuade her decision. Still, if Christine climbed into a vehicle with a john, and the bust was made somewhere else—there stood a good chance that the actual killer might drive by Jack's Joint and not see a working girl on the corner. Cage wanted to have two women undercover. He wanted the second woman to be African American. Cocuzzi agreed. The chief wanted to wait and see how the first few nights panned out. If Christine was spending a lot of time getting picked up, then a second plant might prove necessary.

The plan was simple: bust anyone caught soliciting Christine, get the john to the station, and conduct an extensive background search. The police would have the john's car in possession and the right to search it thoroughly.

Just as Jason Cocuzzi poured coffee into the thermos cap, a small blue, street-salt and grime-covered car pulled up to the curb. Cocuzzi poured the coffee back into the thermos and picked up his radio. "Pete? Over."

"We got him, Cocuzzi. We're recording the conversation. The guy wants to know what a twenty will get him. Unit One, stand by. Over."

"This is Unit One. We're running the plates now. Over."

Cocuzzi watched Christine's performance. She resembled an officially trained thespian. She stood with one hand on her hip and kept tossing her hair back. She gave the apparent impression of boredom. This was another day in a working girl's life. Cocuzzi wished he could hear the dialog to accompany the scene.

"Pete? What's happening? Over." Cocuzzi could not help feeling apprehensive. There would be no way to know for sure if this john was the Johnny Blade. The stakes in the game were high. Police work always involved high stakes. Routine traffic, done day in and day out, sometimes proved deadly. Many jobs caused stress. Being a police officer, the stress started at the beginning of the shift, and often times lasted the full eight hours—and then some. Some police officers, like Cocuzzi, though, seemed to thrive on stress.

"It looks good. Looks like she's going to get in. Over." Peter Cage said as Cocuzzi watched Christine climb into the car. The driver of the dirty blue vehicle looked around, pulled into traffic and drove north down Lake Avenue.

Unit Two, an unmarked squad car pulled out of a spot along the road and followed the blue car. Cocuzzi talked into his radio. "And? Over."

"And," Cage said, "the guy wants her to relieve him while he's driving. He's already got it out." Static and hissing noise emitted from the radio. "I think she's laughing at him. Over."

Cocuzzi smiled. "They're no where near our focal point. Pull them over. Over."

"This is Unit One. We have a make on the vehicle and its owner. The car is registered to a Sonia Baker. We believe the driver might be her teenaged son. Over."

Cocuzzi cursed under his breath. "I want him brought to the station regardless. Same rules. Complete background check, alibis, everything. Clear? Over."

"Will do. Over."

Chapter 41

"Cops all over the place," Fatso said in a whisper as he turned the page of his newspaper.

"What was that?" Michael asked.

"More coffee, please," Fatso said in a voice too loud not to seem suspicious.

As Michael poured fresh coffee into Fatso's nearly full cup, Fatso leaned in closer. "I said, 'cops are all over the place.'" Fatso sat up straight and cleared his throat. In a strong voice he said, "That's perfect, thank you."

Michael could not help but smile. Fatso had succeeded in doing the opposite of what he had attempted to do. Rather than casually warn Michael of the undercover police officers, he attracted everyone's attention. Michael set the pot back on the warmer. "I caught sight of them," Michael said, resting his elbows on the counter. "And right now, most of them are looking at you."

Fatso gasped. "Get out. For real?"

Michael smiled. He could tell Fatso wanted to turn around and see who might be staring at him. It appeared to take every bit of reserve to keep from doing so. "Not anymore."

Fatso let out a sigh of relief. "This doesn't just seem like some bust going down. I get the feeling they're after Johnny Blade." Fatso added sugar and cream to his coffee. "This entire setup has major sting written all over it. In the summer, the cops like to bust the johns. They do these once a month . . . but never have I seen undercover inside Jack's. No, this has something to do with Johnny Blade."

Of course, this was obvious to Michael. "Could be," he simply said, finding it difficult not to stare at the policemen in the diner. They seemed aware of him as well. Michael wanted to find out more. He wondered what might be going on outside. He watched the policewoman dressed like a prostitute climb into a car and drive away. He then noted a car pull away from the curb a few moments later. Though unlikely, it seemed all too possible that the serial killer had just picked up a police officer without realizing it.

"Did you hear about Speed?" Fatso asked. He had folded his newspaper into quarters and set it down on the counter. He wanted to talk now. Michael noted how Fatso could use the newspaper to manipulate a situation. If the heavy man did not wish to be disturbed, he hid behind the creases of a fully unfolded paper. If he wanted to be in and out of a conversation, the paper was folded in half. This let Fatso insert his two cents, and if necessary hide behind the headlines. When Fatso folded the paper into quarters and set it down, then Fatso was ready to chew the fat, regardless of the consequences of the conversation.

"I haven't heard a thing. No. What happened? He get arrested?" Michael thought it seemed like the most logical event to happen to a professional shoplifter. He wondered if Speed had any kind of record. If you stole things for a living, you had to get caught once in a while. Could someone get away with it every time? That did not seem likely.

Fatso pursed his lips together. "I just got this information from Jack, before he left. Seems Speed got busted, big time busted. He was at one of them stores at Midtown Plaza . . . I don't know why that place is still opened." Midtown Plaza was an infamous mall in the heart of the city of Rochester. At one point the place thrived. It boasted prominent department stores and a variety of chain shops. At Christmas time, the mall would be crowded with holiday shoppers. A trolley on tracks near the ceiling gave rides to children waiting to sit on Santa's lap. In the late 1980's and throughout the

1990's the place went to Hell. The mall was full of dangerous vagrants. Armed security guards were added for protection. The large department stores pulled out. For decades, the mall seemed on the verge of closing down. Traffic was slim throughout the year, and even during the Christmas season. For one reason or another, the mall remained open. "I don't go down there. I don't feel safe," Fatso said, and seemed to pause to reflect on this last statement.

"What happened to Speed?" Michael insisted, impatiently. Though curiosity was getting the better of him, Michael found it difficult to stay focused. He watched Felicia watching him. She had a smile on her face that could not be misinterpreted. She wanted him. He wanted her. He displayed a sheepish grin.

"You listening to me or what?" Fatso asked.

"I'm listening. I'm listening," Michael said. "You're just taking forever to get to the point."

As if ignoring the insult, Fatso cleared his throat. "So Speed's on the upper level in the mall, right? And he's in a store filling his bag, or however he does it. When he comes out of the store . . . back into the mall . . . a guard yells for him to stop. See, they can't do anything to you while you're in the store. You can be in a store stuffing jewelry down your pants, but until you leave without paying for it . . . no one can do a thing to you. If they try to arrest you before you've left, all you have to do is tell them you planned on paying for it. Since you hadn't left the store, they can't prove otherwise."

"So Speed was stuffing jewelry down his pants?" Michael asked, teasing.

"No. I'm just illustrating a point."

"Yeah, well now I have a vivid image of Speed's privates decked out in diamonds and rubies." Michael vigorously shook his head as if trying to get the mental picture out of his head. Felicia laughed.

"This isn't funny," Fatso said. He sounded frustrated.

"It is so far. Fatso. You haven't told me anything yet."

"Speed didn't stop when the guard called out to him."

"Why would he?"

"Instead, he took off running, looking back all the time. What he didn't see was the guard coming at him from the side. This guard . . . you've seen the guards there . . . they all look like pro wrestlers. Well, this guard must have been a linebacker or something. He crosses his arms over his chests and barrels into Speed like a fright train. The inertia doesn't stop Speed. It propels him backwards . . ."

"Inertia?" Michael asked, smiling.

Continuing to ignore the interruptions, Fatso presses on. "Speed hits the railing and it gives."

This statement wiped the smirks off the faces of Michael and Felicia's. "Now I have your attention."

"Is he all right?" Felicia asked. She looked worried. Concern was evident in her eyes. They were wide, her brow creased.

"He's all right. He's at Park Ridge Hospital. He's got a severe concussion, a broken arm, and broken ribs. He was lucky. He landed on his side. The police were saying, had he landed on his back, the damage would have been worse . . . and he more than likely would have died. He's under arrest, too. Police even have him cuffed to the bed. When the police got there, they found his pockets stuffed with stolen stuff. Jack said Speed was wearing five stolen shirts and six pairs of stolen pants. The police think all of this extra padding helped keep him from killing himself when he hit the ground. The clothing broke the fall." Fatso was grinning.

"Damn," Michael said.

* * *

Around one, Felicia stood up. "You know, this is crazy. I'm going home." She rolled her head, stretching her neck muscles. "Damned police got nothing better to do than hang out in a diner all night. Hell, Jack don't even sell doughnuts."

Michael smiled knowing Felicia wanted the undercover police to hear her. They appeared to do their best not to. Aside from Felicia and Fatso, the police were the only other guests seated in the dining room. He had filled their coffee cups a few times. They were polite and looked bored.

The cop in costume on the corner had only been picked up three times. Michael had to assume the three johns were arrested, and none of them was the serial killer. The woman working the street had to be cold. The sound of the wind caused the building to moan. "It's a bitter-looking night," Fatso said.

Michael did not want Felicia to leave. It was unrealistic to think she would stay the entire night. He had things in his car and wondered when he might be able to give them to her. As he stood by her, but behind the counter, he tried to talk without drawing attention. Fatso made no game about it. He was not only staring at them, he was anxiously waiting to hear what Michael had to say.

It was an awkward moment. Only Felicia seemed to be enjoying it. She smiled at Michael as he searched inside himself for the right words. "When I get out of here, I got something I'd like to give you."

"I'll bet you do, kid," Fatso said and grunted out a laugh. He looked around the diner to see if he had scored one with the undercover police officers. They seemed more like fixtures, rather than people. They barely moved, each looking out the front window, eyes clearly focused on their fellow employee, the streetwalker.

"Fatso, you mind?" Michael asked. "Huh?"

"Hey, sorry, kid." Fatso picked up his paper. He unfolded it some. He held it up, but peered over the paper's edge. When Michael continued to stare at him, he lowered his eyeballs and mumbled. "Sorry. Geesh!"

Michael lost his motivation. He felt dumb, foolish like a schoolboy. This was not the image he wanted to convey. He had never considered himself shy around women. Felicia did something to him, though. And yet, part of him wondered about something else. Maybe he felt funny asking her to do something in front of other people because everyone here knew she was a prostitute. It was possible. The fact that she was, did bother him. He still found himself very attracted to her. He wanted to spend time with her. Crude as it sounded, there was no getting around the fact that she earned her living screwing guys for money.

"What, Michael?" Felicia asked. He looked into her eyes and

knew immediately that she wanted him to keep going, to find the strength and ask her out.

"Nah, it's nothing. Some books I have in the car. I'll catch up with you. Don't worry about it." It hurt saying this. He wanted to say so much more. He had hurt her, too. The look in her eyes changed. She was no longer looking at him in the same way. The longing look had vanished. Now she looked sad. Her eyes looked shiny and wet. "You'll be in tomorrow?"

Felicia tossed a few bills onto the counter. "Who knows?" She put on her coat, and while she wrestled with the zipper, she did everything in her power not to look at Michael. "Good night. Good night, Fatso, and good hunting officers."

She pulled open the door, capturing everyone's attention. As she left, she managed a quick glance over her shoulder to let Michael see she was crying. He was about to say something—though he had no idea what to say—but it did not matter. She left. The strong winds kept the diner door from closing. The bitter wind easily found its way in to Jack's, and a sudden and violent chill worked its way down Michael's spine.

As the door slowly closed, Fatso set down his newspaper, once again. "Way to go, lover-boy."

Michael pulled out his pack of cigarettes. He lit one, ignoring Fatso, and watched Felicia walk by the undercover whore and disappear around the corner. He had blown it. "Dammit."

* * *

When his night shift ended, Michael Buzzelli felt like crap. Jack's Joint remained dead for most of the night. It was almost as if the clientele knew the police had the place staked out and therefore, stayed away. The highlight of the evening happened on the three occasions where the woman, Christine Wrzos, came in to get warm. She played her part to a tee, talking a line of crap, keeping Michael and Fatso entertained. When she was inside, the undercover policemen relaxed. It was a break for them too.

Jack was pissed when he showed up. The register was bare. Michael left out the back door while the old man was still cussing away.

Michael knew what he wanted to do. He wanted to stop by and talk with Felicia. He knew she was mad at him. She might not want to see him. He could drive home, get ready for bed, write a little or watch some television, but decided against it. If he tried writing, his heart would not be in it. The articles he worked on were very important. If he could not write with all of his heart and concentration, then the articles would need to wait. Though he did not need any heart to watch television, the thought of lying on the sofa watching television did not sound appealing.

After getting his car started and wiping the accumulation of snow off the front and rear windshields, Michael sat behind the wheel and thought about what options he had left. Only one remained.

He pulled onto Lake Avenue and headed for Felicia's house. It was a beautiful morning. The freshly fallen snow was white, and not yet tainted by car exhaust. As he left the city, the scenery around him became more extraordinary. The snow was several inches thick and sat like white rising shadows on each tree branch. The sight of winter can be exhilarating, and Michael understood this perception to be part of a good omen, a sign reflective of glorious things to come.

What he did not know was that his interpretation of the omen could not be any further from the truth.

Chapter 42

Saturday, January 26

Valerie Wringer stood by the kitchen counter washing the breakfast dishes. A wet soapy semi-ring started around the mid-section of her violet shirt, making the ring a deeper and darker shade of purple. While she washed, she stared absently out the window over the sink admiring the way the day was starting out. The fresh falling snow blanketed the yard, filling in any footprints. She especially liked the way the trees looked, covered with powdery white snow.

As she finished washing out a glass once filled with pulpy orange juice, Valerie called out to her daughters. "Girls if you're almost ready, we'll get going." On Saturdays, Veronica and Victoria bowled on a youth league. Veronica was twelve, and the oldest. Victoria was ten, and Valerie thought, a much more accomplished bowler. Valerie knew part of the reason. While Victoria was competitive and focused, the boys on the league had easily distracted her older sister.

Things in the house were much more difficult, and Valerie often times found herself crying for no apparent reason. But that was not exactly true. There were plenty of reasons to be upset. The thought of Veronica interested in boys was reason enough. In two months Veronica would become a teenager. The girl had begun having periods when she was eleven, and though as mother and daughter they had discussed some of the birds and bees, Valerie knew a much more content-oriented talk would be necessary.

Valerie let the water out of the sink. As it drained, she used her blue sponge to wipe down the sides of the sink. She used a few sheets of paper toweling to dry her hands and wipe down the counter. “Girls!”

“Coming!” The unanimous reply came and was immediately followed with the sound of feet pounding down the hallway and down the stairs.

“I’m not ready. I can’t find my brush,” Veronica said. She stood at the bottom of the stairs, pouting. She had her hip cocked, and for no reason at all was staring daggers at her mother.

Victoria was sitting on the floor next to her big sister, trying to keep her balance on her rump as she struggled to fit her foot into her snow boot without first untying the laces. “Why are you looking at me that way? I didn’t take your brush . . . and Tori, untie the boot first.”

“I don’t have too,” Victoria said as she managed to shove her foot into the boot. She reached for the other one, and the wrestling process started up again.

“Did you check in the bathroom drawers?” Valerie asked, feeling compelled to offer a solution. They did not have time to argue. It was nearly ten o’clock, and the girls began bowling at ten thirty. Valerie wadded the paper toweling up and tossed it into an over-filled pail under the sink counter. “Let me take a look.”

As she walked toward the stairs, Veronica did not move. She made a harsh face and had no problem sharing it with her mother. Her upper lip was raised, as was her left nostril. The heavy lipstick and thick application of eye shadow and mascara made her look like a simple-minded clown. Though this should have made Valerie laugh, it did not. She was instead enraged. “What is your problem, young lady?”

Veronica crossed her arms over her chest. “Nothing.”

Poor Victoria scooted out of the way on her rump. She stopped trying to get into the second winter boot. Valerie knew that Victoria hated the fighting. However, Veronica seemed to thrive on it. Though she wanted to blame all of this on her ex-husband, she knew to be fair, she could not. She remembered having similar run-ins with her own mother. She also remembered after a run-in with her mother, she would go to her daddy for comfort and an understanding ear. Veronica did not have that luxury.

Knowing all of this did not defuse the situation any. "I was about to go upstairs and look for your hair brush . . . *your* hair brush . . . and you're going to give me an attitude? I don't think so. If you can't find your brush, then tough."

"Then I'm not going bowling," Veronica said as if she were punishing her mother.

"Go on and stay home, then," Valerie said. Inside her heart ached. She hated to fight with one of her daughters. She did not want Veronica to miss a week of bowling. The girls enjoyed bowling, sometimes for different reasons, and it was a perfect way for them constructively to spend a Saturday Morning.

"Veronica," Victoria said simply, in a pleading voice. She had untied her boot and was in the process of loosening the laces. She stuffed in her foot and stood up. "Don't be this way. Mom didn't loose your brush."

"Shut up, Tori!"

"Don't talk to your sister that way," Valerie shouted.

"It's okay, Mom," Victoria said. She bent forward, and while she tied her laces, said, "She doesn't mean it, Mom. I know that."

Again, a pang of needle sharp pain pierced Valerie's heart. She did not know much about psychology, but she was certain any one-oh-one textbook on divorced families would have a way to categorize all three of their behaviors. "Whether she meant it or not, I will not allow her to tell you to shut-up," Valerie said, then turned her fury onto her oldest daughter. "Your sister didn't want you to miss out on bowling, she does nothing but try to look out for you, and this is how you treat her?"

Something in Veronica's expression softened. Veronica looked past her mother and over at her kid sister. "I'm sorry, Victoria. Mad at me?"

"You know I'm not," Victoria said, smiling. She shrugged her shoulders. "Still want to miss bowling?"

Veronica looked at her mother. "Mom? I'm sorry."

Valerie wanted to hold a grudge. She found it a real challenge to switch on and off her emotions. She needed to remain levelheaded. All three of them were stuck going through major changes. The girls were without a father, and she was without a husband. None of this was easy. Valerie took a split second to remember one thing. Right now, all they had was one-another. Valerie knew she needed to be a mom and a dad to these girls, but she would also need to be their friend. They needed to trust her and feel like they could come and talk to her. She did not want them to think that she was unapproachable. This argument was silly and hardly worth battling over. Veronica had sincerely apologized to them. "Okay dear," Valerie said as the two embraced.

There was a knock at the door as Valerie ran up the stairs. "One of you get that, and I'll look around for the brush."

In the bathroom, in the drawer, under a wad of hair Scrunchies, Valerie found Veronica's brush. She looked at herself in the mirror and saw the woman behind the façade. Who was she fooling? No one. Here she was a single mother of two and forced to go back to work. What did she know how to do? She was without any kind of training. She could barely use a computer. She was this close to applying for help from the state. It was a last resort and she dreaded the need to turn to it.

Taking a few squares off the roll of toilet paper, Valerie dabbed at her eyes. She was not going to let herself start crying. The girls were waiting for her. She had to take them bowling. She could wait in the car while they bowled and cry for as long as she wanted, but she would not start crying now. Not now.

"Silly daughter of mine, your brush was right where I said it might be," Valerie said, rounding the hallway corner and starting down the stairs. She stopped in mid-step when she saw her ex-husband sitting on the sofa with one daughter bouncing on each knee. Both girls stared expectantly up at their mother. They looked confused, yet happy. They missed their father so much, but they knew that mom did not want them talking to their dad, and knew that mom would not let daddy near the house. They knew all this, but they did not really know why. Why did mom want to keep them away from their daddy?

She could not tell them that their daddy was not a good man and that he had a severe drinking problem. She could not tell them that their daddy beat up his supervisor at work. She could not tell her daughters that their daddy was having sex with whores and contracting diseases. They did not need to hear all that, not now, and maybe not ever. Regardless of all his wrongs, he was still their daddy. Valerie loved her own father so much. When he died, a part of her had died. She had been daddy's little girl—and being daddy's little girl was one of the strongest and best emotions she brought with her from childhood into adulthood. The experience was so strong and positive that if her daughters could know even a fraction of that kind of love, then she did not want to be the one to spoil it.

"Valerie, my dear, how have you been?"

Forcing a smile, and perhaps wishing the brush in her hand were a knife, she answered his question with one of her own. "Martin, what are you doing here?"

Chapter 43

"You know, I feel like I can't get rid of you," Felicia said. She sat down across from Michael at the kitchen table. She rested an elbow on the table, trying to keep her eyes focused on her cup. The coffee was freshly brewed and she reluctantly poured him a cup. He had a big bag filled with books, but had yet to explain why he chose to bring them into the house. He knew she was not glad to see him. He could tell by the look in her eyes. They looked dark and beady. He kept on smiling. He wanted to get over this hurtle, to work past this block in their relationship.

"I'm sorry about today," Michael said. He did not want to avoid the issue. He was wrong, and knew he was wrong. Ignoring that there was a problem, that he had a problem with Felicia's profession, would not solve anything. Apparently his feelings on the subject were stronger than anticipated. He wanted to see the relationship progress, but did not think that was possible, not with Felicia still working as a prostitute. A part of him knew it would be unfair to ask her to change her life for him. The other half knew changing her life around could be the best thing for her. What kind of future did she have to look forward to?

"I have no idea what you're talking about," Felicia said sternly, leaning over the table as she spoke. "The only thing I know for sure is that you're a class 'A' jerk. You haven't got balls enough to be a man. What would have been so difficult, Michael, about asking me out, huh?" Felicia asked. Now her voice trembled. "I am still a girl."

The fierceness to her was gone. Tears where just blinks away from being shed. Michael did not want to upset her. The time for speaking the truth was now. He needed to explain his feelings, but more than that, he needed to share his intentions. If he backed down now, then he knew he would have no right to bring this subject up again in the future. "Felicia, I think I might love you."

* * *

Valerie Wringer felt every muscle in her body tighten. Over the years, Martin had gradually changed as his drinking increased. He had become progressively more mean and resentful. He spent more time alone, watching television up in their bedroom and working in the shed out in the backyard. When she learned he had lost his job, she had not been surprised. He had been going into work inebriated for many months. She knew it was just a matter of time before it all caught up to him. She made the mistake of warning him once. That had been the first time he struck her. It was a hard open-handed slap. She had said, "Martin? Martin do you think you should drink so much before work? I mean, you know you can get in trouble. You can lose your job if you show up to work drunk."

He had stared into her eyes, and she had watched any warmth drain from them. She was so intent on staring into his frigid, icy eyes that she never saw the slap coming. It rocked her, knocking her off balance. The stinging in her cheek burned as if on fire. She used both hands to cup her face. The tears came immediately, almost on contact. She could think of nothing to say. He did not defend his actions, or apologize for them. Instead, Martin had left the house, slamming the door on his way out.

In hindsight, that day had been the beginning of the end. And now that it was over, she wondered why this man—this stranger—was sitting in her living room holding her daughters on his knees. "Martin, what are you doing here?"

Martin smiled, while his hands massaged the backs of his daughters. Valerie kept from cringing. The way her husband was staring at her gave her the creeps. He looked the way Jack Nicholson did in the *The Shining*.

"What do you mean, 'what am I doing here?' I live here. I'm home," Martin said. He was smiling, and talking to his girls while he spoke. The looks on their faces changed, brightening. Then Martin stared challengingly at his wife.

"You're home, Daddy? For real? You're staying home?" Victoria said, wrapping her arms around her father's neck. Her long hair covered most of Martin's face.

Veronica parted her kid sister's hair away from her father's face. "You're not kidding, Dad? You're not teasing us? You're coming back home to live?"

Someone had Valerie's heart and was running it through a meat grinder. Still frozen in her stance on the stairs, she felt helpless and terrified. What kind of crap was Martin trying to pull? They were divorced. She did not want him in her house and she did not want him doing what he was doing to her children. It had been difficult enough for them the first time she threw the bum out on his ass. Now he was playing them, playing into the needs of all children. What child from a broken home would not jump at the chance at having their mom and dad back together?

"Mom?" Veronica, the oldest, asked. She gave Valerie such a hopeful look, there almost seemed no way out. Veronica was old enough to know that her father could not be telling the truth, but young enough to want to try and believe it. The girls wanted their father back. They wanted normality restored. They thought having their father back in the house would make things better, would make things right. Having Martin back would make things the way they once were, that was for sure. It would not make things better or right. Martin moving back in would make things worse. She could not allow that. She would not allow that.

"No, dear. No, honey. Your father is just teasing. He is not moving back in here." She said this with conviction, and yet remained stuck like a statute on the stairs. She knew why she had not moved. She felt scared. He terrified her. This man was all muscle. and if he wanted, he could inflict real damage on her body. If she thought he might harm her girls, Valerie would charge like a rabid bull. Thankfully, this was not the case. He genuinely appeared to love his daughters.

Victoria began to cry. She looked like she might be hugging Martin too tightly. Her arms, securely wrapped around his neck, had to be cutting off oxygen. The thought almost brought a smile to Valerie's lips. However, the situation was too serious and Valerie recognized the potential danger. He was in the house. Getting Martin to leave would not be easy. Getting him to leave without becoming enraged might be utterly impossible.

Chapter 44

"Do you think I'm some kind of dumb asshole?" Felicia was standing. She had jumped to her feet so quickly and defiantly that she had knocked over her chair. Now she stood there with her hands rolled into fists, and those fists were planted firmly on her hips. She resembled a warrior, despite the gray sweatpants and white T-shirt attire. In one swift motion, she used her arm like a broom, sweeping the stack of books off the table and onto the floor. "Do you really think you're that much better than me? Get out of my house."

"Felicia, you're taking this wrong. You're not letting me explain," Michael protested calmly in his defense. "This has nothing to do with me thinking I'm better than you. I think I can help you, though. I want to help you study and earn your high school diploma." He smiled, certain Felicia would now see and understand where he was coming from.

"Get out of my house now, Michael!" Felicia looked angrier than she had a moment ago.

Michael was not sure, but somehow he was going about this in the wrong way. He never envisioned this kind of response, thinking his proposition would have been the opportunity she had been waiting for. He refused to even stand up. "Don't you see that I love you? I don't care if you have a high school diploma or not."

Felicia stood like a soldier, fists on her hips. “Oh no? Well you could have fooled me.” She kicked the books, scattering them. “First of all, you even thinking you’re in love with me is a joke. You think because I slept with you, I love you in return?” She forced out a grim laugh.

“It’s more than that,” Michael said calmly. He would not lose his patience, knowing she needed to attempt to prove him wrong and would use everything she had before even beginning to let him into her life.

She held onto the back of her chair in a white-knuckle grip. “You know what? I asked you to leave and I want you out of my house right now.”

Michael leaned back. “I want us to talk about this.”

“There is nothing to talk about, and if you don’t move your ass, I’m going to whack you over the head with a frying pan.”

Michael could not help himself. A laugh escaped him, and he lost his collective composure. Immediately, he knew the damage caused by his lack of control and was not surprised as Felicia strode purposely past him. He heard a cupboard door open. Without turning around, he knew she was fetching a frying pan. He told himself to keep cool, and when she warned him again not to laugh . . .

But there was no warning. A memory flashed like thunder through his mind. He had been five and riding a two-wheel bicycle for the first time. He lost his balance and was heading for the road. His mother, who had been running along side him, grabbed him by the shoulders and yanked. She kept him from rolling into the street, but did not have a strong hold and let him fall onto the driveway. His head banged the ground with such force he had blacked out.

As he opened his eyes, expecting to see his mother, Michael was more than pleasantly surprised to see Felicia hovering over him. She looked terrified and concerned. “Oh, I’m so sorry, Michael. I didn’t want to hit you with the frying pan. Really I didn’t.”

Closing his eyes, because it hurt too badly to keep them open, Michael managed to mumble. “I suppose I deserved it.” When

Michael tried to sit up, he felt dizzy. He ran his hand along the back of his head. There was a bump, but he did not think he had bled any.

Felicia helped him to his feet. She had him in her arms. They stood like that for a minute, each taking the time to study the face of the other. Michael leaned forward and kissed her. "I'll tell you what. Let me ask you three questions without you interrupting me. Let me get the questions out and then I'll leave. All right?" When Felicia remained silent and continued to stare into his eyes, he asked, "Is it wrong of me to want to help you get your diploma? How about, if I love you, is it wrong that I don't want you to be a prostitute anymore?" She continued to stare. She wanted to argue. He could see it in her eyes. He saw something else there, too, aside from the building need to bicker and banter. He saw a spark, as though he had made some kind of connection. "My last question. Even if you think you might like me a little, or even if you can't stand the sight of me, isn't it worth it for you to get out of your line of work?"

Michael pulled out of her arms, despite feeling suddenly cold, and knelt by the table. He gathered the books and set them in a neat stack on the table. "Just think about it," he said and left.

Chapter 45

There was no alcohol in the house. Once Martin was out, Valerie had gotten rid of it all. At the time, nothing could have pleased her more than pouring the contents of his bottles down the kitchen sink drain. Never in her life did she imagine she might regret doing so. She tasted blood and knew her bottom lip was swelling, could feel it puffing up. "I'm okay kids. Why don't you both go up to your rooms, all right?"

Veronica stood behind her kid sister, but held onto the child's shoulders with a maternal-like grip. Veronica's eyes were wide with fear. Valerie knew the children were frightened. They had never before witnessed this kind of behavior. Thankfully, Martin had only done this kind of thing when they were alone. Valerie always feared telling her girls the abusive truth. It would have been so easy for her to explain to them how mean and rotten their father was. She could have turned the girls away from him in a heartbeat. Of course, it could have had the reverse effect. Valerie's girls could have wound up resenting her for talking bad about their father. No longer would she need to worry. Veronica and Victoria, unfortunately, were seeing first hand the kind of freak their father truly was.

Before Martin struck again, Valerie pleaded with Veronica. "Please, take your sister with you upstairs."

Victoria, crying and shook her head. "What about bowling?"

"Come on," Veronica said. Valerie knew it was not easy for them to go upstairs. She knew Veronica wanted to help, but was too young and afraid to do anything. In a way, Valerie was thankful. She did not want Martin to focus any of his attention on the girls. He was off the wall, and whereas she had thought the children were safe from his delusional wrath, she no longer knew what to believe.

With the children safe upstairs, Valerie knew she had to act in order to gain some kind of control over the situation. "I'll tell you what, Martin. Let me drop the girls off at bowling while you make yourself comfortable. On my way back, I'll stop at the liquor store and pick up a new bottle for you?"

He nodded in agreement. "That sounds great. Wonderful." When he slapped her again, she fell to her knees. Both nostrils were bleeding. "You take me for some kind of retarded jerk-off?" When he kicked her, the toe of his boot caught her in the Solar Plexus. The air rushed out of her lungs, and she gasped struggling to breathe. "You run out with the girls and I'll relax on the sofa and wait for you to return." He squatted down next to her, resembling a baseball catcher. "You'd return all right. You'd bring me a bottle of here's-the-police!" He slapped her on the head, almost playfully, before grabbing a fistful of hair and bringing her back up to a standing position. "Guess what?"

Pain was coursing through her body. Her chest hurt from the kick and her heart beat so fast she feared it might explode. Her swollen lip throbbed. It felt as if blood was gushing from her nose. She could not think straight. She needed to get the girls out of the house, but had no idea how she might accomplish that. Right now she worried about his question, "Guess what?" Did he want an answer, or was it rhetorical?

Still holding that clump of hair near her forehead, Martin forcibly tipped her head back. Valerie felt tremendous pressure on her throat, and swallowing became suddenly difficult. Through clenched teeth, with rancid breath and through a mist of spittle, Martin asked his wife one more time. "I said, 'guess what?'"

"What?" Valerie managed. "What, Martin?"

"I have whiskey hidden in places you're too dumb to have checked." He discarded her, pushing her head away from him. He moved past her to the door leading to the basement. He opened the door, but did not descend down the steps. "Go fetch it for me, dear," Martin said with a sneer.

Valerie caught sight of the girls from where she stood in the kitchen. She saw them through a crack in a partially closed bedroom door. They were frightened and watching. Valerie found the strength to smile. "Sure, Martin," she said. Valerie knew the girls could see her and this would mean they could see all the blood. Their father had no idea what kind of traumatic scarring he was causing in his daughters. And if he did have a clue, he did not give a damn about it.

Thankful to be out of her children's line of sight, Valerie's smile vanished. Martin said, "In the clothes locker, under the summer shorts and stuff, there's a bottle. Bring it up."

Valerie stood tentatively across from Martin and close to the basement door. She did not want to go into the basement. Bringing him a bottle of whiskey would be synonymous to asking him to stay and torment the family. Knowing this, however, was futile. What other options did she have? She moved sideways by him and started down the stairs. At the bottom of the staircase, a naked bulb sat in a ceiling mounted fixture. The pull-string dangled. She tugged on it, and light lit the dank washroom.

She looked back up the stairs. Martin looked like a psycho. Like a crazy man. He had his arms down straight, hands at his sides. He stood slouched forward, shoulders sagging. She noted his fingers. They worked like spider legs climbing his thighs without moving anywhere. It was the menacing smile, the twisted and contorted expression on his face that frightened her the most. His lips were stretched into a flat smile, making them too thin-looking to be lips. His left eye kept twitching, almost as if he were winking at her. Martin, clearly, had lost his mind.

"Go on, dear. Believe it or not, I haven't got all day. Wait a minute. Yes, I do." He let out a roaring laugh. "Because I'm not going anywhere!"

Swallowing hard, trying to fight off crying, Valerie moved

deeper into the basement, past the washing machine and dryer. She walked between two laundry baskets and closer to the steel gray clothing cabinet. She opened the doors and ignored the musty, pungent smell. In a few months she would be washing the clothing in here and stuffing the winter clothing away. Right now, sunny and blue-sky days were furthest from her mind.

Piled on the bottom of the cabinet were shorts and tank tops. She ruffled through the stacks and found the bottle Martin had hidden some time ago. A sudden explosion of ideas rocketed through her mind. She saw the opened box of rat poison on top of the cabinet. She could add a few pellets to the liquor. It might kill him, though. Hating him the way she did, she did not want to kill him. Killing him would bring in the police, only the police would be against her. The state might take away her daughters. If she ended up in jail, who would look after Veronica and Victoria? She could water down the whiskey—but how? He would hear the water running.

"Find it?" Martin called out impatiently. She could see his bulking shadow cast down the basement stairs. She could not tell if he was drunk now. He was not acting drunk, despite his irrational behavior. How much worse would he become after guzzling down alcohol?

"Yeah. Got it," she said. She knew how he got when drunk. He wanted sex. It had been one thing to accommodate him when they were married. She started to pray. Would Martin want her? He had to know they were no longer married and she would not have sex with him simply because he wanted to have sex, right?

As she walked slowly back toward the stairs, she stopped to pick up a wet towel. She wanted to wipe away some of the blood from her face, but stopped. She decided to leave the blood. It would make her look less attractive, perhaps repulsive. It might be the only defense to keep his sexual desires at bay. Reflexively, bile came up her throat, the acid burning in her mouth. She thought she might vomit from just the thought of him touching her. When she dropped the towel back into the laundry basket, she saw something on the shelf over the dryer.

"Did you find it, or not?" Martin called. He sounded angry.

Looking to the stairs, to make sure he was not coming down, she reached over the dryer for the screwdriver. Her fingers felt along the shelf's surface, touched the handle, and closed around it. She moved fast, going to the stairs and grabbing the screwdriver and stepping around the second laundry basket, when the screwdriver slipped out of her hands. It banged against the dryer and fell to the floor. She did not dare pick it up now.

She went to the stairs. Martin looked like he had not moved. She tugged on the cord to turn the light off and climbed up the stairs toward him. Each step she took, she thought she might die of a heart attack. She did not think the organ could take much more. In a pathetic, fleeting thought, she wondered if her death might be the best—the quickest and safest escape.

She looked up at the cobweb-covered ceiling and pictured her girls. She could not let herself get killed. Veronica and Victoria needed her to be strong and to find a way to get this asshole out of their house.

At the top of the stairs, she held the bottle out to him like a peace offering. He crossed his arms over his chest, then nodded his head up and down, as if catching on to some inside joke. His tongue, thin and pink, darted out of his mouth and licked his lips in a slow deliberate way.

"Whatcha got hidden, darling?" Martin asked. He snatched the bottle out of her hand with lightening speed. His fumbled briefly with the cap, but then easily loosened and twisted it off. He took a quick swallow. When he was done, he smacked his lips and let out a satisfying, "Ah!"

She tried to ignore the question. He had his whiskey. Though he looked crazy, he suddenly looked happy. "Hungry?" she asked. It might be the perfect opportunity. Feed him a big meal while he's drinking and he'll get sleepy. He would be drunk and tired and much easier to get away from.

"I said, whatcha got with you? A hammer? A razor? What?"

She put up her hands. "Nothing. I don't have anything."

"You must really think I'm freaking stupid, don't you?" He pivoted his body to the left and carefully set the bottle down on the kitchen table, the way a mother might lay an infant down in a bassinet. When he turned back, he did so with purpose. He stood like a boxer, his stance suggesting his eagerness to fight. The punch came and connected with her gut. For the second time, the air rushed out of her lungs. Valerie doubled over. She felt his hands on her. He was feeling her up. He grabbed at her ass and thighs, and ran his hands up and down her legs. "My fault. Thought you had a screwdriver or something."

Slowly, she stood up as straight as she could with her hands protectively placed on her belly. Her hair stuck to the sweat and blood on her face. Her eyes were open wide, filled with terror. This man in front of her was out of control. She did not know him at all.

"Did you say something about fixing me something to eat?" Martin asked, picking the bottle of whiskey up off the table and bringing it to his lips. After a long swig, he wiped his mouth on his sleeve. "Because, my dear, I'm starving."

Chapter 46

Jason Cocuzzi had forgotten what it felt like to sleep. He was up and around, but thought he might resemble a zombie more than a homicide detective. He was not complaining. He could go home and sleep for a few hours any time he wanted and no one would say a word about it. What surprised him most was his affiliate partner, Peter Cage. The man had unsurpassable stamina. Cocuzzi did not know why, but could not deny the competitiveness inside him. Cage, several years younger, should have more energy. Knowing this, however, did not make it any easier. In many ways, Cage was a lot like Cocuzzi, and at this point, Cocuzzi was not exactly sure how he felt about that.

Cocuzzi was late for the meeting he had called. When he entered the tiny conference room, which resembled a classroom with rows of school desks with chairs, several plain-clothes police officers began to applaud. “Glad you could make it,” one of the officers called out, heckling. This brought around a much-needed bout of laughter.

Cocuzzi, holding a piping hot cup of coffee, spotted Detective Cage at the front of the room, sitting on the edge of a desk. Christine Wrzos, the undercover prostitute, was in a chair in the first row, smiling at him. She was still dressed like a whore. For reasons he could not explain, seeing her dressed that way—or maybe it was just because he was seeing her again—excited him.

"All right, all right. Knock it off." He made his way to the head of the room. He set his coffee down on the desk as Cage stood up and took a seat along-side Officer Wrzos. A pang of jealousy tightened in Cocuzzi's stomach. As a professional, Cocuzzi pointed a finger at Peter. "You should be up here with me."

Peter Cage smiled and shook his head. He was making eyes at Wzros, but only so Cocuzzi could see. "Nah, I'm all right. I'll listen from here." He winked at Cocuzzi, the way a buddy might wink at his friend, as if saying, *Watch me. I'm going to make it with this chick.*

"Detective Cage, up here. Now." It was an unnecessary order. There was no reason for making the Irondequoit detective stand at the front of the room. Cocuzzi knew he was acting foolishly, like a child. Maybe it was because he felt so tired. He only hoped no one else was smart enough to sense his jealousy.

Once again, Cage took his place sitting on the desk. Officer Wzros was looking at Cocuzzi and he suddenly felt uncomfortable. It was evident by the look on her face that she knew exactly what had just happened.

Deciding he had better move on, and quickly, Detective Cocuzzi cleared his throat. "Things went well last night. Though, to the best of our knowledge, we have not apprehended our infamous Johnny Blade . . . we did make nearly a dozen arrests. Officer Wrzos, nice work."

Playfully obnoxious cheers and whistles overtook the room. "Settle down," Cocuzzi said. Cage was smiling at Christine Wrzos, and Wrzos was seductively smiling at the other officers in the room. Aside from Cage's presence, Cocuzzi was pleased with his group. They got along and worked well together. "Extensive background checks are still being run on the twelve men arrested last night."

"And one woman," an officer added.

"And one woman," Cocuzzi said, sheepishly.

"But she looked like a man," the same officer commented.

Everyone laughed, including Cocuzzi. "Okay. We're going to

set up the same sting and run it just like last night. We'll only get so many consecutive nights of this before word spreads and the johns quit coming around.

"I want to take a serious second here and thank all of you for your hard work and professional abilities. Last night went smoothly because of the abundance of talent in this group," Detective Cocuzzi said. Those in the room clapped and whistled. "I know most of you, like myself, are putting in long hours on the case, and I appreciate that. It's important to me to express these feelings. You are all outstanding officers. Regardless of how things pan out, I want you to know I think this is a perfectly assembled team full of more ability than should be allowed in one station."

More applause erupted. It felt like a high school pep rally. Cage wore a grin that suggested as much. He kept looking from Cocuzzi to the other officers in the room. Caught up in the moment, even he was clapping his hands.

"What's with the spiel?" an officer asked. "Yeah. What gives?" another called out.

"On Monday, the FBI will be in town and more than likely they will pull rank and jurisdiction," Jason Cocuzzi said, cautiously. His words were like a pin. The team's balloon quickly deflated. "Listen, though. Listen. It doesn't mean we're off the case. And even if we get taken off the case, the key thing here is that the serial killer be caught and stopped. That's the key thing. We can't let pride . . . my pride, and your pride . . . keep us from working together with the FBI to achieve a common goal. Johnny the Blade is loose and on a rampage. Innocent women are being brutally murdered. If the FBI can lend us a hand, or if we can lend them a hand, and we solve this case . . . then the reward for our efforts is solid. We will have made the streets safer for the people in Rochester. That's our job, ladies and gentlemen. Our job is simple. We need to work to keep the streets safe, and the added bodies from the FBI will only make our mission in this instance that much easier. Our objective can only become that much more attainable, obtainable . . . whichever, whatever."

For a minute, the room remained silent. Detective Jason

Cocuzzi had everyone's attention, but no longer held their enthusiasm in his hand. It was not until Christine Wzros began to clap, slowly and methodically at first, that the others joined in. The clapping came out like a chant or a bass drum beating in time with an increasing tempo.

Peter Cage stood up, swept away by the moment. He clapped in time with the others. "You know what?" he shouted. "You know what this means? This means we need to catch this bastard before the weekend is over. We need to show the FBI just what kind of law enforcement team we have here in Rochester!"

Peter Cage spoke words moving the police team into a frenzy mode. Christine Wzros stood up next to Cage and clapped even faster. Cocuzzi controlled a sudden urge to knock the young detective on his ass. His speech had done fine. The team had responded. He did not need Cage stepping in to steal his thunder. Damn him!

As the police officers filed out of the room, Cocuzzi stood with his back to the desk, sipping his still piping hot coffee. Wrzos and Cage were still huddled close together and talking. Cocuzzi almost spit out his coffee when he heard detective Wrzos giggling. Before she walked out of the room, she turned and waved. Part of Cocuzzi believed that the wave was for his benefit, as if she might be teasing him.

"Man, she's hot. Isn't she hot, Jason?" Peter Cage asked when the door to the room closed and the two officers were left alone. He stood with his hands in his pockets while chewing on his lower lip. "Think I should ask her out?"

"I think you should keep your mind on your work. We've got a near-impossible task in front of us. We need to stay focused. Getting all messed up like . . . look at you? You resemble a school boy with that dumb look on your face," Jason Cocuzzi said. He felt disgusted.

"I could be in love," Cage said in a serious voice. "This could be it, and I'm not kidding around here."

Cocuzzi wanted to say, "It could never work." He wanted to tell the Irondequoit cop to forget about it, that Detective Wrzos was out of his league. None of these things were true, though.

Cocuzzi knew he was just feeling jealous and sorry for himself. Wrzos was more Cage's age. They would undoubtedly have more in common. Cocuzzi kept his mouth closed and left the room, taking his cup of hot coffee with him.

Chapter 47

Michael Buzzelli sat at his computer. The articles he had been tenaciously working on neared completion. They were the personal pieces on the locals at Jack's Joint. It took some doing, but Michael was able to contact Jeff Marks, a friend of his who was interning at Strong Memorial Hospital. He left a message on the young doctor's pager. When the telephone rang, Michael was a little annoyed with the disruption. The piece he was working on flowed. He hated to lose that train of thought.

"Hey Mike, what's going on?" Jeff Marks asked. The voice sounded tired. Michael could only imagine what it must be like working in a hospital, based on the drama shows he had watched on television.

"Thanks for calling back. How have you been?" Michael asked. Small talk was a necessity, something he had learned about when working on the college paper. You wanted everyone to feel like your close personal friend. It just so happens Jeff had been Michael's close personal friend all through high school. "How's the internship coming along?"

"It's rough. You know how I debated between law school and medical school? Sometimes I wonder if I made the right decision," Jeff said. Michael now wished he had gone to see Jeff, instead of contacting him by phone. He cringed as he realized who he reminded himself of—Matthew Sinopoli.

"You wouldn't want to be a lawyer . . . they have no ethics, no values. How would you feel defending a guilty man? What if you got some homicidal maniac off of murder charges on a technicality? Could you live with yourself knowing a killer was free just because you were good at your job?" Michael tried to rationalize. As much as he understood why every defendant deserved a lawyer, he never liked the idea of killers getting off on a technical issue. It was a disturbing flaw in the system.

"Looking at it that way, no. I guess I wouldn't want to be a lawyer. It's just they got me working in the ER and . . . take last night for example, we had to turn away a person who was without insurance. The lady wasn't hurt, like with an injury, but she was clearly suffering from manic depression. In my opinion, this woman was suicidal. Her showing up at the hospital was a cry for help. Why shouldn't she feel that way, right? You need help, you're in pain, where do you go? The hospital. And what did we do? We sent her back out into the streets because she wasn't injured and because she hadn't actually tried to commit suicide, there was no immediate danger. I think the receptionist gave her a flyer for a help line, or a clinic, or something," Jeff Marks said.

Michael was at a loss for words. He could not know how his old friend felt. "It's got to be tough."

"Yeah, and the night before last, a three year old died under my care. It was a little boy. He got into the cupboards under the kitchen sink. He swallowed like a gallon of paint thinner. The cupboards had this kind of plastic lock that goes around the two handles, but the parents must have gone under there for something and disengaged the thing. Now three is pretty old. So the kid drinks the stuff, I mean it smells sweet, right? And he's smart enough to put it back and close the cupboards. By the time the parents realize the kid is sick, a lot of time has gone by. Even more time goes by before they bring him here. There was nothing we could do. Nothing. I had one of the nurses lead the parents into a conference room, and then I had to tell them that their boy was gone."

Michael could not help feeling like crap. "Are you all right?"

“I will be. They tell me this all takes time. I have to work on separating myself from the patients. It feels like an oxymoron. My job is to help the patients, to know them better than they know themselves, but then I’m not allowed to get close,” Jeff said. “Look, I’m sorry. I know this isn’t why you called.”

“Forget about it, Jeff. It’s no problem. We ought to plan to get together sometime, drink some beers, or something. Sounds like you need a night out and away from the job.”

“It sounds great. I have no idea when, with school and the internship . . . my life is more than full, but I’d like to get together when I have a free night. You’re right. It’s something I could use. Now, why have you called? I got your message, and you’re right, the name ‘Speed’ isn’t anywhere in any admittance forms,” Jeff said.

“But the scenario?”

“The scenario isn’t on any forms . . . the way you told it, either. However, we have a few patients at the hospital brought in under arrest. Is this a young, black male?”

Michael picked up his pen and prepared to write on his tablet. “Yes.”

“He went over a railing at Midtown Plaza not too long ago?”

“Right.”

“His real name is Harvey Brown. Aside from some injuries, he’s fine. He has already been released from the hospital.”

“Police have him in custody?”

“Don’t know. You’d have to ask them. Look, I hate to dump on you and then cut out, but my pager just went off again. I’ll give you a call sometime, all right?”

“That would be great Jeff. Thanks for the help.”

“Anytime. Take care.”

“Yeah, Jeff, you too.” Michael hung up the telephone feeling a little depressed. For a while he sat still and thought about the situations Jeff had described. Day in and day out he saw people suffering. Most of the time he would be able to help those people, and that had to feel wonderfully gratifying. There had to be times, like with the three-year-old boy, however, that made you wish you went into sales instead.

When the telephone rang a few moments later, this time Michael was thankful for the interruption. He needed a break from his thoughts. “Hello?”

“Michael? It’s Felicia.”

Michael thought his heart might stop beating. He sat up straight in his chair, as if she might be able to see his poor posture. “Mad at me?”

“Mad? No, not really. It’s why I’m calling.” Felicia let silence fill the line. Michael respected this and waited. He knew when she was ready, she would tell him what was going on. “You know how my father’s sick? Well he’s been home for a few days.”

“How’s he doing?” Michael asked. He did not want to interrupt her, but needed to ask. Though his parents were relatively young, it could only be a matter of time before they began to experience health problems. He did not care to imagine losing either his mother or father.

“Better, much better. The doctors have him on this bland diet. He hates it,” said Felicia with a little laugh. “You know, I haven’t even seen him yet.”

“Not at the hospital?”

“I waited there, but when he was well enough for us to visit, I just couldn’t bring myself to go in,” Felicia said in a somber tone of voice.

Michael knew she had to be smiling and wished he could see her face. “I’m glad to hear that . . . that your father is doing better, not that he hates his new diet.”

“My mother just called. She and I, and even Marcia—my kid sister, have been talking on the phone a lot these past couple of days. I think I got so mad at you because of them. They’ve been saying the same things to me, you know, about going back to get my diploma and everything,” Felicia said.

“I didn’t mean to be a bother to you. I just care. I can’t help that,” Michael said.

“I know, and I believe you. I believe them. So, anyway, after you left I was pissed off at you and my mother and sister, and I was ready to throw those books you left for me in the garbage, but I stopped. I dropped them and crumbled to the floor. I was so beside myself, I didn't know what else to do but stay on the floor and cry," Felicia said. She was crying now, Michael knew. "It hit me, Michael, like a bolt of electricity in the ass, it hit me. I'm a two-bit whore and why? Why should I be doing this? Forget all the things I said to you back at the restaurant. Why am I a whore now? Why am I being so stubborn?"

"Felicia . . ."

"Let me finish, please. Let me just say these things. If you weren't too mad at me, if you are still interested, I would appreciate your help. I want to earn my degree and get into some other line of work," Felicia said.

Michael thought he might cry. Hearing Felicia say these things made him feel wonderful. "I would be delighted to help you."

"Delighted? People say that word?"

Michael laughed. "Just dorks like me," he said.

"One other thing. I've kinda mended some wounds at home. My mother wants me to come to dinner tonight. I told her I would. She asked if I wanted to bring you. She and Marcia like you, I guess, though I can't understand why," Felicia said. "I have never brought a guy home, and I know it sounds stupid . . . going to have dinner with my parents, so if you don't want to . . ."

"Hey, Felicia, are you trying to un-invite me before you even invite me?" Michael asked. "Because if you're inviting me, I'd love to go."

"You would? For real?"

"Tell me what time."

"Five."

"I'll pick you up at four-thirty," Michael said, and hung up.

Chapter 48

Veronica and Victoria sat huddled close together on their bed. Veronica kept a protective arm wrapped around her sister. They both had stopped crying, but neither could stop trembling. Veronica could not get the image of her mother covered in blood out of her mind. She never knew her father could be so vicious. She knew when her father lived home her parents fought a lot, especially in the last few years, but she had never seen her father strike her mother. The more she thought about it now, the more she realized that the violence had to be going on. It explained a lot.

Veronica could remember one day in the summer. Her father had come home early from work. He was drunk. Veronica could always tell. He would talk and walk funny. When he would catch her looking at him, silently questioning his behavior, he would stare her down—challenging her to say something. She never did. The look in his eyes was enough to keep her from opening her mouth. On this one summer day, when he walked into the house, he sent Veronica and Victoria to their rooms. She and her sister stayed by the door and listened to the argument. Their father was home from work early because of the lunch their mother had packed for him.

"Peanut butter and jelly?" he had said. "Am I some kind of kid?" With each sentence, his anger intensified. He had raised his voice, but was not quite yelling. "I'm working my ass off . . . slaving my fingers to the bone, and when I go to lunch and expect a satisfying meal, I find a peanut butter and jelly sandwich on plain white bread. You know what the guys did? They laughed at me. One guy, Stan, he asked me why I didn't have you cut the crusts off the edges."

Then Veronica had heard it, a cracking sound. It had to have been a slap. But her father had not stopped complaining, and she did not hear her mother cry out, so it could not have been a slap.

"How am I supposed to stay at work if I lost the respect of the guys I work with?"

"I'm sorry, Martin, I didn't know. You eat peanut butter and jelly here, so I figured it would be okay for your lunch. I haven't had the time to go grocery . . ." and there it was again, the slapping sound. ". . . Martin please. I know now that you don't want those kinds of sandwiches for lunch . . ."

Veronica knew her mother had been getting slapped, but had chosen to ignore the fact. The coming to terms with this was an emotional breakdown. Veronica could not stop crying. Victoria wrapped her arms around her big sister. "Don't cry, Veronica. We'll help Mom."

"How?"

"We can call the police," Victoria said, providing an easy and obvious solution.

"But that's our father," Veronica pointed out.

"Yeah, and he's hurting our Mom." Again, the voice of wisdom had spoken.

* * *

It was nearly two o'clock. The girls had to be so worried. Valerie was at a loss. She wanted to go upstairs and check on her daughters, but did not want to direct Martin's attention anywhere near them. Sooner or later the bastard would have to fall asleep. She could hear the television in the other room while she washed the plates from his lunch. Martin, watching the news, had the volume turned up loud. The reporter was talking about the serial killer, Johnny Blade. Periodically, during the report, Valerie heard her husband grunt as if he might be laughing. Leave it to Martin to find murdered women funny. She could not help but wonder if Martin had slept with any of the prostitutes that were killed. And with that thought, another, more frightening thought came to mind. She wanted to dismiss it, but could not. Not easily. It was ridiculous to think Martin Wringer, bastard that he was, could be responsible for the murders.

Still, she found herself looking at the telephone on the wall. She sucked in her lips and chewed on them. She looked over toward the living room. Martin was on the sofa watching the news. The only way he could see her using the phone would be if he got up and came back into the kitchen. If she dialed 9-1-1, she would not even need to talk. The dispatcher would send out a car, just to make sure things were okay.

She moved the nozzle on the faucet so the water would come out harder and faster. She wiped the sweat from her palms onto her apron and walked quietly toward the phone. She kept looking toward the living room. She reached for the phone. She could feel her heart slamming around wildly in her chest. As her fingertips touched the telephone, she heard the sound of him getting up. She dropped to her knees and pulled open the cupboard under the counter. When she emerged with a can of pie filling, he was standing at the threshold between the kitchen and the living room, watching her. “I thought I might bake a pie,” she said, hesitantly.

He patted his belly. “Sounds good. What have you got?”

“Cherry?” She held up the can, showing it to him. He nodded and went back into the living room. Valerie felt her hands shaking. Every muscle in her body seemed to ache. She thought she might drop the can. She set it down on the counter. As she fished the manual can opener out of the silverware drawer, she cried. *How did I get trapped in this nightmare*? she wondered as her hand-spun the crank on the opener.

She worked diligently to bake the pie. She had pre-made crusts in the refrigerator. She unfolded one in a pie tin. She turned on the oven. As she added the pie filling, she again found her thoughts plagued with indecision. She wanted to poison him. She did not want to kill him. In the cupboard with the glasses she had allergy medication with strong antihistamines in them. She ran the water to drown out the sound of her removing tablets from the package. The tablets were solid, like aspirin. She put three tablets into a spoon. She placed another spoon on top of the other to grind up the pills. She sprinkled the tablets over a specific area, shaped like a pie slice. For good measure, she ground up three more pills and spilled the dust of the dosage in the same triangular area. She put the box of allergy medication away, then washed the spoons and her hands in the water before shutting the water off.

She put the top on the pie, and carefully marked the slice heavy with antihistamines with the fork. Setting the pattern of the tines into the top at a different angle from the rest. She sprinkled sugar onto the top crust and placed the pie in the oven.

Chapter 49

Detective Jason Cocuzzi sat with his elbows on his desk. He had his hands cupped and his face buried in his palms. He knew how to gauge his weariness. He used his mood. He had blown up at Detective Cage for no good reason, and had perhaps made an ass of himself in front of the team, not to mention, in front of Christine. The pressure was getting to him. The thought of the FBI moving in on his case felt unsettling. Thinking they would catch the serial killer before Monday morning was ludicrous.

Cocuzzi looked up when Detective Peter Cage dropped a six-inch stack of manila files onto the desk butted up against his. Cage sat down and let out a disgusted sigh. "Nothing," Cage said. He ran his fingers like a brush through his hair. He leaned back in the chair, and tossed a foot up onto the desk. With his hands locked behind his head, he stared at Cocuzzi with a blank expression.

"Those the arrest files?" Cocuzzi asked, though he knew the answer. "Background checks on those johns turned up nothing?"

"Just married and, or, lonely men out looking for an expensive relief," Cage said. He took his foot down and leaned forward in his chair. "I don't know why, but I felt certain we had him. I figured he had to be one of the guys we picked up."

Cocuzzi nodded his head in agreement. "It would have been nice."

"It would have been a lot better than 'nice.' Look, I like working with you and everything, but I want to go back to my job. Maybe I wasn't working on a murder over in Irondequoit, but I was working on cases," Cage said. He stood up and anxiously stuffed his hands into his pockets. "I hope that doesn't sound heartless."

Cocuzzi smiled. He wanted Cage to go back to the other side of the river, too. "About earlier . . ."

"What earlier? You mean at the meeting this morning? You know, I was going to ask what got into you, but didn't. We're all under stress, no big deal. Let's just forget about it." Cage shrugged his shoulders as if he had already dismissed the issue.

Cocuzzi had to admit that at first he did not like the young detective, thinking him too young and cocky. He was not particularly fond of the cop's attitude, or with the way he treated people. Over the last several days, things have changed. Cocuzzi might not admit to liking him, but he would admit he respected the guy. "You know, that would be all right if you and I were partners for years, but that's not the case." Cocuzzi stood up. While talking animatedly with hands, Cocuzzi continued. "Stress may be what caused my outburst, but it does not explain why I treated you with any less respect than I would have given to another police officer. I think you're a good cop, a smart guy. You see what I'm saying? Truth is, I have no good reason for talking to you the way I did. I'd like to say I'm sorry," Cocuzzi said. The reason he had talked the way he had to Cage was because of Christine. However, he was not lying when he told Cage he had "no good reason." Cocuzzi held out his hand. Without even a slight hesitation, Cage shook it. "Thanks, man."

"You're all right, Cocuzzi, and like I said, I like working with you," Cage said. "But I want to wrap this mess up and get back to my department, you know?"

Again, Cocuzzi nodded. "Got any ideas?"

"Aside from what we're doing, at this point, I got nothing. We need a solid lead on this guy. We need to get the profile out on the streets. We should let some things slip to the press, you know? Maybe have them rerun some pieces on Shawcross that we might feel apply to this case. Like, they say in the profiling that serial killers are usually male, white, and between the ages of, what was it, twenty-two to fifty?"

"I see what you're saying. Let me think about it. It might be a good idea," Cocuzzi said. Alerting the press could be a tricky move. Potentially, it could save lives. If the prostitutes and barfly women knew the general things to keep in mind before hopping into a vehicle with a stranger, then they might not wind up a statistical notch in the killer's blade. However, this could also prolong the capture of the killer. Johnny Blade might be forced to move to another city where his profile had not been splashed all over everything by the media. Cocuzzi was not thrilled with that thought. He would not want simply to push his problem into another city. "We'll think about it."

They had a few hours before setting up for the sting. Cocuzzi glanced at his watch.

"I'm getting hungry. What do you say we run out and grab a bite or something?" Cocuzzi asked with a warm smile. He felt confident that things would work out well between them and, given enough time, a strong friendship just might grow from it.

"Man, I'd love to, but I kind of made plans to eat with Christine," Cage said, hesitantly. "You know, you could join us if you'd like. I don't think she'd mind at all."

Deflated, Cocuzzi sat back down. "You know what, the more I think about it, the more I know I'd better go through these files again . . . you know, fine-tooth comb and all. You two go have a good meal, but hey, don't over-eat. Last thing we need is a beer-bellied prostitute on the street corner. Fine lot of johns she'd attract." He picked up the stack and removed the rubber band.

"Cocuzzi, you can look at those files in the car while we're staking out the place. You're going to have to eat something, right? Just come with us. I'll even let you pick where we go," Cage offered.

"Nah, but thanks. I appreciate it."

"I'll pick up the bill. How can you say no to that? You pick the place and I'll pay the tab. You gotta love that offer."

Cocuzzi pretended to consider this. He pursed his lips, then shook his head. “No. I’d better get through these files. Reading in a dark car will give me a pounding headache.” He opened the first of many files and leaned back in his chair. He let his eyes roam left to right, left to right as if he were immediately engrossed in the work. From his line of peripheral vision, he saw Cage stand there watching him for several seconds before turning and walking slowly away.

When Cocuzzi was certain Cage had left, he tossed the file back onto the top of the stack, and rested his elbows on the table. He cupped his hands and buried his face in his palms.

Chapter 50

Michael let his cigarette sit in the ashtray on the counter in the bathroom while he brushed his teeth. With only a towel wrapped around his waist, he watched himself in the mirror as he worked the toothbrush, back and forth, up and down, in his mouth. He spit the foam into the sink, turned on the water, cupped his hands under the faucet, and slurped up a mouthful. He swished the water around and spit it out. He turned off the water, wiped his hands on his towel, picked up his cigarette, and went into his room to get dressed.

On the bed was the newest pair of jeans Michael owned. Setting his cigarette in an ashtray on his dresser, he chose a gray wool long-sleeved V-neck shirt. He put on a fresh white T-shirt, first. While he put on his socks, the doorbell rang. "Just a minute!" Michael put on his boxer shorts and socks. As he made his way to the front door, he managed to get his legs into his pants. With his towel slung over his shoulder, he answered the door.

Standing in the doorway, fidgeting like a child, stood Felicia. "Before you ask, I couldn't wait. I've been ready since three."

Michael shrugged, moving to the side. "Well, come on in. I'll be ready in a couple of minutes."

She followed him to his room. She sat on the dresser, picked up his cigarette, and took a drag. Felicia stared at him while he finished getting dressed. “You know, if I weren’t so nervous I’d want us to have sex first. But I think I might throw up.”

“Because you're nervous, or at the thought of having sex with me?” Michael asked.

Felicia laughed. “You seem to always know how to make me feel better.”

“It’s good to know.”

“But I have to tell you something. I’m scared.”

“That’s not a big surprise,” Michael said, softly. “This is going to be a big change for you. Good or bad, change is hard.”

“You aren’t kidding. It’s like quitting smoking. Smoking is bad for you, even though you enjoy it,” Felicia said, rolling the butt of Michael’s cigarette around between her fingers. “Smoking is bad for you. I know it is and you know it is and still we both smoke anyway. The big change would be to quit smoking. It would be good for us to do this . . . but not easy.”

Michael felt himself get tense. He thought he might sense Felicia’s intentions. “Ah, I don’t think so,” he said backing away from Felicia. The twinkle in her eye told him he was right.

She slid off the dresser and stood with the cigarette in her hand. She took a long drag. “I say, you finish this one and that’s it. You have to quit smoking.” Her words had the desired effect. She was challenging him.

He pulled his wool shirt over his head, fixed the sleeves around his shoulder, and just stood there shaking his head. “You’ve got to be kidding me.”

“You think so? Well, I’m not. I want you to quit smoking.” She made and kept eye contact with him. Michael knew if he looked away, he would lose. This had a comical feel to it. “Well?”

Michael walked toward her. He reached for the cigarette in her hand. When his fingers wrapped around it, he smiled, never looking away. She smiled with the challenge still evident on her curled lips. “Well?” She asked for a second time.

He took the cigarette and took a long drag. He inhaled the smoke and held it in his lungs for several long seconds before exhaling a small cloud of smoke into her face. He put the cigarette back in her hand and spun around. “I’m done,” he said.

"Done? You mean you quit?"

He had given it a lot of thought. She was not asking for much. She wanted him to commit to change so she would not be the only one. "I mean, I quit. Done."

She crushed the cigarette out in the ashtray. "It's not going to be easy."

"I know. I've tried quitting before."

"Make love to me," she said.

"But you might throw up," he said back, teasing. She ran at him and wrapped her arms around his neck. "Want an antacid or something first?"

"Shut up," she said, and forced him onto his back onto the bed.

Chapter 51

"Why don't you call our girls down. They've been upstairs a long time. That pie smells so good, I'll bet they could go for a piece," Martin Wringer said. He was seated at the kitchen table next to his bottle of whiskey. He kept his hand around its neck in a firm grip. "Girls!"

Valerie cringed. She felt a tight knot wadding itself up and growing in the pit of her stomach. "Martin, they're resting. They're tired. We'll give them some pie afterwards."

The expression on Martin's face changed. A split second ago, despite being drunk, Martin was acting as if he belonged in the house, as if everything were all right and back to normal. Now, he regarded Valerie differently. He looked at her suspiciously. He stood up and walked over to the bottom of the stairs. Not once did he look away from his wife. "Girls! Veronica? Tori? Come on down here."

Valerie heard the bedroom door open and watched as her two frightened children slowly came out of the room. "Yes, Daddy?" Veronica asked. She stood like a protective shield in front of her little sister.

"Your mother made some pie. Would you like a piece?" Martin asked in a tender voice, just lightly flavored with suspecting sarcasm, and yet he still did not look away from

Valerie. "Come down here, girls."

Valerie looked over her husband's head and up the stairs. Veronica was shaking her head "no." She did not want to come downstairs. It broke Valerie's heart to see her twelve-year-old's lower lip quivering, trembling with fear and uncertainty. "Martin, they're not hungry," Valerie said, making an attempt to divert her husband's interests.

"Shut up, bitch!" Martin said. He pointed a threatening finger at her. His lip was curled in a snarl, reminding Valerie of a snake ready to strike. She kept her distance. "Girls!"

It was the tone of his voice that demanded respect this time, and Veronica and Victoria came down the stairs together. Valerie watched as her daughters carefully moved around their father into the kitchen. Veronica left her sister's side and ran into her mother's arms. "Oh, Mom," she cried. "Are you all right?"

Before Valerie could answer, Victoria had locked her arms around her legs. Valerie put a hand on the head of each girl. "I'm fine girls. I'm fine." Martin was watching them. He did not look happy with the display. The sight of it appeared to be making him angrier. Before he could snap, Valerie said, "Go sit down girls. Would anyone like a glass of milk?"

No one answered. "Martin? Milk?"

"No," he said, sounding like a Neanderthal.

Valerie picked up the pie knife. She had to close her eyes tightly to keep the vivid images of slashing Martin's throat out of her mind. She did not want to hesitate. He might take the knife from her and serve the pieces himself. "Everyone take a seat," she said as pleasantly as possible. Veronica watched her mother with such intensity that Valerie worried about the trauma the girls were undergoing.

She cut and served a piece of pie for everyone. The piece for Martin contained the antihistamines in the pie filling. Valerie could sense Martin's weariness without even having a taste of the pie. The alcohol was knocking him out. It always did, eventually.

Knowing he suspected something foul about the pie, she used her fork and chopped off the tip of her slice. She scooped it into her mouth and was amazed at how good the pie tasted, despite the seriousness of the situation she was in.

Veronica and Victoria followed their mother's lead. They all tried the pie. "This is real good, Mom," Victoria said.

Seemingly satisfied, Martin broke off the end of his pie with his fork. He raised the food to his mouth, but paused. Valerie knew she had been watching him too closely. Martin held out his fork. "You try it," he said, smiling.

"I have a piece," Valerie said as if her husband were acting silly.

He thrust the fork closer to her face. She did not hesitate and ate the pie. She then made a face as if to say, See, you're being ridiculous. Martin grunted and went about eating his slice. "You're right, Tori. This is good."

Inside, Valerie felt relieved. The tiny piece of pie she had eaten off Martin's fork, even if saturated with the allergy medication would not effect her. Antihistamines had the exact opposite effect on her. They made her wired and jumpy, as if jolted by a lightening bolt of caffeine.

Like an animal, Martin ate his way up to the crust, then stopped and set down his fork. He used his finger to probe around at the filing along the edge of the crust. "Stop eating, girls," he said. "Stop eating." He reached out and grabbed Veronica's hand before Veronica could eat her next piece of pie. He slid her plate closer to him and inspected what was left, using his fork to peel off the top crust layer. He looked closely at the filling, then moved onto Victoria's piece of pie. He began laughing as he did so.

"Martin?" Valerie asked. Though she felt her heart beating like a boxer's fist against her ribs, she thought for sure the organ had stopped altogether. She found it difficult to breathe. "Honey?"

"Did you poison me and the girls? Did you put something in our pie?" He touched his finger to the filling on what was left of his crust. He rubbed his finger and thumb together and a powdery substance snowed onto the table. "You son of a bitch. You son of a bitch," Martin said, slamming the palms of his hands down onto the table as he pushed himself up onto his feet. The chair he had been sitting in tipped over and banged onto the linoleum floor. Using his arm like a broom, he swept the plates and flowery centerpiece off the table. The noise was clamorous. All three girls stiffened, unable to anticipate what might be coming next.

Though she thought she had braced herself for the attack, she was not ready for the punch Martin threw. It connected squarely with her jaw. The power behind the blow knocked her out of the chair. She found it difficult to focus. Her vision was blurry. As she tried to stand up, her head filled with fog. When she opened her eyes, she realized she was still on the kitchen floor, holding her chin. "Martin," she said, pleading. "Not in front of the girls."

Though her heart pounded so hard all she could hear were the beats in her ears, Valerie could see the terrified faces of her daughters as Martin's foot shot out, kicking her in the thigh. An intense pain rocketed its way toward every nerve in the area. She clung to her leg as she attempted to scramble away from the maniac. She knew she was in trouble when her backward retreat was stopped solid by the oven. "Martin," she screamed out as he kicked her again.

Veronica and Victoria left the kitchen in a hurry. Martin was too preoccupied to notice. Valerie felt a small sense of relief as she heard the front door opening. They would be safe. They were out of the house.

Martin knelt down next to Valerie and stared at his wife with a pathetically sympathetic look. "I just want to come back home. I want things to go back to normal. I miss you and the girls. The girls need their father. You saw them today, sitting on my lap. It's not right for you to deny them their father."

Valerie lowered her head, crying. She felt terrified. *How could he be talking to me like this . . . as if everything were all right*? she wondered. "It can't work, Martin. This can't work."

He clenched his teeth and tried to smile. "Valerie . . . Val . . . honey . . . we can work all of this out. We're not the divorcing kind. We're the in-love kind. I'm still in love with you. Don't you feel the same way about me? Don't you miss having me home?"

She saw the muscles in his jaw working as he ground his teeth. Maybe she should agree with him and say whatever she could. "I don't think so. I don't see how."

Martin grabbed a fistful of hair, pulled her forward, and

slammed the back of her head into the stove. As a loud thunderous boom exploded inside her brain, and as Valerie's ears began to ring, Martin stood up, lifted his leg, and aimed the bottom of his boot toward Valerie's face. She wondered about her own safety and thought for sure that her life was about to end. As his foot crunched against her nose, and as tears immediately poured from her eyes and mixed with the blood flowing out of her nostrils, Valerie said a quick prayer hoping God would somehow save her from such a primitive and barbarous fate, then lost consciousness as an odd light shown in her eyes—glittering, almost.

* * *

The smell overtook her nostrils, more powerfully than if she had placed her head in a bucket filled with ammonia. It was like a volt. Her eyes popped open and she screamed into the face of the man hovering inches over her, at the same time, bringing her arms up defensively. Panicking, she tried to gouge out her husband's eyes, but the man was strong, catching and holding her wrists.

"Ma'am, it's okay. It's all right."

Valerie shook her head, clearing her vision and saw that a police officer was kneeling next to her. Martin was not in the kitchen. She sat up slowly, and with the officer's help. "Where's Martin? Where's my husband?"

"We have him outside. An officer is taking his statement. If you are feeling all right, I'd like to have a word with you. Are you feeling all right?" The police officer had a warm, wet kitchen towel in his hand. "If you'd like to keep this pressed against your nose. The bleeding has stopped."

Valerie took the blood soaked hand towel and pressed it against her nose, gently. It ached and throbbed. It felt huge. It had to be swollen. "Can I get up?"

"Can you? Let's try." The police officer took her under the arm and helped her to her feet. "How's that? How does that feel?"

"I'm a little queasy. I think my nose is broken," Valerie said.

"I think you're right. We have an ambulance on the way," the police officer said.

"Chet?" A man called from the living room. "Can you come out here?"

The police officer offered Valerie a comforting smile. "That's my partner, Harrison. I'm going see what he needs. Have a seat at the table, and I'll be right back. Okay?" Officer Chet bent down and picked up the fallen chair. Valerie sat down. Chet, in a most tender way, placed his hands on her shoulders. "I'll be right back."

Valerie looked at the mess on the floor. Dishes and pie were all over the place. She cried into the towel. She felt so ashamed and so embarrassed. The entire day was a nightmare she would never forget. And as she cried, relief began to flood through her. God had answered her prayers. The police were here and she was safe. Martin had not been able to kill her. *My girls*, she thought worriedly. *They must have run to a neighbors and called the police.*

When Chet returned, his demeanor appeared different. He now stood by the table with his thumbs hooked through his belt loop. The other police officer, Harrison, entered the kitchen and stepped over the mess on the floor. He held a brown lunch bag. Using a fork off the floor, he scooped most of the pie into the bag.

"What's he doing that for? I'll clean it up," Valerie said, suddenly feeling anxious.

"Mrs. Wringer . . ."

"It's Miss. I'm not married anymore," Valerie said. The knot was back in her stomach. She had a bad feeling.

"You and your husband were recently divorced?" Chet asked. Valerie watched Harrison.

"That's right."

"Why?"

"He was an alcoholic. He was screwing around with hookers," she said. She lowered her head so that she was not making eye contact with either of the police officers. "He beat me."

"When Martin came here today, did you let him into your house?"

"No. One of my girls must have."

"Did you ask him to leave?"

She had not. "No."

"Why not?"

"I thought he might have been drinking. He's violent when he's drinking. I didn't want to do anything to upset him."

"Did he harm you in anyway?" Chet asked.

Now Valerie looked at the police officer as if he were an imbecile and lowered the hand towel away from her face.

"I mean before you tried to poison him?"

Valerie gasped. "I didn't try to poison him."

"Didn't you get him a drink, making him feel welcomed?"

"He had a bottle of whiskey hidden in the basement. He forced me to bring it up to him," Valerie said, defensively.

"Did you, or did you not ask him to stay for lunch."

"No . . . I mean, I did, but I was trying to distract him. My girls were hiding in a bedroom upstairs. I didn't want him to harm them."

"Had he ever harmed them before?"

"No."

"What made you think he might harm them today?"

Valerie remained silent. "This is ridiculous."

"Harrison ran a check. We don't have any record on domestic calls being dispatched to this house. Nothing was ever filed by you. Are you sure your husband beat you before you tried to poison him?"

"It's an antihistamine. I wanted him to fall asleep so I could get my girls and get out of the house. He had beaten me well before lunch." She wanted to yell, ask my girls, but did not want to involve them. Not yet, not if she did not have to.

"Where did you get the medication?"

"It's in the cupboard, over the sink."

Harrison opened the cupboard. He produced another lunch bag and, with the fork, knocked the box of medicine into it. "Did you put anything else in the pie?"

Valerie looked at Harrison with disgust and shook her head from side to side.

"Are you sure?"

"Pie filler," she said.

"Still have the can?"

"It's in the trash."

"Ms. Wringer, let me ask you a serious question, all right? Did you feed this pie to your daughters?"

Valerie felt tears brim in her eyes. "I did, but not the piece with the medication."

"How can you know that?"

"I marked the pie crust. I pressed the fork tines into the crust at a different angle. I knew which piece to give to Martin. I knew which piece he had to eat." Even as she said it, even though she knew she was right, she knew how it must have sounded to the police officers. "I want to file assault and battery charges against my husband, and I want a restraining order. I don't want him near my kids, this house, or me! Never is he to come near us again."

While Harrison dug around in her garbage, Valerie went back to crying. She heard the front door open. Two paramedics, dressed in white shirts and navy blue pants, walked into the kitchen carrying medical bags. Valerie felt thankful for their interruption. While they inspected her, she thought about the best way to handle the situation. If necessary, she would not say another word until she contacted her attorney. She would call her sister and have the girls picked up until things were straightened out.

Chapter 52

They stood hand-in-hand on the front step. Felicia could not hold still. She kept shifting her weight from foot-to-foot. Finally she gathered up enough courage to ring the doorbell. "Are we terribly late?"

Michael shook his head. "Five minutes."

"My dad hates when people are late."

"Relax. He's going to be just as nervous as you are," Michael said.

"You think so?"

"I know so. I know I would be."

She kissed him quick. "Thanks for coming with me."

He squeezed her hand. "I love you."

Her eyes twinkled. She did not say it back, but Michael was all right with that. It would take her time. He was in no hurry.

Marcia, Felicia's younger sister, opened the door. Michael remembered her from the hospital. Tonight, however, the pretty young lady wore a smile. "Dad's so nervous," Marcia said, stepping aside to let the couple in.

Marcia and Felicia kissed and hugged hello. "So am I," Felicia confessed. "Do you remember my friend, Michael?"

Marcia nodded. "Hi again."

"Hi," Michael said. He wanted to compliment the way she

looked, wearing an ankle length dress and her hair up, but thought it inappropriate. "It's good to see you again," is what he said instead.

At the end of the front hall, Michael saw Felicia's mother. She stood anxiously with her hands clasped together. The scene reminded him of a story out of the Bible. The prodigal daughter was returning home. The occasion called for a feast. If Michael was not mistaken, he smelled turkey.

After her mother's warm welcome, she led them all into the family room where Felicia's father sat on the sofa, pretending to watch television. It was not hard to pick up. Tension filled the room. Neither father nor daughter seemed to know how to react. It would be difficult for both of them, for different reasons, Michael knew.

Felicia took a step forward. Michael caught her father's eyes as they moved to see what she was doing. "Daddy?"

Her father rolled his lower lip over his upper. He had one hand on the arm of the sofa, one on his thigh. His fingers rolled into loosely balled up fists, then unrolled, only to roll up again. "How are you?" the man managed.

It was enough. Felicia went to her father's side and dropped to her knees. She hugged him and cried into his chest. Her father looked at his wife and at his other daughter. Slowly his hand left his leg and worked its way onto his oldest daughter's back. Once contact was made, the hug became more sincere. In less than a second, he was holding her ferociously tight. And maybe he did not want anyone to see, because as he began to cry, he turned and rested his cheek on top of Felicia's head. Michael could hear him mumbling. "I've missed you. I've missed you."

Like a spectator, Michael looked over at Marcia and her mom. They were holding each other and crying. They all looked happy, and hopeful. It was when Marcia held out a hand toward Michael that he became caught up in the wave of emotions. He held her hand. She gave it a squeeze.

When the reunited hug between father and daughter ended, Felicia lifted her head. Her father cupped her by the ears and stared into her face. "I love you, Daddy."

"I love you, too," he said, and they kissed. Then he held her head out and stared at his daughter for a moment longer before saying, "Okay. Let's eat."

* * *

Valerie tried not to seem so weak and out of control, but she could not contain herself. She was furious with the police for their silent accusations. She was furious with herself for letting them get to her this way. Once she was able to tell the entire story, everything would get cleared up. She needed to keep reminding herself of this fact.

Officer Harrison had his brown lunch bags in his hands and was looking around the house expectantly. "I think I got everything."

"Where's Martin Wringer?" Officer Chet asked. He had his notepad out and was scribbling profusely. "Mind if I sit?" Chet asked Valerie.

"No. Please, make yourself comfortable," she replied with a strong flavor of sarcasm.

Chet thanked her and sat down. "Look, Ms. Wringer, I know this isn't easy," Chet said. "We're going to follow you to the hospital and get this cleared up."

"Am I under arrest?"

"Right now? No." Chet closed his pen and slipped it into the breast pocket of his uniform.

Harrison came back into the kitchen. "Chet, we've got a problem."

"What is it?"

"Wringer. He's gone."

Though the two police officers looked panicked, Valerie felt relieved. Martin's screw up would only help her prove how crazy the man truly was.

"Did you ask him to hang around?" Chet asked. He was standing up with his hands firmly planted on the weapons on his belt.

"Yeah. Sure I did. He asked if he was free to take off. I told him I'd be inside for a minute, to wait here, and that you and I would be back out to talk to him in a couple of minutes. I also told him I knew he'd been drinking, so I didn't want him behind the wheel," Harrison explained.

Valerie thought he looked too young to be a police officer. She had trouble recognizing his authority, whereas Chet looked much older and possessed a much harder look to him. "He's dangerous," Valerie said. "He sweet-talked you outside, but when you came in here to get my side of the story, he got nervous. He probably figured I would tell you my side and you'd find out the truth, so he got scared and took off."

"Ma'am, we don't need your opinion right now," Harrison said. He was looking at his partner for support.

Chet had his hands on the radio clipped to the shoulder of his uniform. "This is two-one-one-two, over."

"Go ahead two-one-one-two."

"What was your husband driving, Ms. Wringer?" Chet asked. When she told him, he talked into his radio again. "We need to contact the DMV for plate numbers on a white conversion van registered to a Martin Wringer," he said, and provided an address to the police dispatch. "Will hold for information, over."

"And I remember something. Before I blacked out, right after he kicked me in the face," Valerie said, cringing as the memory replayed itself in her mind's eye. "I remember just before I closed my eyes that he, Martin, had taken out a knife," she said, more to herself, in realization. "I think he was going to kill me."

Chapter 53

"That wasn't just good, that was great," Michael said to Felicia's mother. He wanted to lean back in the chair and pat at his belly. Luckily, the table manors instilled in him since childhood prevented the obnoxious behavior.

"So tell me, Mike, your family live around here?" Felicia's father asked. He had a slice of French bread and was dipping the crust into the gravy on his plate.

"Yes. In Gates," Michael answered. Rochester was a large city and housed many suburban towns. Gates, not only a suburb, also seemed to be home to a large number of Italian families. "They've lived there forever. Well, when they first got married they had a small house in the city on Isabelle Street. As soon as I was born, they bought a house off Spencerport Road."

"Nice area," Felicia's father said. "And what do you do?"

"Daddy," Felicia called out, offended.

"What? I'm just asking."

"It's not right," Felicia's mother said.

"What's not right. Mike, you mind if I ask you what you do for a living?"

"Of course not," Michael said, smiling. He was not prepared for the question. "I work part time as a cook at a diner."

"What diner?"

"It's a small place. It's called, Jack's Joint."

"Never heard of it," Felicia's father said. "So you do that part time, huh? What do you do full time?"

"I work for the Rochester City Chronicle," Michael answered and caught the look Felicia flashed him. "I write the obituary columns."

"Lively job," Marcia added. Michael smiled and pointed at her.

"You go to college?"

"Brockport. Got my degree in journalism," Michael said, only now he was looking at Felicia. She looked confused. She was, after all, hearing this for the first time.

"Going to be a writer?"

"Someday, yes. I hope to be," Michael said. He smiled, thinking Felicia would be pleased to hear his goals.

* * *

Felicia's father fell asleep on the sofa after dinner. "He's been doing that a lot lately," Marcia explained.

"Mom, I don't want to eat and run, but . . ."

"Oh sure, honey. I'm just so glad you came tonight," Felicia's mother said. They hugged. Michael watched with approving eyes. As they were leaving, Marcia hugged her sister and gave Michael a warm handshake.

Once outside, Michael said. "I think your sister is starting to like me."

Felicia slapped him hard in the chest.

"What the hell was that for?" Michael asked.

"You have a college degree from Brockport and work at the paper? How could you not tell me all of that? I mean, don't you think those are the kind of things I should know about you?" Felicia did not wait for an answer. She stormed away toward the car. "I can't believe you didn't tell me you were a college graduate!"

"How about, I can't believe you're mad at me about it. Why are you so upset? I don't get it." Michael walked with his hands in his pockets. "Believe it or not, this is a good thing. A good thing. If we wind up together, I'll be able to support you," Michael said smugly as he stopped in front of her by the car.

She smiled. "Oh, now you plan to support me, too?"

Michael kissed her. "Maybe."

She kissed him. "You went from planning on supporting me, to maybe? What's the deal with that?"

He kissed her, harder. "You want me to support you?"

"I don't know yet. What other surprises do you have that I should know about?" Felicia sounded scared and insecure.

"Nothing. I'm not keeping any secrets from you," Michael said.

"Promise?"

"Promise," he answered and kissed her more passionately. When finally the kiss ended, he sighed. "I have to be to work in a little while."

"How are you going to support me, if you have to work two jobs now?" She laughed and opened the car door. Inside the car, they strapped their seatbelts on. "No really, why do you need to work two jobs? You're not married or something? Paying child support or something, are you?"

Michael laughed. There was a sudden ripple in his perfect evening. "Paying off my student loans is more like it," he said, lying.

Chapter 54

Christine Wzros wore an excessive amount of make up. She dressed in tight blue jeans and high heel shoes. She sat with Detective Jason Cocuzzi in his unmarked squad car. Detective Pete Cage was in the surveillance van parked across the street. "Tell you what," she said to Cocuzzi. "I like this undercover work. It's pretty exciting, but I can't stand the cold."

"You're doing great," Cocuzzi said. He wanted to ask how lunch was, but let it slide. "To be honest, tonight might be the last night for this operation."

"The good thing would have to be the amount of married scum we busted," Officer Wzros said. She looked under her long red fingernails. "You were married once, weren't you?"

"No. Never."

"Why not?" Officer Wzros asked.

"You're a cop, you know what it's like. It's hard to find a woman who will understand what I do for a living. It's even a little unfair to ask a woman to try and understand. I mean, unless you are a police officer, you have no idea what kind of career you're in for. When I'm working a case, I'm consumed. Look at how we've been this past week. I think I've been home six times. Mostly, I just showered and changed clothing. What wife would want that kind of lifestyle? None, I tell you. Even if they think they know what they are getting into . . . they have no idea until they experience it first hand. And it's not easy on the wife, either. Think about it. If you're married to a guy who works at, let's say Kodak, every morning he gets up and goes to work at eight, right? Then at five, it is reasonably acceptable to expect him home any minute. Sure, the guy could have a deadly car accident on his way home, but probably that won't happen. A cop goes to work . . . especially a cop with crap for seniority, and he's working the graveyard shift. The wife is at home on pins and needles for eight hours a day, for forty hours a week. She's wondering night after night if her husband will pull into the driveway at the end of his shift. She wonders, every time the telephone rings, or every time there is a knock at the door, if it will be that one feared time she will hear the words that her husband has been hurt, or shot, or dead . . ."

"Your dad was cop, huh?" Wrzos asked intuitively.

"Yes. He and my mother divorced when I was fourteen," Cocuzzi said, slapping the steering wheel like a shy teenage boy. "They kept telling me I was at an age where I'd be old enough to understand what was going on. They kept telling me that they didn't hate each other, but that my mother couldn't keep on living that way."

"I'd think you're never too old to be hurt and effected by your parents divorcing," Wzros said.

Cocuzzi shook his head in agreement. "I remember saying to my mother, 'So then you still love him, Mom?' And she told me that she did. And I said to her, I said, 'So if after you're divorced . . . if he gets killed at work, are you going to feel any differently about the news than you would if you were still married?'"

"She didn't have an answer to that?"

"No. No answer. It made her cry, though. I didn't mean to make her cry, but maybe I felt a little better knowing I wasn't the only one hurting so bad." Cocuzzi found himself staring into Wrzos' eyes. *Why did I say all that*? he wondered before she leaned over and kissed him.

The pounding on the windshield startled them both. They pulled out of the kiss and searched around them. Detective Pete Cage was standing by Wrzos' door with the palms of his hands pressed against the glass. Cocuzzi rolled down the window. "Hey love birds. Just to shed some perspective on that tender moment. She's wired for sound," Cage said, pointing at Officer Wzros. "Your chief is going to wind up hearing that entire heartfelt confession."

Aside from feeling humiliated, Cocuzzi wanted to deck Cage. It took every bit of self-control to keep from getting out of the car and starting a fight. "You can erase that part of the recording, detective."

"I'll see if we can do that," Cage said, mockingly. He turned his attention on Wzros. "We still on for tomorrow night?" Cage winked, clearly teasing.

Bastard. "Get back to the van," Cocuzzi said before Officer Wzros could respond. "It's almost time to start the night."

Chapter 55

"You know, as long as you don't mind, I'd like to go with you to work tonight. I want to talk with Sandy. She might like to hear I'm getting out. Believe it or not, she's been begging for me to leave this kind of life since forever," Felicia said. "I really consider her a good friend. I don't have, like, a best friend. If I did, I think she'd be it."

Michael wondered about Sandy. She was a young woman, also worth saving. He felt like a failure, which was ridiculous. He could not be expected to get women out of prostitution. His motive for working on Felicia was purely selfish. He loved her. "Yeah. Hang out at the diner. Hell, I'll even buy you a cup of coffee," Michael said.

"Coffee? You treat me like gold," she said, teasing. As if suddenly content with the world around her, she unfastened her seatbelt and slid closer to sit next to Michael. She rested her head on his shoulder. "What about your parents?"

"What about them?" Michael asked. "When will you get to meet them?"

"Exactly," Felicia said.

"I was thinking about that. How about next Sunday? They have sauce around two. I haven't been there in the last few weeks, and I think my mom's a little upset with me. They'd love to meet you, too, I'm sure," Michael said. Although he knew how much his family liked Ellen the attorney, he felt confident they would take to Felicia in the same way. At least he prayed they would, though, for obvious reasons, he would want to keep her previous job a bit of a secret.

"Sounds perfect. I'll check my calendar, but I know I can at least pencil you in for next Sunday."

"Why thank you, ma'am." Michael spotted the police set-up as he drove down Lake Avenue. "We should screw with them."

"Who?"

"The police." Michael debated pulling up to the curb and throwing out an offer to the undercover prostitute, but passed. The police were leaving him alone. He did not need to infuriate them. Instead, as they made a right off Lake, toward parking in the rear, Michael flashed a friendly wave that the female officer ignored.

Like déjà vu, Michael and Felicia walked around to the front of Jack's Joint, passing the undercover officer without so much as a word. Felicia held on tightly to Michael's arm. "You know what?" she asked as Michael pulled open the diner door.

"What?"

"You can't understand the tremendous amount of relief I feel. I didn't think I'd feel this way, but I do. I feel great," Felicia said, standing outside the doorway. "I'm glad we're together."

"Me, too," Michael said as they stepped inside.

Fatso sat at the counter with the newspaper, but was talking to Jack Murphy. "What I'm saying is, it's not only rattle snakes that rattle. All snakes do this. When a predator is close, ready to strike, a snake . . . any snake . . . will rattle its tail to draw the attention to its rear. If something bites, chomps, or crushes the snake's tail, the creature won't die. It's better than getting a bite on the head, right? And, while the predator is preoccupied with watching the snake's tail, the snake can strike."

Jack shook his head. "I knew that. I told you I knew that. Why do you have to insist on telling me something I already know?"

"I don't know Jack," Fatso said. He looked sad and hurt.

Jack must have picked up on this. "But it is useful information, Fatso. Sometimes I know things, but forget about them, you know?"

Fatso smiled. "Sure. Not like the elephant, though."

Jack held up his hand. "Stop. All right. Just quit it." He smiled at Michael. "Thank God, you're here."

Michael smiled and went around the counter to relieve Jack. "Long day?"

Jack looked at Fatso, shaking his head. "Long enough. Hey, I wanted to tell you what a fine job you're doing. The customers say good things about you . . . and that's not something they normally do. Things keep like they are, we can talk about an increase in pay in a couple of weeks. What do you think? I gave you a lot of responsibility, right from day one. You've handled the job well and have shown me I can trust you."

They shook hands. "I'm touched," Michael said. "Thank you."

"Next week, next Sunday, we'll talk. All right?"

"Sounds good. Thank you," Michael said again.

"All right, well I'm out of here." Jack turned to those listening. "Ladies and gentlemen, have a nice night."

A few people replied. Michael tied the apron around his waist.

Felicia leaned on the counter. "I wonder where Sandy is?"

"She was here earlier," Fatso said. "She got pissed and left when the police people showed up. Two nights in a row and she was flaming. She didn't have any problem yelling at the undercover people sitting in the booths."

Michael watched out the window by the pinball machines as a luxury sedan parked along the curb. Marcus got out of the car and entered the diner with a folder in his hand. He stared directly at Michael as he went to his usual booth and sat down. Once seated, he continued to stare at Michael, who in turn felt a little unnerved by the unasked-for attention. Michael looked away from Marcus, and then back to him. Marcus had not looked away.

"How about that coffee you planned to buy me?" Felicia asked.

Michael, becoming increasingly uncomfortable, wanted to ignore Marcus. "Sure, sweetheart."

"Sweetheart?" Fatso teased.

"Yeah," Felicia said. "A lot has changed."

* * *

Detective Jason Cocuzzi found it difficult to concentrate. The stakeout did not demand much attention as long as no one pulled up to the curb. However, he did not like the way his mind roamed. He felt giddy and that, being so unnatural to him, felt disgusting. Christine's kiss had moved him like nothing had in a long time. His body had responded immediately, but more than that, he had responded emotionally to the kiss, to the warmth. For the longest time, he realized, he had denied himself any kind of closeness. The fact that he opened up to Officer Wzros still amazed him. The fact that everyone in the surveillance vehicle overheard him was disturbing.

When the van pulled up to the curb, Cocuzzi snapped back to attention and was pleased with his ability to focus when needed. He clicked on his radio. "Getting this? Over?"

"Recording. He's called her to the window. Over?" Detective Cage said.

It started to snow large fat flakes. The wind was picking up. The nice day had ended, making way for a snowy night.

"Unit One, be ready to roll," Cocuzzi instructed. "Over."

"Unit One on stand-by. Over."

* * *

Michael noticed one of the undercover police officers, posing as a diner, raise a finger to his ear. The movements and the way the man's face contorted reminded Michael of the Secret Service agents that guard the president. Though it was the ear toward the wall, Michael squinted in order to see a tiny wire lead down the collar of the man's shirt. Looking outside, Michael saw the van at the curb and the policewoman at the passenger window.

Fascinated, he watched as the lady cop opened the door and climbed into the vehicle. A buzz of activity had to be running through the wires as the police officers at their posts waited anxiously for the sic 'em command. Michael instinctively reached for the pack of cigarettes on the counter, but stopped himself. He shot a side-glance over to Felicia who seemed to be monitoring him as closely as the police were monitoring the woman driving away with the john.

"The habit is going to be the hardest part," Michael confessed. He knew he could quit. He was not thrilled about being forced to quit, but he could not look at it that way. He wanted Felicia out of the prostitution business because he cared about her. She wanted him to quit smoking, perhaps, for the same reason. No one was forcing him to do anything. Ultimately, the choice was his.

* * *

"We lost contact. Over." It was Detective Cage. He sounded frantic. "Read me Cocuzzi. We lost contact. Over."

Jason Cocuzzi had heard the broadcast the first time, but had frozen. Now his mind reeled. "All units, follow in pursuit. We're looking for a rusted van." Cocuzzi proceeded to read of the plate number. He repeated the message.

Cocuzzi felt dizzy as he started up his engine. He threw the car into drive and peeled out of his parking spot, the tires screaming in protest. While he drove north down Lake Avenue, he fumbled for the siren switch on the dashboard. The screaming of his siren joined the screechy chorus of the other police cars involved in the search. "Posts One and Two, join in pursuit, join in pursuit!"

Chapter 56

When the two men with booths by windows jumped up, Michael knew he had been right. Both held a finger to their ear as they raced out of the diner without ever looking back. The silent night was shattered as sirens from everywhere, all at once, exploded into existence.

A story was breaking, Michael realized, as he took an order from a young black man at the counter. It was possible, probable and likely that the police were chasing down Johnny Blade. Many people made fun of the police, but Michael knew the job before them was more challenging than most. Officers had to work with their hands tied.

Michael remembered a recent drug bust. The police stormed a known crack house. A gunfight broke out. A nineteen-year-old woman, with thirty-five bags of crack in her pockets, was shot and killed. The woman did not, however, have a gun. The woman also happened to be African American. The people of the city of Rochester cried out about injustice and unfair racial treatment, never mind the fact that the woman should not have been at a crack house. Never mind the fact that she had more drugs on her than most drug dealers carry around at a given time. Never mind the fact that the people crying out injustice were the same people who cursed the police for not closing down all the city crack houses. No, Michael knew the police operated on a highly Catch-22 policy.

"Damn," Fatso commented. "Think they got him?"

"They might," Felicia said. "The bastard."

Michael wanted to leave, run to his car, and follow the police pursuit. Every instinct in his body told him to do just that. He wanted the story so bad he could taste it. His mouth had started to salivate. Matthew Sinopoli, at the paper, would be out of his mind with jealousy if Michael not only covered the story, but also was actually present for the arrest.

Rubbing his hands anxiously up and down the thighs of his jeans, Michael's mind was made up. The story was important. Out there—out in the city, the climax to a serial killer's rampage was being uncovered. The identity of a prostitute-murdering madman might be revealed at any moment. Jack's Joint was a job to get him closer to his career goal. If he stayed behind the counter and Johnny Blade was apprehended, he would no longer need to continue his employment with Jack Murphy. The story would be, in essence, over, and he would have passed on a prime opportunity—a once in a lifetime chance—to witness a notorious takedown.

He leaned over the counter, holding Felicia's full attention. "You know what? I'll be right back."

"Where are you going?" Felicia asked.

"Yeah. Where are you going?"

Michael turned around. Marcus was at the counter. Marcus wanted to know where he was going, too. Marcus' eyes, like black beady marbles, had locked on him, his brow furrowed, and his jaw muscles worked back and forth, sending waves of tension through his cheeks.

* * *

Feeling like a re-born child, Martin Wringer drove with both hands on the wheel. After leaving his wife's house he pulled into a gas station and used the rest room. Like a drunk, he got down on his knees and hovered over the bowl. He inserted his middle finger into his mouth and pushed it back far enough to tickle his tonsils. Gagging on the finger more than once, he eventually forced himself to vomit.

He hated vomiting. It felt terrible. You could not breathe as the surge of chunky, undigested food flowed like water through a fire hose up your throat. He hated the feel of those chunks as they scraped the roof of his mouth and tongue as the liquid mess spewed forth. He hated the wretched sound of retching. He hated the smell, but when he was done, he felt re-born.

He wore a smile and could not, for the life of him, get rid of it. He felt the way a man feels after drinking a bunch of beers. Not drunk, but tipsy. His smile had warmth about it and the warmth spread throughout his body. The closure he had received today was the answer. Spending all his time wondering had been driving him crazy. Should he go home? Should he move to another state? Should he drive off a cliff? All of those questions and so many more jumbled ones had been spinning around in his head for so long, he thought he might explode.

There would be no explosion. Now, with the closure he needed, he was satisfied he knew what course to plan out for his life.

Canada. He would head up to Canada and see about becoming a Canadian citizen. They offered free health care to their citizens. The entire country was beautiful—even up in those snowy, freezing northern areas. He could be a Canadian. He loved beer and hockey. He could work an occasional "eh" into his conversations. Martin also felt confident the Canadians would love him, too. And prostitution in parts of Canada was legal. Legal prostitution meant the government regulated the women. In regulating the women, Martin could enjoy their services and not have to worry about catching any sexually transmitted diseases.

Knowing that he did not want to move back in with Valerie, the bitch, made everything easier. He was glad they had had the chance to talk things out. Sure, she wanted him back. His girls wanted him back, but it would be better for everyone if he just let them learn to adjust for a while, without him around. They needed that time. Hell, he needed that time. He was only human. Even he hurt sometimes, and pain, he knew, needs time to heal.

With him in Canada, when the girls were ready, they would have a wonderful place to visit. They could tell all of their friends they were going up to Canada for a few weeks to spend time with their dad. What kid would not want to say something like that? *It even sounds cool. My dad lives in Canada.* And this was why Martin could not frown away his shit-faced grin.

Nothing was keeping him in the States. Canada, if he hopped on the Parkway and headed west, was little more than an hour's drive away and he would find himself at the Rainbow Bridge. Cross that and he would be in Niagara Falls. The thought of heading to Niagara Falls got him thinking about the casino. It could not hurt to stop in and play some slots, even just twenty dollars worth. He felt lucky.

He felt lucky. He felt like getting lucky one last time with an American girl before he bid the grand USA farewell.

* * *

Immediately he shivered as if the fingertip of an icicle traced its way down his spine. "What do you mean?" Michael asked Marcus. Everyone in the diner was focused in on the conversation. Marcus' demeanor demanded that kind of attention.

"I mean, where the hell are you going? Are you going to follow after the police?" Marcus asked. He spoke calmly, despite his choice of verbiage.

Michael wondered what the Mafia-wannabe might be up to. He did not want to deny anything, but neither did he wish to admit to anything. He wanted to plead *no contest,* but said, "Why would I do that?" Answer a question with a question. It was the best technique to keep from saying anything. Politicians were notorious for this kind of reply.

"I don't know. Why don't you tell me, or us, since we all have a place in your story," Marcus said. The silence that ensued meant everyone was chewing on that comment. "Well?"

Marcus knew. Somehow the little Guido-bastard had found him out. "What are you talking about?" He knew as soon as he asked that he had made a mistake. Bluffing was futile, but he had played the hand and would now have to suffer through the consequences.

"You want, I should tell everyone? Gladly." Marcus was getting ready to roll. When he next spoke, he spoke with a grin that frightened Michael. "Michael Buzzelli, our Michael . . . Jack Murphy's Michael . . . works for the Rochester City Chronicle."

No one gasped, or even seemed surprised. Fatso just shrugged. He had been at the counter when Michael interviewed with Jack. Michael had told Jack he worked for the paper. He would not doubt Fatso overhearing the entire conversation. He also would not doubt after leaving that day, that Jack discussed his resume and application with everyone in the place.

Felicia just smiled at Marcus. "So?"

Marcus smiled back, as if not at all fazed by the placid effect of his announcement. "Maybe he told you that his position at the paper is menial and flat . . . working as a journalist writing the obituary ads, huh? Sounds right?"

He talked directly to Felicia, his intended target. Michael understood what was coming. He had no idea how Marcus obtained any information, but he knew beyond a doubt that Marcus was armed with bullets and was ready to blast them at Felicia and anyone else in their path.

"Marcus," Michael said. He did not want to sound like a beggar, but knew in order to get the man's attention, he would have to appease the situation. "Marcus, please."

Marcus stopped talking and folded his hands in front of him as he shrugged. "You want to finish? See, if you don't, I will. I'll let you have the choice, though, because I can't decide. I can't decide if this coming from me will be more damaging, or if it comes from you. See my dilemma?" Marcus spoke using animated hand gestures. His fingers pointed and curled and spread while his wrist rolled and his hands flipped and flopped. Normally Michael made eye contact with people when talking with someone. However, Marcus's hands, much like his demeanor, demanded attention.

"What's he talking about?" Felicia asked, suddenly suspicious. Fatso was quiet, but sat at the counter with his back straight, eager to find out what was going on.

Michael, looking at Marcus, faltered. "Felicia, I told you I work at the paper, you know?"

"Yeah, I know. What's the big deal? What's going on?"

Marcus had left the folder on the table. Michael could only assume what documents it might contain. If he assumed the worst, he was going to be in trouble. The last thing he wanted to do was volunteer more information than needed. If he did not say enough, and Marcus had conclusive evidence to nail his shortcomings, Felicia would be pissed. "Well, writing the obituary columns sucks."

"I imagine it would," Fatso said.

"Shut up," Felicia ordered. "Go on, Michael."

"I didn't go to school to write an obituary column for a paper. I went and earned a degree so I could become a reporter, a real journalist," Michael managed.

"Well, no kidding," Fatso said.

"I said, 'shut up,'" Felicia repeated her order. Michael noticed the fearful look in her eyes. She could not anticipate his next words. Everything right now, for her, was a dark mystery.

"I took this job, here at Jack's, to get closer to the Johnny Blade story."

Confused, keeping her emotions at bay, Felicia asked, "What? Like undercover work?"

Michael had been watching Felicia's reaction, but turned to study Marcus, to see if he was happy with the anguish he was inflicting. "That's right, undercover work." He wanted to explain more. He wanted to tell her that he knew Johnny Blade would come back and strike again, but refrained. Revealing that thought would serve no purpose.

Felicia sat deadly silent on the counter stool, obviously assessing her feelings. "I guess that's kind of exciting for you. Ambitious," she said cautiously. She sounded leery.

Marcus cleared his throat, catching everyone's attention. Felicia looked at Marcus with one of the hardest, most evil looks Michael had ever seen. He thought she might be able to kill him at that moment. She knew Marcus' intent. To crush Michael, and ultimately destroy her new found world.

Strolling casually back to the table for his folder, Marcus said, “Pretty close, Felicia. You seem to have a good grasp on handling the situation . . . that is, if you had all the facts.”

Felicia turned on Michael. “What other facts? What else is there?”

Michael was looking directly at the folder in Marcus’ hand as he walked back to the counter. He set the folder down on the counter. In black marker, in big block letters, someone had written OBITS. That was the name of the file on Michael’s work computer’s desktop. It was his personal file, one he thought would be safe. If Marcus had obtained the documents from that file and had hard copies in his folder, all Hell was only seconds from breaking loose. He had written drafts of personal pieces on nearly everyone in the diner and now it all made sense.

Maybe Marcus did some background checks on Michael. Maybe he found someone at the paper with access to his work computer. Obviously he had been able to get documents from that computer. Maybe Marcus would not have cared if there had not of been a piece written about him.

Michael knew what he had written about Marcus had been harsh, but had to be, because it was the truth. Marcus was a mystery man, and that was how the piece was built. The man, a loner, had to have a concealed past. The incident with the robbers the one day in the diner should have thrilled Marcus. For that portion of the piece, Marcus was displayed as a hero. However, Marcus did not want any noted involvement and had fled when he had had the chance, before having to talk with the police.

Michael knew the problem. He had invaded the privacy Marcus had so carefully constructed around himself that this was a way for Marcus to get back at him. Exposure. “Marcus, come on,” Michael pleaded.

“It’s been fun watching you squirm, but you take too long, see? So forget about it. I’ll take it from here.” Marcus moved to open the folder. Michael slapped his hand down on the folder. Marcus, through clenched teeth, said, “Move it or I’ll break every bone in your stick-like body.”

Michael knew he was not being threatened. Marcus was only saying what would happen. Reluctantly, he removed his hands. Marcus opened the folder and handed out copies of documents to Fatso and Felicia. “Since Speed’s going to be in jail a while, he’s not going to be able to enjoy the article Mr. Buzzelli has written about him, but maybe I can send him his copy.”

“These aren’t going to be published in the newspaper,” Michael said. He knew he sounded extremely defensive. “I’m a writer.”

No one was listening, each engrossed in reading what had been handed to them. Silently, Felicia was crying. Fatso kept sighing.

“What the hell is this, kid? I thought we were friends.” Fatso slapped his document down on the counter. “You put a knife in my heart, kid. Right in my heart.”

Michael felt so ashamed. No words would come to him, so he stayed quiet. He watched Fatso slide off the counter stool. He left his paper, he left the piece Michael had written, and walked out.

Felicia, done reading, cradled her forehead between the web of her thumb and finger. Mascara streaks made a path down her cheeks. “Is this what I am to you? Am I something for you to study and psychoanalyze? Was this whole thing . . . us? Were we . . . was I part of your study? All of us here, us poor people, we were a stepping stone to you? A freaking stepping stone!”

“My editor never even saw those. He doesn’t know I wrote them,” Michael managed to say on his behalf.

“You think that’s the point? I don’t care if your editor assigned you to write them. You wrote them. You watched us, you took notes,” she said softly and threw a trembling lip. “I have no idea who you are. You fooled me. And let me tell you something Michael. I don’t fool easily. I never let my guard down. Never. But you . . . you got it down. You got to me. And now I have to question everything that has happened in my life these last few weeks. I thought everything was so wonderful, sunny . . . changing. I can’t believe how wrong I was. I can’t believe how cheap you’ve made me feel.” She laughed. “Imagine that . . . you made a whore feel cheap.”

Michael found it difficult to swallow. He could not even be

angry with Marcus, because he knew everything Felicia said could not be far from the truth.

Felicia set down her document, then stared at Michael for a several seconds, long enough for a black tear to drop from her cheek and splash onto the front page of the piece. "I thought I loved you," were her last words before standing up and walking out.

Michael wanted to go after her. He peeled off his apron and ran around the counter. Marcus, an obstacle, stopped him. "I don't want you doing articles on my life, you got me?" Marcus said, giving Michael a shove. "I don't know who you think you are coming in here, pretending to be . . . what? A low life piece of crap like Fatso, like Felicia there, like me? You think I'm a low life piece of crap, Michael? Is that what you think about everyone here? You went to college, landed a cushy job on a big city newspaper, so you're better than me? See my car?" Marcus pulled out his keys and dangled them in Michael's face. "See the car I'm driving? I seen the car you drive. I seen the piece of crap car you drive, Michael, and you've got to ask yourself who's making the better living here."

Michael heard Marcus, but was distracted. Felicia was by the pole, her head hung low. She was hurting and he knew he needed to get to her. "Please, Marcus . . . can we discuss this later?"

"Later? What, like we should check our calendars?"

When the white van pulled up to the curb, Michael's heart stopped. Felicia looked back into the diner and then at the van. She went up to the passenger window.

Michael's heart sank. He did not want her to go back to being a prostitute. Despite everything that transpired, he was not phony with Felicia when it came to his feelings. He wanted to help her—he loved her.

When she got into the van, and the van pulled away, Michael felt as if he had stuck his finger in an outlet. A shock of recollection sped through him and charged his brain. In his mind he could see Vanessa. She was out by the corner. A van stopped and she climbed in. It was the last time he saw her. The van Felecia just climbed into was identical.

But the police were in the process of apprehending Johnny Blade. Or were they?

"Marcus, I need the keys to your car. Now!" Michael felt a surge of energy, emotion, and adrenaline race through his body.

Marcus, smiling smugly, shook his head. "What kind of drugs are you on?"

Michael sucker punched Marcus in the gut. As the Mafia-wannabe bent over, Michael snatched the car keys from his hand. "Call the police, Marcus! Call the police!"

Chapter 57

Martin Wringer pulled away from the curb. He had only stopped because he recognized the whore. "What was with that girl the other night? She didn't seem right," Martin asked.

"Very perceptive," the American whore said flatly. "She was an undercover cop. They're looking for that Johnny Blade guy. I think they got him tonight, though."

Martin grinned. "Is that so?"

The whore was looking at him. He could feel it. He kept his eyes on the road.

"You know what? I've changed my mind. I'd like to get out," the whore said. Martin did not think she sounded afraid. Maybe she suspected he was the infamous Johnny Blade, but he did not think so. She just sounded disinterested.

"Too bad," Martin replied. "I've had a busy, busy day. Tonight I'm leaving for Canada. I'm going to live there. And you, my dear, are my last American adventure." He smiled knowing the whore would feel honored.

"I'd rather you let me out. Anywhere is fine." The whore fidgeted in her seat, twisting away from him with one hand on the doorknob.

Using the back of his hand like a hammer, he pounded her in the face. It did not knock her out. The whore screamed, throwing open the door. Martin reached across the seat, catching her by the back of the pants. He kept her from jumping out of the van, and increased his driving speed, just in case she came loose and fell out.

With as much strength as he could manage, while still steering the van, he pulled her back in. Having never let go of the door handle, the abrupt tugging also caused her to pull the door closed. This time, Wringer used his elbow and smashed the side of her head with a crushing blow.

* * *

Michael took a quick moment to use his arm like a broom sweeping snow off the front windshield. It was coming down. The wind had picked up. It felt like a hundred below. He jumped into the car, started the engine, and worked the automatic windows. As they lowered for both front doors, snow fell into the car. He put the windows back up—free of snow—and switched on the defrosters as he pulled away from the curb.

The van was nowhere in sight. Michael drove as fast as he could up Lake Avenue. The snowflakes resembled a massive swarm of fat white bumblebees blanketing the night. Visibility was limited. Michael switched on the car high beams, and switched them off again. The high beams made it more difficult to see. The snow was relentless, panicking Michael. There was little he could do if the van pulled off the main road and went down a side street. He tried to look down each street as he concentrated on the road in front of him. Thankfully, the road looked pretty free of traffic at this time of night

In a way, he wanted a police officer to stop him. None were around.

As he headed toward Ridge Road, he felt overwhelmed. The van could easily have gone east, toward Irondequoit, or west toward the town of Greece. The van could have stayed on Lake heading north or could have turned off anywhere at any time.

Not too far in front of Marcus' car, Michael saw a van swerving back and forth between two lanes. He sped up. When the passenger door to the van flew open and he saw someone hanging out and then sucked back in again, he quickly closed the distance between them as they raced toward the intersection at Ridge. Michael knew it was the van with Felicia in it. Despite the prevailing weather conditions, he drove faster.

At the intersection, an oncoming car slammed into the side of Marcus' car sending the sedan spinning. The jarring accident forced the glove compartment to pop open at the same time the air bag exploded in Michael's face. The sound of brakes resounded off the pavement like werewolves howling in heat at the moon. Michael held onto the steering wheel with both hands. His face, firmly pressed into the air bag, was warm with blood. The bag had most certainly broken his nose.

When Michael opened his eyes, he was facing south on Lake. His eyes were watery. His nose throbbed like a son of a bitch and the bag was still inflated. The damned bag was not deflating. He pushed on it with his forearms, hoping to force the air out, though to no avail. In the sun visor Michael found a pen. He raised it above his head and swung it like Norman Bates in the movie Psycho during the shower scene. It took several jabs before the pen penetrated the material. The bag deflated.

Two cars blocked any path forward. People were getting out of their cars. No one looked happy with Michael. He had run the red light.

He slapped the car into reverse and pulled away from the accident. "Get my license plate number," he yelled out the window. Marcus would be pissed, but he was going to be pissed anyway.

He had lost sight of the van, but could not be more than a few seconds behind. Michael kept his eyes riveted to the road while he waited for the gong-like ringing in his head to subside. His ears throbbed from the deafening noise still going off in his head. Instantly, an ache began to ebb its way down his neck and across his shoulders.

The light from the glove compartment caught his eye. He looked down and was not surprised to see a Glock next to a cell phone.

Michael took the cell phone from the compartment and dialed 9-1-1. He waited impatiently for someone to answer. On the third ring, when the dispatcher greeted him, Michael went off. "Listen, I'm in hot pursuit of Johnny Blade, the serial killer. Right now we're going . . ."

"Sir. Sir, please. Where are you calling from?" the dispatcher asked.

"I'm trying to tell you. I'm on a cell phone speeding up . . . north . . . up Lake Avenue. I just passed through Ridge Road."

"We have an accident report that just came in. Ridge and Lake."

"That was me. I caused that accident," Michael said. He felt frantic. "Look, this van . . ."

"Sir, I need you to return to the scene. Police are already arriving at the scene."

They should be. The precinct could not be more than fifty yards from the accident. "Listen to me! I'm chasing Johnny Blade, the serial killer. He's in a van."

"Hold on one moment, sir."

Michael stared at the phone in disbelief.

"What kind of van?"

"White . . . a white van with dark tinted windows."

"Hold, sir." There was a solid minute of silence. Michael used the time to concentrate on relocating the van. Up ahead, a vehicle passed under a streetlight. It was too far ahead to be certain, but Michael thought it might be the van. "Sir? We have Detective Jason Cocuzzi on the line with us."

Michael heard, "Detective Cocuzzi here?"

Chapter 58

They were on a side street off Lake, by a small residential park. Police officers had the driver of the van face down on the cold pavement. The side of his head was full of blood. Officer Christine Wzros had done a job on him with her nails.

No weapons were in the van. The driver, Mark O'Connor, was drunk. He had a record of physical domestic violence. He had a record for soliciting prostitutes. No one was sure or not if O'Connor was Johnny Blade, although it seemed probable.

Wzros seemed okay. She looked a little shaken, but did her best not to let it show. She had her arms crossed in front of her, snuggling herself, and bracing herself from the cold.

When his cell phone rang, Cocuzzi stepped away from the scene to answer it. "Detective Cocuzzi here."

"Detective, it's me. It's Michael Buzzelli, from the paper?"

"Look, Buzzelli, I'm kind of busy here . . ."

"No, detective, wait. It's about the killer, about Johnny Blade," Buzzelli said, sounding out of breath.

"This is off-the-record, but we may just have him in custody," Cocuzzi said with a confident tone. He was getting cocky, but felt he deserved the right to do so. The bastard on the ground with Christine's claw marks through his face had put him through hell. Now that this might be over, he would not have to deal with the

FBI and could perhaps look forward to a sound solid night's sleep.

"It's not him, Cocuzzi. You don't have the right man. I know. I'm following the sick bastard right now. He has a woman in the car . . . Felicia!"

Now, as he was connected with the reporter from the Rochester City Chronicle, the detective's mind spun with uncertainty. He imagined Johnny Blade to be an out of reach psycho—one that they might never catch. He did not want to believe what he was hearing. Surely, Buzzelli was off his rocker. They potentially had the serial killer and were cuffing him and reading him his rights. The nightmare was potentially over, potentially done. Potentially. "What the hell are you talking about? Buzzelli, what the hell is going on?"

"I was following the van that Felicia climbed into. About . . . I don't know, a mile past the diner . . . the side door flew open and Felicia was hanging out of it. Then she went back in and the door closed again. I got in an accident on Ridge, but I left the scene."

Buzzelli was not making any sense. He did not have time for this nonsense. "Why do you think this is Johnny Blade, and not just Felicia working a john?" Detective Cocuzzi asked. Detective Cage had sauntered up next to him with his hands in his back pockets, looking annoyed with the bust at hand. Cocuzzi held up a finger, letting Cage know something might be up.

"When I saw her climb into the van," Michael explained, "it was like déjà vu. I saw Vanessa, the other victim, climb into that same van the night she disappeared. I'm certain of it. Same exact van!"

Cocuzzi looked at the creepy guy being placed into the back of a squad car. For some reason the arresting officer was being gentle with the hood, making sure O'Connor did not bump his head. They were wrapping things up. The thought of the killer still lose, still out on the streets and perhaps with a potential victim caused a rumbling in the detective's belly, an ulcer in the making. Buzzelli was wrong, plain and simple. The reporter had a thing for one of the prostitutes. *She keeps on working, Buzzelli gets jealous . . .*

Cocuzzi looked at the man who had attacked Christine. He sat in the back of the squad car, staring out the window. He had to be

Johnny Blade. Potentially. "And where are you now?" Cocuzzi asked Michael Buzzelli.

"Me? I'm . . ." The line went dead.

* * *

Michael let out a scream. The cell phone's battery died. He could not even get the light inside the phone to glow. "Dammit, dammit, dammit!" He threw the phone at the passenger door. The plastic smashed.

He could no longer travel at fifty miles an hour. The roads felt slick. With the way the wind was now blowing, black ice could be under snow spots on the road. Trying desperately not to become discouraged, he followed Lake Avenue for another few miles, heading toward Lake Ontario. When he spotted the van stopped, only yards in front of him, he thought his heart might stop beating. The van was making a left. Michael signaled his turn and hopped onto the Parkway behind the van. The Parkway was like an expressway. It was two lanes of traffic that led all the way to Canada without any traffic lights or stop signs. The fifty-five speed limit made for happy travelers.

Aside from feeling utterly terrified for Felicia, he knew she had to be all right since the maniac was driving the van. That is, as long as she was still alive.

Michael wondered about heroics. He could use Marcus' gun and shoot out the tires. If the Blade lost control of the van and crashed and Felicia was hurt . . . No, he would not do that. Nor would he attempt to run the van off the road.

The van kept at a steady speed. Michael followed, keeping his distance. He knew the driver had to be Johnny the Blade. If he had been a normal john, he would have pulled over somewhere on Lake Avenue. Maybe he would have gone to one of the nearby motels. *The question now . . . where is this maniac headed*?

* * *

Martin Wringer paid little attention to the whore. Though the pig was still unconscious, she would not be that way for long. He had hit her, but not that hard. When she eventually came to, she might attack him while he concentrated on his driving. He could not have that. His knife, by the bed, left him with no weapon readily accessible. He was not sure how to proceed. The roads were terrible. Rochester weather made him sick. In his mind he had to ask himself if going further north still made sense. What's more, he suspected the piss ant in the sedan was following him and that was beginning to get on his nerves. Martin had yet to see another car on the parkway, and no street lights either, for that matter. Martin let the van slow down some. The sedan began to catch up. Martin slowed slightly more, keeping the van at fifty. Any slower and the driver in the car might become suspicious.

When the car slowly caught up to him, Martin checked all around him to make sure no cars were around, and then slowed even more. He wanted the sedan to try and pass, then he would steer into the car and force the driver off the road.

* * *

Michael did not know what to do. The van kept slowing down. If he did not pass, the driver would know something was up. If he passed, then the van could exit anywhere and he would be stuck. He could not pass the van and drive at fifty without adding to suspicion.

"Dammit," Michael said, looking at the shattered cell phone in pieces on the car mats. He took the gun out of the glove compartment and set it in his lap. He had fired a gun before. During college he had hung out with many criminal justice majors. A lot of them did co-op for the local police station. On the weekends they would go as a group to the firing range in town. This was no firing range. He was not sure he could even use a gun. This was not like a movie where the star kills everyone and makes one-liner jokes about it. The thought of shooting another human being was furthest from his mind.

He pulled into the left lane and sped up.

As he came along side the van, he found he could not see the driver. The van door filled the passenger side window in the sedan. Michael would need to lean across the front seat and look up and out the window to catch a glimpse of the driver. Instead, as he started to pass the van, he lost control of the vehicle.

It was not until a split second later that he realized what had happened. The son of a bitch was trying to force him off the road. The contact sent the sedan to the shoulder. Michael slammed on the brakes just as the van veered toward him a second time. The van wobbled back and forth as the driver corrected his actions after missing the car.

Michael sped up and slammed the nose of the sedan into the van's rear. This jolted him and he slammed his forehead into the steering wheel with such force he was sorry he had punctured the air bag. Every part of his body seemed to be aching. The steady buzz in his ears had done nothing but increase. Michael ignored everything and floored the gas pedal, sending the sedan into the van again. This time Michael thought he might be prepared for the crash, but was not. He was so tense the pain in his arms, shoulders, and neck only intensified. The seatbelt felt like it had burned and cut through the flesh around his neck.

When the van slammed on its brakes, Michael was completely caught off guard. He felt the tail end of the sedan rise in the air, and watched in horror as the hood of the sedan crumpled into a pointed triangle. Michael thought the entire dashboard had lunged at him, and feared the engine block might wind up on his lap.

Freeing himself from the seatbelt, Michael threw open the door and jumped out of the car.

The van tried to pull away, but the fenders were hooked together.

Michael found it near impossible to move. The snow-covered ground felt wonderful on his painfully aching bones and muscles. His head was spinning and he could not think, or see clearly. The blizzard around him gave the illusion of being lost in a dream sequence. Michael knew his arm was broken. Pain was coursing its way from the elbow directly to his head. Finding words to describe that kind of excruciating pain would be difficult. It was like taking a big tree branch, leaning it standing up against a wall, and then kicking the branch in two. That was how his arm felt—kicked in two.

He heard the van's engine whining and racing. The tires spun uselessly on the pavement, unable to gain enough traction and force to separate the van from the collision. Slowly, Michael rolled over onto his side and saw the van's driver side door open. He felt like everything around him was moving in slow motion.

Trapped. He felt as if he were lying on a ground covered with molasses. His head hurt badly. His nose ached. For some reason, lying down and going to sleep was a comforting thought.

The sedan's one working headlight hung by wires, sending enough light around to produce odd-shaped shadows. The car's directional blinked on and off, signaling a turn the car would never make.

Michael saw Johnny Blade had Felicia by the hair. Johnny Blade dragged her out of the vehicle. She was alive, screaming, and kicking. Michael watched as Johnny Blade punched Felicia in the face. The punch sent her reeling and into a snow bank, not too far away.

Johnny Blade got back into the van, but did not shut his door.

The gun, Michael thought. *The gun.*

It could still be in the car . . . on the seat. It could be lost somewhere in the snow. He did not know where to look. *The damned thing could be anywhere.*

When he saw Johnny Blade come out of the van, he saw the glimmering reflection of a knife's blade. They were going to die out in the open. Out on a main highway, and there was nothing he could do about it.

Where is the gun? Michael kept asking himself. He tried to pull himself up to his knees. He thought his right arm might be broken. The pounding in his head was like thunder claps with each heartbeat. He knew he might pass out. He knew if he closed his eyes, the pain would go away.

Felicia screamed.

The charge of her scream triggered Michael into motion, and he reached out with his left arm. Digging his fingers into the snow, he pulled himself a little closer to where Johnny Blade stood over

Felicia.

A horn honked, and he turned his head to look at the car headed east on the Parkway. Hoping to see the car stop, he quickly said a prayer that it would. When it drove on by, he swore under his breath.

Would he have stopped? Not likely.

Johnny Blade dropped to his knees.

Michael got up to his knees. An impression was in the snow. He fell forward, reaching with his good arm. His hand went elbow deep into the snow. The cold seemed to burn his exposed flesh. He found the gun.

* * *

Martin Wringer dropped to his knees with a smile. He would kill the girl, kill the jerk from the sedan, and flag down some road assistance for help. When the car stopped, he would kill the driver and get the hell out of Dodge.

It was a shame to kill this whore without having had her first, but he saw no other choice. And really, it did not matter. Canadian whores, US whores. They were all North American, right?

He could feel his smile getting bigger as he held the knife to her forehead and pressed the tip into her skull. He heard the distant sound of thunder and almost laughed as he was knocked backwards. The knife had fallen. He knew he had been shot. He could feel the warmth of his blood spilling out of his arm. There was no pain though, so he stood up.

The whore had rolled over and was trying to crawl away. He grabbed her leg with one hand while the other patted around in the snow in search of the knife. He tugged on her leg, and twisted it. She spun around, almost willingly. From the angle of the headlight, he could see her face clearly. Blood dripped from the cut on her forehead, running down her face like a fast-flowing stream. She was snarling, and when he saw her right arm arcing toward him, he knew why.

She had the knife, and before he could turn away, the tip of the blade sliced a painful path through his eyes and across the bridge of his nose. He let go of the tramp's leg and tried in vain to protect his face from the blow he had already received. His palms were pressed hard against his eyes.

The intensity of the wound amazed him. He wanted to pass out, but his screaming kept him from doing so. He fell onto his back and rolled around in the snow.

The snow under his head turned from white to red in seconds.

He knew he could not stay on the ground. The police would be coming and he needed to get away. The police would never understand everything he had been through. They would not take the time to listen to him. He had done nothing wrong, but felt sure the police would turn everything around and make him out to be the bad guy—like some kind of monster.

He managed to get to his feet.

"Don't move," the man who had shot him called out.

Martin ignored the sound of the man's voice. He could hear the sound of an approaching car. The snowflakes kept landing on his eyelashes. The coldness felt wonderful on the slashing wounds, but he could not see where he was going.

"Everything all right?" Martin heard someone call out. It had to be that the driver of the approaching car had stopped. Martin ran toward the front of the van, since the sound of the driver's voice came from somewhere behind him.

"If you could call the police and for an ambulance," Martin presumably heard the man from the sedan with the gun say.

"I'll go right now! Hang tight," someone said. "I'll go to a phone and call the police!"

Martin ran out into the road. The driver would stop. He would hop in, and the driver could get him to a hospital—and then off to Canada.

He heard the horn as he felt the grill of the vehicle crash into his thighs. This hurt, but was nothing compared to the feeling of falling backwards and slamming his head onto the pavement. He felt like a bowling ball dropped onto a lane. His head felt as if it were rolling down the lane and simultaneously smashing into all ten pins at once.

His eyes shut immediately. One fleeting prayer whisked its

way through his mind. “Please God, please let me be dead.”

Chapter 59

Michael sat on a gurney at Park Ridge Hospital. He'd spent over an hour in the waiting room before being sent to sit and wait in the ER. Not one doctor had been by to check in on him. He thought about calling Jeff Marks, the intern, to talk about the way he felt he had been forced to wait with a broken nose and arm, but thought better of it, knowing Marks had more important issues on his plate. The admitting nurse had given him a towel to press against his nose. For the most part, the ambulance drivers had gotten the bleeding to stop. The place buzzed with hyperactivity. The bad weather was responsible for several major car accidents, despite the time of night. Many people out at this hour were drunk. Drunk driving was a challenge all in itself. Throw a Rochester snowstorm into the equation and the drunk driver had not a prayer.

The time left alone felt good. Michael's mind had been a whirlwind. He could not think straight when they brought him in. Though he had some time to reflect, he still was not sure about everything, it had all happened so fast. All he knew for sure was that he was worried to death wondering how Felicia was doing.

Nearly an hour ago doctors rushed by Michael with Johnny the Blade on a matching gurney looking frantic and panicked. Michael wondered if the doctors were even aware of who they were rushing off to the operating room. Should it make a difference to them anyway?

"Mr. Buzzelli?" It was Detectives Cocuzzi and Cage. Cage had both hands in his pocket and was looking around the ER as if distracted. Cocuzzi had been the one speaking. He stared at Michael, a look of genuine concern in his expression. The use of Michael's name had an unasked question attached to its tone, "Are you all right?"

"Hey guys," Michael said, shaking his head. "I'm all right."

"You did an amazingly commendable and stupid thing tonight," Cocuzzi said. "We ran the van's plates, checked with his ex-wife, and we're pretty sure this Martin Wringer is now our prime suspect. We found a knife that's been bagged for evidence, we also found a gun. Did you fire that gun?"

"I did."

"Who's gun is it? Is it yours?"

Michael had no idea what kind of history might be attached to that weapon. He did not want to incriminate Marcus. Marcus would want to kill him by now anyway. He worried about anything else the police might find in Marcus' car.

"It's not mine. I know that, but I can't remember where the gun came from." The answer was lame and immediately attracted Cage's attention.

"You used a gun to shoot Martin Wringer, but you don't know where you got the gun from?" Detective Cage asked. He was standing there with one hand on his hip pointing a finger at Michael.

"That's right," Michael said, lifting the hair off his forehead. "See that bump? Amnesia, I think."

"Bullshit!" Cage spat.

Cocuzzi put a silencing hand over Cage's arm. "We'll worry about the gun later. What about the car you were driving?"

"What about it?" Michael treaded water carefully.

"Where did you get it?"

"What do you mean?"

"He means the car was reported stolen earlier in the day. Except for your prints, we got nothing. Did you steal this car?" Cage asked.

Michael knew one thing immediately. The gun could not be traced to Marcus, because the car could not. If he had to he would bet the cell phone in the glove compartment would turn out to be stolen, too.

"The keys were in it," Michael said. "So I guess you could say I stole it."

Cocuzzi did not look concerned about the theft, since the car had been reported stolen well before Michael stole it again.

"How did you know the keys would be in it?" Cage asked.

Again, Cocuzzi quieted the detective with a touch. "How's the nose?"

"Throbbing, but I'm okay."

"The head?"

"I'll live."

"Still plan on doing the story if I give you an exclusive?" Cocuzzi said without a smile.

"Yes, sir."

"Get the nose bandaged, get some rest, and call me in the morning. I won't be going home anytime soon." They shook hands. Cage shrugged and gave in. He shook hands with Michael, too. "And Buzzelli?"

"Yeah?"

"You did a nice job. Thanks."

Chapter 60

Thursday, January 31

Homicide Detective Jason Cocuzzi felt like crap. He had been stuck in meetings all week long. The FBI agents showed up on Monday anyway. That day and most of Tuesday had been spent briefing them. Pete Cage had made a funny comment. “Two days we've been going over this crap. What’s brief about it?”

On Wednesday Cage went back across the river. It did not seem to matter much to his captain that a journalist cracked the case and a prostitute caught the serial killer. Cage would be treated like a hero in Irondequoit. It did not matter. What did matter to Cocuzzi, like him or not, was the fact that he did not want to have to work with that arrogant, cocky son of a bitch ever again.

Though the case was solved and now in the hands of the media, Cocuzzi planned on taking some time off. Aside from feeling like crap, he also felt tired. He was sick of the weather, the slate gray skies and unpredictable storms. Most of him loved the city. He could not imagine himself moving to another. A small, nagging part of him wanted out. Not just out of Rochester, but out of the police business. If he left before landing twenty years on the force, his pension would be a laughable joke. Early retirement was out of the question. He did not want a paper-pushing job, he realized as he leaned back in his chair behind his desk. The top was covered with papers and he did not have the energy or drive to work on the reports.

So a vacation made the most sense. He had accumulated the maximum weeks of vacation and carried them over from year to year. A month off—spent in a tropical paradise—sounded so good. He laced his fingers and put his hands behind his head while closing his eyes and picturing Nassau in the Bahamas? The Florida Keys? He had never been to either location and always dreamed of going.

Then he felt it, the odd sensation of someone watching him. Slowly he opened his eyes. He removed his hands from behind his head when he saw Christine Wrzos standing alongside his desk. "I'm sorry, I was just thinking," Jason Cocuzzi said, almost defensively, as if his mother had caught him flipping through the pages of a dirty magazine.

"Happy thoughts, I could tell," the young female officer said.

"Can I help you?" It sounded curt and rude. He felt uncomfortable around her now. He did not know how he should behave. What did she expect of him, if anything, after that kiss. Should he expect anything of her? Calling her a few nights back had been one of the only things on his mind. Actually doing so was another story completely. His stubborn head told him just to forget anything happened and ignore everything else. But with her standing next to him, that stubborn advice seemed futile and useless.

"So formal," she said. "Well, if you want to put it that way, then yes. You can help me. I'm hungry and would like to be taken to dinner tonight."

"Wzros, it's ten a.m."

"So. After lunch. I know I'll be hungry again around super time. Is it a date, or no?" Some of her self-confidence was wearing. It had to be extremely difficult for a cop to ask out a superior.

"Sounds like a date."

She smiled and simply walked away from his desk. Scratching his head, he wondered where she lived. Should he plan to pick her up? What time would be good for her? What the hell would he wear? *My God . . . where in the hell can I take her*?

Chapter 61

Saturday, February 2

Michael was home sitting at the computer. He worked mostly from home all week long. A few times he ventured down to see Detective Cocuzzi, but mostly he could do what needed to be done by phone. He sent his feature articles by e-mail and the editors were thrilled to receive them. Conducting business this way, Michael could not help but compare himself to Sinopoli, giving the reporter more credit than he had in the past. Since Martin Wringer did not die, and this crazy mess would soon come to trial, Michael had been given the luxurious assignment to cover the course of events.

Yesterday he mailed a letter to Jack Murphy at Jack's Joint. This piece had been the most difficult thing he has had to write to date. He saved a copy and sat now reading it to himself.

> To Everyone at Jack's Joint,
>
> Many of you are mad at me. I can't blame you. I was deceitful and dishonest. I don't expect any of you to forgive me, though it is forgiveness I am seeking.
>
> The things you read—that I wrote about you—will never be published. The files have been trashed. I was wrong to think I could further my career at the sake of my

friends. I consider you—all of you—as friends.

Sincerely,

Michael Buzzelli

Michael switched off the computer just as someone rang his bell. As he went to the door, he half expected to see his old girlfriend, Ellen. She had been calling him lately, having read about his adventures in the paper. She was also impressed with his stories covering Johnny Blade.

Maybe something still existed between them. She was a promising attorney while he was a recently famed journalist. Their lifestyles complemented one another. Though he felt nothing for her any longer, she was attractive and had a nice family.

When he looked through the peephole he smiled. Ellen was not on the other side of the door. Felicia stood there, grinning, holding an armful of books. "Open up!" she said, her muffled voice making its way through the door.

He let her in.

She stood near the kitchen table and set the bag of books down.

"Hate me?" Michael asked.

"Yes. Heard about your letter."

"And you forgive me?"

"No. I signed up for my high school exam. It's late next month." Felicia looked at the ground. "I haven't been back to Jack's. Sandy called me at my mother's. I moved back home. I plan to finish high school and enroll in junior college in the fall. I'm thinking I might want to go into law enforcement or something."

Michael closed his door. "You, a cop? I can see that."

"Can you?"

"Most definitely." Michael went to the fridge and removed two cans of soda.

"Will you . . . what I wanted to ask is if you'd still consider helping me study?"

Michael set the cans on the table. He touched Felicia's arm. "I'd be honored, officer."

She laughed and playfully slapped at his chest. "I'm sorry . . . "

"You're sorry? What are you talking about? I'm sorry. I'm the one that's sorry. That entire night would never have happened if I had been straight from the beginning."

She stood on the tips of her toes and kissed him softly on the lips. "Who knows. If you had been honest from the beginning, maybe none of this would have happened."

The End

OTHER BOOKS AVAILABLE FROM BARCLAY BOOKS, LLC

Check Out Our Website To Learn More About These Available Titles:

http://www.barclaybooks.com

(The) Apostate by Paul Lonardo: Mystery\Suspense\Sci-Fi ISBN 1931402132

(The) Burning Of Her Sin by Patty Henderson: Mystery\Suspense ISBN 1931402264

Dark Resurrection by John Karr: Horror\Suspense ISBN 193140223X

Death On The Hill by James R. Snedden: Mystery ISBN 1931402051

Do No Harm by James R. Snedden: Drama Intrigue ISBN 1931402272

(The) House On The Bluff by Elena Dorothy Bowman: Mystery\Fantasy ISBN 1931402000

(The) Institut by John Warmus: Suspense ISBN 1931402094

Island Life by William Meikle: Suspense\Horror ISBN 1931402205

Memory Bank by Sandi Marchetti: Sci-Fi Suspense ISBN 1931402124

Night Terrors by Drew Williams: Horror\Suspense ISBN 1931402248

Phantom Feast by Diana Barron: Horror\Suspense\Fantasy ISBN 1931402213

Psyclone by Roger Sharp: Horror\Suspense\Sci-Fi ISBN 1931402019

Riverwatch by Joseph Nassise: Horror\Suspense ISBN 1931402191

Soft Case by John Misak: Mystery (Detective) ISBN 1931402108

Spirit Of Independence by Keith Rommel: Horror\Fantasy ISBN 1931402078

Third Ring by Phillip Tomasso III: Mystery\Suspense ISBN 1931402116

Time Stand Still by John Misak: Mystery\Suspense\Sci-Fi ISBN 1931402183

Vultures In The Sky by Shields McTavish: Action\Adventure ISBN 1931402027

Appointment In Samara by Clive Warner: Action\Adventure ISBN 1931402256

Accidents Waiting To Happen by Simon Wood: Suspense ISBN 1931402302

(The) Workout Notebook by Karen Madrid: Nonfiction Diet\Exercise ISBN 1931402035

Here Are A Few Sample Blurbs

CATHOLIC CHURCH COVER-UP AND SCANDAL!

A Must Read Novel of Suspense

The Institut by John Warmus

LaRochelle, France: 1938: "Gently," Inspector Edmund Defont ordered the body to be cut down. Those who did not know him would suspect he feared he might hurt the dead girl—or wake her. The two policemen who worked silently under his command knew his sole intent was to preserve the crime scene. Thus, begins Edmond Defont's police investigation into the nightmares of David Proust, a young, affable priest who dreams and women die. When Defont's prime suspect and best friend both disappear in the middle of the night, his search takes him to the Institut d'Infantiles: an ancient Roman fortress in the middle of the Carpathian Mountains in the wilds of Poland: a place that conceals the mysteries of centuries.

ISBN: 1931402094 NOW AVAILABLE

* * *

A Must Read Page-Turning Drama Of Intrigue

Do No Harm by James R. Snedden

Three young men with totally different aspirations meet in medical school where they form a lasting friendship. The author follows their lives, cleverly weaving their stories of intrigue and sex, probing the events influencing their lives, ambitions, and careers.

Charles, poor boy from up state New York, whose goal is wealth and social status. He sets up practice in the City of New York; however, when legitimate means don't produce financial rewards quickly enough, he resorts to criminal activity, consorting with members of the underworld and making himself vulnerable to blackmail.

Abner, a farm boy from rural Illinois, inspired by the doctor who cared for his family, has his altruistic motives turn to disappointment when reality replaces dreams. Returning to his hometown, he is met with resentment and hostility and must decide to leave or stay and fight.

David, the rich boy from San Francisco. The only son of a wealthy businessman, he chooses medical school to escape his parents and their plans for him to carry on the family business. An adventurer and ladies man, tragedy strikes just as he finds purpose to his life.

ISBN: 1931402272 NOW AVAILABLE

Published By Barclay Books, LLC

http://www.barclaybooks.com

COULD THE APOCALYPSE BE ALREADY HERE?

The Apostate by Paul Lonardo

An invasive evil is spreading through Caldera, a burgeoning desert metropolis that has been heralded as the gateway of the new millennium. However, as the malevolent shadow spreads across the land, the prospects for the 21st century begin to look bleak.

Then three seemingly ordinary people are brought together:

Julian, an environmentalist, is sent to Caldera to investigate bizarre ecological occurrences.

Saney, a relocated psychiatrist, is trying to understand why the city's inhabitants are experiencing an unusually high frequency of mental disorders.

Finally, Chris, a runaway teenage boy, happens along and the three of them quickly discover that they are the only people who can defeat the true source of the region's evil, which may or may not be the Devil himself.

When a man claiming to work for a mysterious global organization informs the trio that Satan has, in fact, chosen Caldera as the site of the final battle between good and evil, only one question remains . . . Is it too late for humanity?

ISBN: 1-931402-13-2 **NOW AVAILABLE**

* * *